HIGH
COUNTRY
FALL

Also by Margaret Maron
in Large Print:

Bootlegger's Daughter
Home Fires
Southern Discomfort
Storm Track
Uncommon Clay
Last Lessons of Summer
Slow Dollar

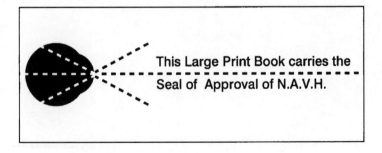

This Large Print Book carries the
Seal of Approval of N.A.V.H.

HIGH COUNTRY FALL

Margaret Maron

Thorndike Press • Waterville, Maine

Published in 2004 by arrangement with Warner Books, Inc.

Thorndike Press® Large Print Mystery.

The tree indicium is a trademark of Thorndike Press.

The text of this Large Print edition is unabridged.
Other aspects of the book may vary from the original edition.

Set in 16 pt. Plantin by Minnie B. Raven.

Printed in the United States on permanent paper.

Library of Congress Cataloging-in-Publication Data

Maron, Margaret.
    High country fall / Margaret Maron.
      p. cm.
    ISBN 0-7862-6936-7 (lg. print : hc : alk. paper)
    1. Knott, Deborah (Fictitious character) — Fiction.
2. Summer resorts — Fiction. 3. North Carolina —
Fiction. 4. Mountain life — Fiction. 5. Women judges —
Fiction. 6. Large type books. I. Title.
PS3563.A679H54 2004b
  813'.54—dc22   2004055241

In memory
of
Sara Ann Freed (1945–2003)
who graced so many lives.

As the Founder/CEO of NAVH, the only national health agency solely devoted to those who, although not totally blind, have an eye disease which could lead to serious visual impairment, I am pleased to recognize Thorndike Press★ as one of the leading publishers in the large print field.

Founded in 1954 in San Francisco to prepare large print textbooks for partially seeing children, NAVH became the pioneer and standard setting agency in the preparation of large type.

Today, those publishers who meet our standards carry the prestigious "Seal of Approval" indicating high quality large print. We are delighted that Thorndike Press is one of the publishers whose titles meet these standards. We are also pleased to recognize the significant contribution Thorndike Press is making in this important and growing field.

Lorraine H. Marchi, L.H.D.
Founder/CEO
NAVH

★ Thorndike Press encompasses the following imprints: Thorndike, Wheeler, Walker and Large Print Press.

Author's Note

I am a flatlander, born and bred, so there is no way I could have sent Deborah Knott to the mountains of North Carolina without the generous help of many people. I am particularly grateful to Harriette Buchanan, P. M. Sharpe, Celeste and Johnny Blankenship, and especially Kaye Barley, who not only brought key newspaper articles to my attention, but also gave me a grand tour of her part of Appalachia and answered a hundred e-mail questions.

Special thanks also to Davidson Neville, who very patiently explained the intricacies of business-related insurance policies.

Without the watchful eyes of District Court Judges Rebecca W. Blackmore, Shelly S. Holt, and John W. Smith of the 5th Judicial District Court (New Hanover and Pender Counties, North Carolina), Judge Deborah Knott would probably commit reversible errors every time she held court. I am forever in their debt.

Lafayette County is an amalgam of several regional counties, and Cedar Gap is a completely fictional town there. Any resemblance to a particular town or county is strictly coincidental. (I know I've said the same about Colleton County, but this time it's true!)

Margaret Maron
Johnston County, NC

The Great Smokies are the largest single mountain range in eastern North America. Even so, they are but a small piece of the jigsaw puzzle that makes up the Southern Blue Ridge Province.

So, if you live in the Smokies region, you can wake up every single morning and say to yourself: "Well now, here I am in the general area of the Great Smoky Mountains, a mountain range on the western front of the Southern Blue Ridge Province, a part of the Blue Ridge Province, one of the four provinces in the Southern Appalachians, a part of the Appalachian Mountains, which are probably named after a Florida Indian tribe."

George Ellison
Smoky Mountain News
Waynesville, NC
14 February 2003

AUGUST

Fog was so thick in the lower elevations that Dr. Carlyle Ledwig had his windshield wipers on the slowest setting to swish away the fat droplets that formed on the glass and obscured the road ahead. With visibility almost down to zero, he crept along at thirty-five miles an hour, though he often hit sixty on these straight stretches in nicer weather.

From beside him, Norman Osborne chuckled. "All you need's an orange on your license plate and they'll think you're from Florida."

Ledwig grinned "I *am* from Florida. Remember?"

"Yeah, that's right. Well, from New York then." The big man sat back in the passenger seat of Ledwig's SUV as if he were lounging in his leather executive's chair down in Howards Ford and looked over at

11

his friend. Ledwig's hair wasn't nearly as gray as his, but neither of them was young anymore. "Driving in fog's like a foretaste of senility, isn't it?"

"How do you mean?"

"Can't see behind you, can't see ahead."

"Not the worst way to be."

Osborne gave a sour laugh. "You ever wonder what your old age is going to be like?"

"If I got my dad's genes, I'll be playing eighteen holes of golf twice a week at eighty-five, the way he still does. If I got my mom's, I'm due for my first stroke any minute now."

"Not before we get home, okay?" said Osborne. "I don't want to wind up one of those car wrecks off the side of this mountain, where they don't find us for eight or ten years."

He was silent for a moment, as if contemplating what such a death would mean to his wife. Then he shrugged. "Ah, what the hell? Dead's dead, isn't it?"

"Maybe. But we've both got a whole lot of living left to do."

At that instant, Ledwig drove out of the fog and into sunshine. Above, the sky was a cloud-dappled blue. The road flattened slightly and curved west. To the right, the shoulder dropped off into white nothingness; ahead, tall trees lined the street, and the first hints of autumn colors were beginning to spread their sheltering glory above the immaculate houses on the front edge of Cedar Gap. A huge maple caught the light so that every other leaf seemed veined in gold, but beyond that, a two-hundred-year-old oak was still completely green. It was a scene right off one of the postcards sold in the souvenir shops along Main Street.

"God, I love this town!" said Ledwig.

"It gets prettier every year," Osborne agreed.

"Worth every battle we had to fight," Ledwig said complacently, remembering all the hours both of them had devoted over the years to getting a planning board in place. They'd had to twist a few arms and make a few enemies to convince local businesses to agree to some rules and restrictions for the greater good of Cedar Gap, but this was their reward: a prosperous and picturesque town whose beauty drew thousands of visitors from early spring to late fall, a mountain jewel whose desirability extended to enclaves of expensive vacation homes in the surrounding hills and hollows.

In gardens behind the low stone walls, summer's zinnias had begun to fade while fall's blue asters and clear yellow chrysanthemums headed for their bright peak. The houses became larger and closer together. Small green wooden signs neatly lettered in gold announced that here was an antique store, there was an upholstery shop selling designer fabrics, and over there, three Victorian bed-and-breakfasts in a row. So discreet were the signs, one could almost forget that these were now commercial establishments, no longer private homes.

Ledwig rounded the curve where Main Street formally began and his complacent smile darkened into a scowl as it always did the moment he saw that dilapidated log building on the right with its raucous red-and-white decorations that would clash horribly with fall's oranges and browns when leaf season began. The shabby cedar siding, the rusting drink signs, the broken paving of the parking strip out front — everything about the place irritated him beyond all reason.

"Want to stop?" asked Osborne. "Make one more try?"

"That's what you said last week," said Ledwig, but already he was slowing and

14

looking for somewhere to park.

The Trading Post was a blatant eyesore that sold fast food and tacky souvenirs. Like a slovenly old moonshiner who sits around in his dirty overalls and dribbles chewing tobacco on his yuppie daughter's white carpet, the place was an embarrassment to the little town's carefully cultivated image of taste and beauty, yet there was seldom an empty parking space around it. As if to mock him, a red Mercedes pulled out from the curb. Ledwig slammed on the brakes and immediately put on his turn signal to claim the spot. It took a little hauling and backing, but he eventually wedged his SUV into the tight slot.

"Remind me what our last offer was," Osborne said as they stepped aside for a knot of tourists munching on hot dogs.

"A million-three," said Ledwig.

"You game for a million-four?"

"Hell, we're neither of us getting any younger. Try a million-five and let's lean on him, tell him what we did to Sam Tysinger."

For a moment, Osborne's mind blanked, then he grinned. He'd always had an infectious smile and several of the tourists smiled back.

They found the elderly proprietor at the back of the store shelving plastic souvenir moonshiner jugs filled with honey from local bees. He wore a red plaid flannel shirt, bib overalls, and clodhopper shoes, in a deliberate parody of a flatlander's conception of a mountain hillbilly. As they tendered their newest offer, he continued to shelve the honey with unconcealed impatience until Ledwig made a less than subtle reference to the planning board.

"You threatening me?" he snarled then.

"Not threatening, Simon," said Dr. Ledwig. "Just pointing out that the town commissioners are not going to let this situation go on forever."

"I was grandfathered in," Simon Proffitt said, swatting the air as if shooing pesky dogflies. "I've got the right setbacks. I ain't encroaching on nobody's property. Hell, I even took down ol' Cherokee Charlie and he were a historical landmark, so you two can go screw each other 'cause you ain't screwing me over another inch."

"Think about it, Simon," said Ledwig in his most persuasive voice. "You're pushing eighty, you have no children. What're you hanging on like this for? You don't have to work this hard. You could take the money, go trout fishing every day, sit on the porch with your banjo, enjoy life."

"I *am* enjoying life." He turned to them with an evil grin. "Twisting you'uns's tails gives me more pure pleasure than your million dollars."

"Enjoy it while you can," said Osborne, dark menace in his tone.

"I surely do intend to." The old man opened his office door, reached inside, and pulled out a double-barreled shotgun. "Wouldn't advise either of you'uns to come back here again. Ol' Jessie here's got something the matter with one of her triggers."

The gun fell from his gnarled hands. It hit the floor and one of the barrels exploded, sending birdshot skittering across the floorboards into his office. One pellet ricocheted back out into the store and pinged off Ledwig's shoe.

"Jesus, Simon!" he yelled.

Excited babble broke out at the front of the store, but the voice of a crotchety woman clerk cut across the exclamations. "Dammit all, Simon! You drop that thing one more time and I'm gonna wrap it around your neck 'fore you kill somebody."

"Ain't nothing but birdshot," Proffitt called down to her. "Ever pick birdshot out of a man's shin, Doc?"

But he was speaking to their backs.

"You're just lucky it landed like it did," his clerk scolded, coming with broom and dustpan. "You could've hurt somebody."

Simon Proffitt just grinned. Luck had nothing to do with the way he'd dropped the gun. He took the broom the old woman shoved at him. Worth sweeping a little birdshot out of his office if it finally made them two think twice about pestering him to sell again.

Sunny waited for him on the large shaded porch with the makings of his favorite drink near the lounge chairs. Her eyes questioned him as he came up the steps and paused to give Ledwig a parting salute before turning back to her.

"Well?" she asked.

They had been married for more than twenty-five years, so Norman Osborne did not need to speak. She read the answer in his face.

"Oh, God!" she whispered, fear tightening around her heart.

"It's gonna be okay, darlin'," he promised, opening his arms to her. He held her close and breathed in the sweet fragrance of her hair. "It's gonna be okay. I'll call Bobby and Joyce tomorrow. Tell

18

'em I'm ready to deal."

"What about Carlyle? Will he — ?"

"Ol' Carlyle doesn't have to know a thing. Who's gonna tell him? Not me. Not you. The Ashes'll keep quiet till it's a done deal, and after that — ?" He shrugged. "After that it won't much matter, will it? And if anybody ever asks, you didn't know a thing. You got that?"

She nodded, trying to hold back the terror she felt, but tears streaked down her cheeks. "I only wish . . ."

Again he put his arms around her. "I know, darlin'. Me, too. But from here on, we suck it up and play all the cards we still got, okay?"

"Okay."

"No more crying?"

"No more crying."

"That's my girl. Now let's have that drink."

Chapter
1

OCTOBER

The trouble with making a public announcement is that the public — in this case, my family — feels entitled to respond. Not only to respond, but to exclaim, to criticize, and, above all, to offer comments and advice. The tom-toms, the grapevine, and yes, the Internet, too, were all working overtime.

From my four brothers who live out of state, to the other seven and their spouses still here in eastern North Carolina — not to mention a slew of aunts, uncles, and cousins all up and down the Atlantic seaboard — half the country seemed to be showering advice on my head.

Real showers, as well.

Bridal showers.

It was early October, three days after I'd begun wearing the ring that once belonged to Dwight Bryant's grandmother; two days after we'd told a couple of friends and both our families that we were planning a Christmas wedding.

I'm a district court judge here in Colleton County. Dwight is Sheriff Bo Poole's right hand and head of Bo's detective division, someone who's known me since the day Daddy piled all the boys who happened to be in the yard at the time into the back of his pickup and hauled them over to the hospital to meet their new sister. Dwight's always thought that gave him the right to act like one of my brothers, too. One of my bossy brothers.

We've both been married and divorced and —

Well, *his* marriage ended in divorce. Mine was merely annulled. (It was years before I learned that Daddy could have saved on lawyer's fees since I'd inadvertently married a hound dog who was already legally married at the time.) Dwight has a little boy up in Virginia; I sublimate with a bunch of nieces and nephews.

I had sworn off men at the beginning of summer, and after yet another relationship went sour on him, too, Dwight proposed that we quit looking for nonexistent soul mates and turn our solid friendship into marriage. That was less than two weeks ago and it seemed like a good idea at first, especially since it turned out that we were surprisingly solid in bed.

With all the hoopla after we announced it, though, I was starting to have second thoughts.

My family's so crazy about Dwight that you'd have thought someone had handed me a cool ten million and it was their duty to help me invest it before I threw it all on the nearest bonfire.

Take Aunt Sister, who about hugged the breath out of me the first time she saw me after hearing the news. "Thank God in glory! I thought you won't never going to settle down before I died." She looked at me dubiously. "You *do* aim to settle down, don't you?", which I think is a little sanctimonious for a woman who spends four months a year on the road in a Winnebago now that Uncle Rufus is retired.

Then there's Nadine, my brother Herman's wife, who belongs to a strict fundamentalist church and has never quite approved of me. "Of course, you can't wear white, but there're lots of pretty dresses in off-white."

"Oh, nobody worries about stuff like that anymore," said April, my brother Andrew's third-time-lucky try at marriage.

Aunt Zell, my mother's sister, couldn't stop beaming. "Now I know you have Sue's silver, crystal, and china," she said, "so why don't I give you a linen shower?"

"And I'll do lingerie," said Portland Brewer, my best friend and prospective matron of honor despite her advancing pregnancy. (Some of my brothers were making book on whether or not she'd deliver before the wedding.) "Black satin teddies. Red silk panties!"

"Kitchen goods!" said Mae and Doris.

"Well, what about ol' Dwight?" said their husbands. "Maybe we oughta give him a tool shower."

"So romantic," sighed my nieces. "All these years of catting around with other guys, then bang!" They had taken to singing parodies of "Brown-Eyed Handsome Man" every time they saw me.

Maidie, Daddy's longtime housekeeper, was writing out family recipes for my edification and Dwight's well-being; while John Claude Lee and Reid Stephenson, my cousins and former law partners, were talking about a formal announcement dance at the Colleton County Country Club in Dobbs.

Dwight's mother, his two sisters, and his sister-in-law had already booked a luncheon date at the University Club in Raleigh for all the women in both families.

Even Daddy. He didn't say much, but his blue eyes twinkled whenever someone mentioned the wedding.

Dwight just laughed and took it all in stride.

I was starting to freak.

"They act like this is the love match of the century instead of a sensible arrangement," I told Minnie.

Minnie is married to my brother Seth. She's also my campaign manager. It was Minnie who advised me that it would be politically expedient to quit looking for the moon and settle down with someone respectably earthbound instead. She was surprised as hell that I'd taken her advice and as pleased as the rest that the someone turned out to be Dwight Bryant.

"Won't hurt you at the polls to be married to a well-regarded deputy sheriff like Dwight," she said, but when she started cooing like our nieces, I immediately disillusioned her.

"Romantic love has nothing to do with this," I told her. "It's pure pragmatism. Sure, we're fond of each other, but it's love based on friendship and mutual history, not romance. He's as tired of channel surfing as I am, so it just makes sense."

"Oh, honey," Minnie said, looking bereft. "No real passion?"

"I didn't say there was no passion," I told her, unable to repress a grin.

"Well, thank goodness for that much," she said, smiling back.

"But it's turning into a three-ring circus. Even at the courthouse. Clerks go out of their way to stop me in the halls and tell me how nice Dwight is. Like he's got a halo and they don't think I'm good enough for him. It's bad enough that Aunt Sister and Nadine and Doris think like that, I don't need it at work, too. Paul Archdale even had the nerve to ask me if I was letting personal considerations color my judgment when Dwight testified against his client this afternoon."

"Were you?"

"Of course not," I huffed. "Paul knows his client's guilty as sin. He was just trying to get a lighter sentence. I may be thinking about marrying Dwight, but that doesn't mean I've quit thinking."

"Dwight's ring on your finger means you're more than just thinking about it," Minnie said gently.

We both glanced down at the ring, an old-fashioned square-cut diamond flanked by two smaller stones. I pulled it off and balanced it on the palm of my hand, where it gleamed and shot out sparks of color in the sunshine.

"I don't know, Minnie. I'm beginning to think this marriage is going to cause more problems than it'll solve."

"No, it won't," she soothed. "You and Dwight will be good for each other, and it would embarrass him to death if you back out now, so you put that ring right back on your finger where it belongs. A lot of people care about both of you, so the two of y'all getting together's bound to be a nine-days' wonder. They'll settle down once they get used to the idea."

"Another week?" I asked glumly. "I don't know if I can take it."

Happily, I didn't have to.

That very evening, there was a message from Roger Longmire, Chief District Court Judge in our district. When I returned his call, he said, "Got anything sensitive or pressing on your calendar?"

"Not that I know of," I told him.

"Good. I've been asked if I could spare someone to hold court up in Cedar Gap."

"Here am I, Lord, send me," I said prayerfully. Cedar Gap is 'way the other

26

side of the state, a good five- or six-hour drive from Colleton County.

Longmire snorted. He knows the Bible even better than I do. "When did you turn into Isaiah?"

"The minute you offered me a legitimate reason to head for the hills."

"Getting a little hot for you down here in the flatlands?"

Was that a chuckle in his voice? I considered for a moment. "Minnie called you, didn't she?"

"Good woman, your sister-in-law," he said blandly. "I owe her a lot. Did you know she was head of the Colleton County Democratic Women the first year I ran for the bench?"

Chapter
2

After Judge Longmire's call on Friday evening, Dwight and I spent half of Saturday walking around my small two-bedroom house out here on the family farm, trying to decide where to add on a new and larger master bedroom so that we could keep my old one in permanent readiness for his son. I hadn't seen Cal since Dwight told him about us, but he's a nice little boy and we get along just fine every time Dwight brings him out to swim in the pond or to ride the horses or the four-wheelers my nieces and nephews are variously addicted to.

Even though my house sits a half-mile off the nearest road, I've never had a chance to feel isolated. The farm is criss-crossed with dirt lanes that the whole family use as shortcuts or racetracks, and April spotted us on her way over to

Daddy's with a sweet potato pie still warm from the oven. April moves walls the way other women move furniture, and my brother Andrew grumbles that he never knows from one month to the next whether he'll get up some night to go to the bathroom and find their bedroom moved to the other side of the house before he can get back. Nevertheless, she made some sensible suggestions about water lines and septic tanks before she left, and so did Seth and Will when they came by after lunch looking for Haywood, who showed up a few minutes later on one of the farm's smaller tractors.

Will's the one who actually built my house, and Seth can find his way around a blueprint, too, but Haywood knows precious little beyond the basics. Didn't stop him from telling us what he'd do if it was him, though. Or Robert either, who had tired of waiting for Haywood to bring the tractor over and had come to find him.

I excused myself to go do laundry and they were still at it two loads later.

Carrying a fresh jug of iced tea and a half-dozen plastic cups, I rejoined them in time to hear Robert say, "— and build it from right there."

"Or we could just build a new house in

Maine," I said, setting the jug and cups on the back of the tractor.

Will and Dwight laughed as I perched cross-legged on the open tailgate of Dwight's pickup to pour them tea. Robert and Haywood didn't get it.

"Maine?" said Haywood. "Now why would you want to build a house 'way up yonder?"

"Get your cup and let's go," Seth told him with a big grin. "I'll explain it to you over at Robert's."

"Sorry about that," I said as the last of my brothers disappeared down the rutted lane.

"Why?" Dwight asked. "Think I don't know the way they like to help and give advice? Besides, you didn't have anything special planned, did you?"

"Well, when you called this morning, you said something about wanting to wet a line and I had my mouth set for pan fish."

"Really?" He moved closer and brushed my hair back from my face with both hands so he could examine my mouth with exaggerated care. "Nope, that's not how it looks to me."

His lips were mere inches from mine and I didn't need a second invitation to put my arms around his neck and let him swing me down from the tailgate, although I could have taken him right there on the back of the truck. Summer had been long and celibate for both of us; and my house here, his apartment in Dobbs, on a couch, on a bed, on a floor or table, we had spent these past ten days making up for lost time. Hard to remind myself that I'd spent my whole life treating him like another one of the boys — not when the mere touch of his hand on my hair was now enough to unleash every hormone in my body.

It was full dark by the time we were ready to think about food again. Much too late to try to catch our supper out on the pond. Instead, we went over to Jerry's Steak & Catfish House and had a waitress bring it to us with a side dish of onion rings and a basket of hushpuppies.

Big mistake.

Every third person who passed by our table was someone who'd known Dwight or me from birth or grade school, and they each had to stop and tell us how surprised they were when they heard we were engaged, "but we're wishing y'all lots of luck and happiness." Whenever I lifted my eyes from my plate, I saw beaming faces watching us.

"Thank God for Cedar Gap," I said

31

when we were back in Dwight's truck, headed for home. "Don't you wish you could get out of Dodge, too?"

"Why?" he asked, sounding honestly puzzled.

"The way everybody's burbling over us? It's not making you crazy?"

He grinned. "Nope."

"Well, it is me. I feel like I'm drowning in a tub of warm honey."

"Not me. I sort of like it that people seem happy for us. Besides, you're the one who thought that getting married would generate some political goodwill, remember? Seems to me it's working."

I sighed and glumly admitted he was right.

At the house, he didn't switch off the truck. "You'll want to pack tonight and get an early start tomorrow and I'd just be in the way."

It was a sensible decision, especially since all our appetites were temporarily sated. Nevertheless, I was irrationally disappointed. We'd been together only a few short days, yet I was already getting used to his comforting bulk in my bed, and when he stayed over, I found I liked waking up to the smell of coffee . . . among other things.

I reached for the door handle. "See you next weekend, then."

"Actually, you won't," he reminded me. "I'll be out that way myself. We'll probably pass each other on I-40 Saturday morning."

I'd forgotten that he was due to spend the weekend in the mountains of Virginia with Cal.

Slow as Dwight drives unless he's expediting to a crime scene, I figured I could be halfway home before he got out of the state. "Want to try and meet up for breakfast in Burlington or Greensboro?"

"Sounds good," he said, "but I plan to get on the road real early."

"That's okay. I'll call you."

He leaned over to kiss me goodnight and I deliberately kept it short and casual so he wouldn't think I was trying to change his mind about staying the night. His smile in the glow of the dash lights was teasing. "Don't go driving off any mountains while you're out there, you hear?"

He knows I don't have a head for heights.

"Don't worry. I'll be hugging the center line all the way."

Actually, except for my ears popping every time the elevation rose too quickly, the drive out next morning was fine.

When I left home at sunrise, the trees along Possum Creek were just starting to turn. Fall was late this year. Sassafras and crape myrtles had been showing a few orange and pink leaves for a couple of weeks, but oaks and maples were still mostly green.

By the time I reached the foothills around Hickory, the gums and tulip poplars were bright yellow. At Morganton, I left I-40 and angled northwest toward Lafayette County and Cedar Gap. As I passed over the eastern continental divide and started down a steep decline, late-morning sunshine lit up the valley from one side to the other and range after range of hills spread out before me in glorious fall colors. Heaven's streets of gold are going to look pretty bland compared to those brilliant oranges and burning reds, the tawny browns and flaming coppers of trees I couldn't begin to identify.

I almost ran off the road trying to take it all in and automatically braked to give myself time to drink in the beauty.

Behind me, a car honked angrily, then zipped around me. The driver gave me the finger as he passed and I heard him yell, "Fricking leafer! Get off the goddamned road!"

Okay, maybe I shouldn't have slowed so abruptly, but he didn't have to go ballistic. Thoroughly steamed, I picked up speed and kept my mind on my driving the rest of the way.

Lafayette County is tucked into a fold of the Blue Ridge Mountains right smack up against the Tennessee border. It's one of the smallest counties in North Carolina. In square miles, its actual footprint is only a sixth the size of Colleton County's, but if you could lay it out somewhere and iron its craggy old hills as flat as Colleton's landscape, it'd probably be half again bigger.

Cedar Gap sits right below a ridge that separates two valleys. It's not the biggest town in Lafayette County — that honor belongs to Howards Ford down in the valley below. Indeed, Howards Ford was the site of the first courthouse, but it was burned during the Civil War when feelings between secessionists and unionists ran high, so the county seat was moved temporarily to Cedar Gap. After the war, the change became permanent. The "new" courthouse was struck by lightning in the late seventies and burned to the ground, which is why the current courthouse is built of native undressed stone and blends into the landscape like a modern, low-slung office building rather than something with Corinthian columns and a Grecian frieze.

I stopped at the grocery store in Howards Ford for some basic essentials and made a mental note of where a drugstore was since I'd been warned that Cedar Gap has none. No Wal-Mart, Kmart, movie theater, no OfficeMax or Home Depot either. A three-lane road winds from the valley up to Cedar Gap — three lanes so that cars don't get stuck behind eighteen-wheelers that can't seem to clock more than twenty-five miles an hour getting up that grade. Here at noon on a beautiful blue-sky Sunday, the road was clogged. Not with trucks, though.

With tourists.

While every third car seemed to have a Florida license plate, I did see plates from several other states, all moving antlike up and down the mountain. Cameras poked from the open windows and I could almost hear the passengers telling their driver to slow down! Wait! Look over there at that bunch of yellow trees! Oooh, see those red maples! Stop!

No wonder that earlier driver had given me the finger.

There are numerous scenic pull-off spots along this road, and every one of them was packed by tourists who hung over the rails with their video cameras to get a better view or a more artistic angle on those spectacular fall colors. The eleven miles between Howards Ford and Cedar Gap took me forever, and when I got there, it was more of the same — every parking spot taken, every sidewalk bench filled. A large bronze monument to World War I sat in the center of a traffic circle on one of the few pieces of purely level ground in town, and the low stone walls that circled it were lined with happy tourists who licked ice-cream cones from the hand-dipped ice-cream shop across the street while they watched the passing show.

As I waited at one of Main Street's three traffic lights, I looked around to get my bearings. Except for the monument and the ice-cream store that was still called Roxie's and still sold hand-dipped ice cream according to the sign in its window, nothing looked familiar, but then I was barely eight years old my one and only visit here with Mother and Aunt Zell.

Mother adored Daddy and she loved her sons and stepsons, yet there were times when she felt suffocated and exasperated by so much testosterone. That's when she'd call her sister, and the three of us would take off for a just-us-girls adventure.

Since I was last here, Cedar Gap had evidently come down with what some of us down east call the "Cary syndrome."

Cary used to be a charming, if somewhat scruffy, little village a few miles west of Raleigh. Then high-end developers moved in, the town was "revitalized," and gradually the town board filled up with such fierce zoning zealots that houses and storefronts are now forced to conform to a limited range of bland colors and architectural styles, signs are discreet and almost invisible, and every lawn is groomed and manicured into such prettiness that all individuality has been tidied away — the Stepford wife of North Carolina towns.

Like Cary, Cedar Gap looked to be well on its way to becoming picture perfect, too. No ugly "big box" stores up here. Huge old sycamore and oak trees almost met overhead, and Main Street consisted of boutiques, upscale souvenir shops, real estate agencies, and restored Victorian houses that had been turned into B and Bs or pricey restaurants that catered to the tourist trade. A handful of law offices clustered around the courthouse just off the traffic circle here in the middle of town. Each sported dark green balloon awnings in keeping with all the other businesses. The whole town is only six or eight blocks long, and cedar-shingled houses and condos stair-stepped up and down the mountain on either side, through thickets of hemlocks and hardwoods. Banks of rhododendron bushes filled all the spaces in between.

Eventually, the light changed and oncoming traffic finally cleared enough to let me make a left turn through a set of gates next to an old stone church.

My cousin Beverly, who lives in Durham, has a condo here and she's always urging me to use it during off-season. Leaf season still had a few weeks to go, so when I called her Friday night, it was only to ask if she could recommend a place.

"Oh, you'd have to pay an arm and a leg for something up there right now," she said. "If you could even find a vacancy. The leaves are supposed to peak this week. But you can use our condo if you don't mind the mess it's in —"

"It's not rented?"

"— *and* if you don't mind sharing it with the twins on the weekend."

"The twins? I thought they were in

school down at Wilmington." Beverly's daughters are nineteen and sweet kids, but not rocket scientist material.

"Nope. They flunked out before Christmas," she said cheerfully. "We've had them at Tanser-MacLeod since last January."

I'd never heard of Tanser-MacLeod and said so.

"It's in Howards Ford. Used to be a junior college up until about three or four years ago. Fred and I thought a small campus might work better for them. Anyhow, we're in the process of renovation and they're doing the painting, which is why the condo's not rented out right now. We need to get it refurbished before it starts snowing. You're more than welcome to use it if you can walk around paint buckets."

Better than sleeping in my car, I assured her.

Beverly said her unit was three levels up from the street. Following her directions, I drove through the gates of the condo, up a slight incline to the parking area that served the first level, then up a steeper drive onto the second level that curved around to a driveway that I swear to God was only about three feet wide and went straight up the side of the hill.

40

No guardrails, just firs with long feathery branches that brushed the car windows.

My sporty little flatlander car took a deep breath — I did, too — and somehow we made it. At the top of the drive, the area leveled out and I pulled into the slot marked F-3 and switched off the ignition.

I do not consider myself a coward, but simply looking back down the way I'd come gave me vertigo. The angle was so acute I couldn't see the bottom and I shivered at the thought of having to drive out again anytime soon.

"Put your faith in the Lord," said the preacher who lives in the back of my head and tries to lead me in the paths of righteousness and sanity. *"If He can move mountains, He can surely help you drive back down one."*

"Or," said the pragmatist who shares the same headspace and who had noticed a set of steep stone steps that led down to the street, *"maybe you could just walk back and forth to the courthouse."*

"Wimp!" sneered the preacher. He took another look at that ski jump of a driveway. *"On the other hand, your hips could certainly use the exercise."*

Chapter
3

The two-story weathered cedar condos were built up the side of the hill so that each had an entry that was close to ground level (or what passes for level ground in the mountains) depending on where the front door was in relation to the driveway that wound past the various units. Two shallow steps led up to a small porch in front of Beverly's. I was unloading my car and stacking groceries and duffel bag by the railing when the door to the next unit opened and a gray-haired man emerged, carrying two large suitcases.

"Ships that pass in the night," he said cheerfully. He pointed his remote toward the blue Grand Marquis parked in the next space and the trunk lid popped open. "You just getting here?"

I nodded. "I take it you're leaving?"

" 'Fraid so." He set his bags in the trunk.

"Are you up for the leaves?"

"Not really. You?" I put the last of my stuff on the edge of the porch, closed my trunk, and fished in my purse to find the notes and numbers Beverly had given me over the phone. One set was for the electronic keypad Beverly's husband had installed so that they wouldn't have to keep replacing the keys their renters lost or forgot to return to the local leasing agent.

"We come every fall," the man said. "Forty years we've lived in Tampa and my wife still misses watching the seasons change."

He smiled at the woman who now appeared in the doorway. "Not that she's ever actually missed them."

"He brings me back every spring and fall even if it's just for a long weekend," she agreed, handing him several shopping bags to stow in the trunk. "Azaleas and dogwoods in the spring, colored leaves in the fall."

I smiled and wished them a safe trip home as I keyed in the numbers Beverly had given me.

Nothing happened.

"Are you sure you have the right place?" asked the woman. "I think that unit's still occupied."

43

I tried the combination again and this time it released the lock. Turning the knob, I pushed open the door. The inside looked as if it'd been hit by Hurricane Fran.

"Oh, my!" said the woman, who stared past me in frank curiosity at the jumbled mess.

The couch and chairs had been shoved to the center of the room and lamps and end tables were stacked on top of them, as is not unusual when a place is being painted. Instead of the usual drop cloths, though, the furniture was covered in a tangle of colorful T-shirts, jeans, sweaters, and dirty socks. A pair of high heels sat atop the entertainment center, and was that a black lace bra draped over a clump of stained sneakers? Through the archway, I saw a dining table piled high with pizza boxes and drink cups.

"I didn't think they looked like they were leaving for good when they went out of here this morning," said the woman. "Somebody must have messed up on your rental."

"No, no," I said. "It's okay. This is my cousin's place and her kids are painting it in their spare time. They'll probably be back soon."

"Don't count on it," said the man.

44

"They haven't gotten in before midnight the whole time we've been here."

I didn't like the sound of that.

"And you've been here how long?"

"Since Friday a week ago."

Ten days? My mind raced through the possibilities. Had the twins lent the place to some of their friends without telling their parents? I gave a mental shrug and began carrying in my things. Beverly had given me their telephone number at the college, and if they didn't show up by the time I was settled in, I'd call and sort it all out.

As I went back to get the last bag of groceries, the man was already in his car with the motor running. His wife finished locking the door and gave me a concerned look. "I do hope everything will be all right for you."

"It will," I assured her. "Y'all drive safely now."

"Don't worry. The only time we've ever been stopped was for driving too slow on the interstate. Can you imagine that? A warning for going too slow? When teenagers are weaving in and out in those little red cars, going ninety miles an hour?"

"Well, you do see more little red cars pulled over than big blue Mercs," I said, thinking how there would probably be more kids than grandparents standing before me tomorrow morning.

The car moved slowly away, then backed up. The man powered down his window and thrust a thin newspaper into my hand.

"The local news," he said. "Only comes out on Friday and if it didn't happen in Cedar Gap or affect Cedar Gap directly, you won't read about it here, but it does carry ads for all the good restaurants here and in Howards Ford."

I had to smile as I watched his car disappear down the slope, brake lights bright red all the way. People accustomed to big metropolitan dailies, like the *Miami Herald* or the *New York Times*, never seem to grasp the concept of small-town newspapers; but Linsey Thomas, who owns and edits the *Dobbs Ledger* back home, explained it to me once when I teased him for running a half-page account of a Scout troop fundraiser my nephews had been involved in. "Big papers sell news," he said. "Little papers like mine sell names. Am I gonna print the names of any little peckerwood that was there? Heck, yeah. Their mamas' and daddies' names, too, 'cause every doting grandma's gonna buy at least three extra copies to send to friends and family who live somewhere else and they're all gonna keep renewing their subscriptions."

The editor of the *High Country Courier* apparently practiced the same policy. The pages were folded open to an article about a patchwork quilt made by volunteers and raffled off to benefit the local hospital. It appeared to name every woman who had worked on the quilt, the winner of the raffle, and a picture of the presentation ceremony at the hospital, wherein an administrator received a check from the officers of the volunteer group. I was surprised to note that they'd raised nearly twelve thousand dollars on that one quilt. At a dollar a chance, they must have hit up every tourist that came through town this year.

I carried the paper inside with me, stepping around an open foam carryout box that contained the dried-up remnants of a sandwich. From the pillows propped against the couch, someone had apparently lounged there on the floor in front of the television to eat and then gotten up and left the box. For a moment, I was almost tempted to phone the nearest motel down in Howards Ford and throw myself on a clerk's mercy. Instead, I picked up the kitchen phone to dial the dorm number

Beverly had given me.

Unfortunately, the phone was dead. No dial tone.

Resigned, I looked a little closer and realized that the place wasn't as dirty as it initially appeared, just a little shabby and a lot cluttered.

Beverly said they were going to junk most of the stuff and refurbish once the painting was done. "If they're going to pay fifteen hundred a week, tourists want everything new and fresh."

Paint buckets sat on newspapers in the middle of the hall and brushes and rollers were soaking in a bucket of water, but so far as I could tell, only the walls of the smaller bedroom appeared to have been painted. Even there, the trimwork was still untouched.

The condo consisted of living room, large eat-in kitchen, a bath off the hallway, two small bedrooms, and a slightly larger master bedroom with its own bath. Since I was the sole legitimate occupant now, I had no hesitation about moving the clothes and toiletries I found there into one of the smaller bedrooms and taking this one for myself. Fresh linens were in the closet and cleaning supplies were under the kitchen sink.

When I went to strip the bed, I stumbled over a telephone receiver on the floor between the bed and the far wall and followed the cord to the unit itself, one of those with a built-in answering machine. The red light was blinking as I pulled it out from under the bed, so I put the receiver back on the cradle, pushed the play button, and heard a young voice with a clipped New Jersey accent.

"June? Marsha. It's Friday night. I guess you're still at the Laurel? Your mom called. She wants one of you to call her back, something about some cousin who's planning to spend the week there? I think you're about to be busted. How's she not gonna know?"

Know what?

That they were lazy slobs who'd barely hit a lick on the paint job they were supposed to be doing?

That they'd lent the condo to friends without telling Beverly?

Busted? For what?

Before I could speculate further, the second message began to play. Beverly's exasperated voice said, "Where *are* you girls? Did you get my message about Deborah coming up on Sunday?"

I lifted the receiver and, as soon as I

49

heard the restored dial tone, found the twins' number again and called it. After four rings, an answering machine kicked in: "Sorry we're not here. Don't you dare hang up without leaving us a message, though, you hear?"

I heard. "June? May? It's Deborah. It's Sunday afternoon and I'm at the condo. Call me."

I set the phone on the bedside table and got on with changing the sheets, trying to remember how long it'd been since I last saw the twins. At Aunt Sister's birthday party back in early August?

Beverly is Aunt Sister's daughter, so she and Fred and the twins would certainly have been there, but we're such a big family it's hard to keep track of who was where when.

Twins run in my father's family, and nineteen years ago, when Beverly knew that she was carrying twin girls, she planned to name them either Hope and Faith or Elizabeth and Letitia — Betty and Letty for short. But the twins were born fifty minutes apart in the middle of the night.

The night of May thirty-first, to be precise.

Beverly being Beverly, she naturally took

50

that as a sign and named them May and June. Sweet girls and identical as Xerox copies. Unfortunately, there are some in the family who think they only got one brain between them. (Of course, there are some who say the same about Haywood and Herman.)

A half-hour later, I had finished doing my bedroom and bath, had kicked enough stuff aside to vacuum a path from there to the front door, and was now ready to tackle the kitchen.

Once I located where the garbage bags were kept, the table and counters were soon cleared of fast-food and drink containers. The dishwasher was full of clean dishes, and after I put those away, I began to refill it with coffee mugs and stray pieces of tableware. When I opened the refrigerator to stow my perishables, I saw several bottles of beer alongside a decent head of lettuce, orange juice, milk, and were those homemade angel rolls in the bread drawer? There hadn't been a baking sheet nor mixing bowl in the dishwasher, nevertheless, these could very well be some the twins had made.

Like Mother, like every other woman in her generation, Aunt Sister had tried to pass the art of breadmaking down to her daughters and granddaughters. I can make decent biscuits, but that's about it for me; and Beverly's not much better. For some reason, though, the twins took to baking like hogs to a mud bath. Whole wheat breads, rye loaves, pumpernickel, sourdough, Irish soda bread, puff pastry — if flour is involved, the twins can make it.

The yeasty fragrance when I opened the plastic bag made my mouth water and reminded my stomach that it hadn't had lunch. I fixed myself a salad, snitched two of those rolls, and carried my food and the *High Country Courier* out to the deck off the dining room. The view was so amazing that for several long minutes I just sat on the lounge chair and stared. Through the hemlocks, looking due east, I could see almost the whole length of Main Street. The sun had begun its slide toward the crest of the ridge behind me, causing long dark shadows in the far hollows down below, but straight ahead, all the near mountaintops blazed in flaming, sunlit colors. Further out, the colors muted until they melded together into a blue smoky haze so that I couldn't tell where the hills ended and sky began.

I will forever be more partial to the

coast, but as always happens each time I do venture west, I start to understand again why so many are drawn to the mountains.

Eventually I turned back to my food and to the front page of the little newspaper. A full half of that page was taken up by a single story. The heavy black headline read "Family Friend Charged in Doctor's Death." Beneath were two pictures. The first was a studio portrait of a pleasant-faced man who appeared to be in his early fifties. The second was a candid picture of two uniformed officers as they led a young man in handcuffs into the sheriff's department here in Cedar Gap.

According to the paper, it was originally thought that Dr. Carlyle Ledwig, fifty-six, had accidentally fallen to his death about two weeks ago while repairing a deck that overlooked Pritchard Cove, wherever that was. "Working with wood helped Dr. Ledwig relax," the paper informed me, lest I should think the late doctor couldn't afford a carpenter.

From the deck to the first rocks below was a thirty-foot drop. His body had been discovered by a Daniel Freeman, twenty-one, a student at Tanser-MacLeod and a friend of the family. He had immediately

53

called 911, but it was too late.

An autopsy disclosed that the doctor's fatal head wound had come not from his fall but from a hammer blow, and a search of the ravine eventually located the hammer, its head still caked with blood. A week later, Daniel Freeman was arrested when a bloody fingerprint from the deck proved to be his. Traces of Dr. Ledwig's blood were also found on the trousers and sneakers he'd been wearing. If the sheriff's department had a theory as to Freeman's motive, they had declined to share it with the *High Country Courier*. Freeman had been released on a $25,000 bond.

Having no hard facts about Freeman other than that he was from Durham, was a senior at Tanser-MacLeod, and had been dating Dr. Ledwig's older daughter, the *Courier* fell back on recapping Dr. Ledwig's life.

I read of his birth in Florida, his degrees from universities in Chicago and New York, his early practice in Florida, his decision twenty years ago to relocate to Cedar Gap, where he headed up the geriatrics department at the local hospital and founded a geriatrics clinic in association with the hospital. His civic involvements seemed to include everything from town and county commissions to sitting on boards here and in Howards Ford. Among other things, he had funded the newly opened Carlyle G. Ledwig Senior Center, had taken active stands on environmental issues, and, according to the reporter, "had possessed the ability to persuade opposing sides to compromise and work together for the common good of Cedar Gap. Even those who disagreed with his stand on certain issues always agreed that he truly loved his adopted town."

I've seen enough of small-town life to read between those lines. The *Courier* evidently considered Dr. Ledwig basically decent, a man who involved himself in community affairs, a man who contributed time and money to good causes, yet also a man who thought he knew what was best for everyone and wasn't above using his influence to get folks to go along with him.

But to be hit with a hammer and thrown from his deck? I cast an uneasy look at the railing where my feet were propped. Was this something else the twins were supposed to be working on? I gave it a good push with my foot.

Rock solid. Well, that was one good thing.

The rest of the paper was the usual assortment of local announcements, ads for rental property (exorbitant!) and real estate (half a million for that dumpy little clapboard house?), and for several restaurants. Eating this late, I could skip the restaurants, but images of that hand-dipped ice-cream shop down on Main Street kept floating through my mind.

Surely a single scoop wouldn't be too self-indulgent?

"Not if you're gonna be walking up and down mountains," said the preacher, for once in complete agreement with the pragmatist.

Chapter
4

Despite the long drive out, my unexpected bout of house-cleaning, and those steep steps, I still felt fresh enough to walk the length of Main Street, browsing the windows, stepping inside the more interesting shops, even buying a sort of burnt orange fall jacket that picked up the gold tones in my tawny hair and didn't fight with my skin when I tried it on. The jacket almost jumped out of its bag when it spotted a handcrafted topaz and beaten copper necklace two windows down, a necklace that cost almost as much as the jacket. They so wanted each other, though, that I immediately whipped out my credit card.

Except for Dwight (or, more precisely, except for sex with Dwight), I hadn't treated myself to anything new in months and I figured I was due.

I managed to resist the designer silk

scarves in fall leaf patterns and colors that filled the window of a dress store, nor did I let myself go into the leather shop although a pair of snakeskin heels winked at me beguilingly from beneath straight-cut leather pants. For a tourist town, there was little that was tacky and tasteless. Even the strictly souvenir stores offered wares a cut above the usual: the T-shirts and sweatshirts were 100 percent cotton and came dyed in restrained earth tones with motifs that were embroidered rather than stamped. If an item could be made of wood or leather instead of plastic, then it was.

I saw a hat that would have looked good on Dwight except that I wasn't sure of his size, and that bothered me. How could I possibly be planning to marry someone whose hat size I didn't know? Yeah, yeah, it was crazy to get hung up over such a silly detail; all the same, I really needed to buy him that hat. Instead, I had to settle for a dark green crewneck sweater that would go nicely with his brown hair and eyes. That size I did know — XL, the same as several of my brothers.

A regional crafts store next door featured handmade quilts and pillow covers in traditional patterns, and, considering the quality of their goods, the gift shops further along the street could have been attached to art museums. Glass, pottery, and wooden bowls evoked the mountains rather than proclaimed it. The only place I could find the Cedar Gap name was on the bottom of a bowl or vase, never splashed across the front.

The sole exception to all this rarefied tastefulness was a ramshackle log building at the bottom of Main Street, something called the Trading Post. The moment I saw it, I immediately remembered walking around inside with Mother and Aunt Zell, the three of us sharing a bag of licorice jelly beans. I also seemed to remember an enormous wooden Indian that had stood out front with a peace pipe in one hand and a tomahawk in the other. He was gone now, probably a victim of political correctness.

Inside were all the geegaws you'd expect to find in a mountain tourist town: Daniel Boone coonskin hats made of polyester plush, Indian war bonnets in neon-colored feathers, dozens of silly doodads labeled "Souvenir of Cedar Gap" or "High Country Heaven," and plastic figurines of hillbillies shooting, fighting, whittling, and swilling moonshine. Part country store, it also carried jeans, bib overalls, work/hiking boots, washboards, kerosene lanterns, flashlights, and a hundred other necessities of bygone years and still useful today, I suppose, if you happened to live in a cabin at the far end of utility lines.

The store was surprisingly crowded. On one side of the front door was a hot dog stand where people stood in line while the lush fragrance of hot chili and onions swirled around them. On the other side, even more people were browsing through a candy section where small wooden nail kegs were filled with lemon drops, sassafras sticks, peanut brittle — every old-timey candy imaginable. Customers were encouraged to fill a plastic bag with any assortment they wanted because the price per ounce was the same for all, and yes, I did buy an ounce of licorice jelly beans for old time's sake.

Back out in the cool evening air, the sidewalks were becoming less congested as twilight fell. Cars still jostled one another for parking spots, and couples dressed in resort-style chic converged on the restaurants. Old-fashioned streetlights glowed softly beneath the trees, and inconspicuous spotlights illuminated the bronze soldier in the middle of the traffic circle.

When I reached the circle on my return walk back up the street, I veered off to check out the courthouse. A small arrow pointed to public parking down a sloping drive to the rear. On the side, though, I saw slots reserved for the various court officials, including one for Judge Rawlings, the judge for whom I was subbing while he sat court down at the coast, where gray trout were supposed to be running this week.

According to Longmire, Rawlings had traded with a Beaufort judge whose wife wanted to see leaves. Unfortunately, it was discovered at the last minute that she needed major surgery, so he would be spending this week either sitting at her bedside or playing Mr. Mom to their two children. Because Rawlings had already rented a place on the beach and because the Beaufort judge needed a sub anyhow, the call had gone out about two hours before Minnie's call for someone to replace Rawlings.

"Pure serendipity," Longmire had said, and standing here on the traffic circle in a town where no one was likely to come up and burble at me, I couldn't agree more.

I crossed the street, got in line at Roxie's, and ordered a scoop of fudge ripple, which

I savored all the way back to the condo.

Darkness had fallen completely now and those steep steps were poorly lit. Halfway up, I sat down on a ledge to finish the cone, and when I tilted my head back, I saw that the stars had come out, sharp and crisp against the deep blue. I know the mountains have been having trouble with air pollution, smog, and acid rain, but tonight was so clear that even the Milky Way swirled across the sky more brightly than I had seen in ages, despite a moon that would be full in another night or two.

Impulsively, I pulled out my cell phone and called up the menu for Dwight's number. It rang twice, then a recording informed me that "The wireless customer you have called is not available. Please try your call later."

I could call his pager, of course, but what was the point? Just to tell him I'd arrived safely? Or to ask him his hat size?

It wasn't as if we'd be murmuring sweet nothings in each other's ear, and he'd think I was crazy if I said the only reason I'd called was because the moon was making me lonesome for the sound of his voice.

When Dwight suggested that we get married, we had sensibly decided that long-standing friendship and newfound sex were all that we needed for a stable marriage. I told myself it would be childish and greedy if I started whining now because we didn't have stardust and moonglow, too. Nevertheless, as I gathered my bags and trudged on up the steps, I couldn't help sighing for all those times I'd been so deeply, desperately, insanely in love that I didn't care whether or not the guy thought I was crazy for calling.

The minute I opened the condo door, I realized someone had been there in the two hours I was gone. Lights were on in every room.

"June?" I called. "May?"

No answer.

It seemed to me that there were now fewer jeans in the stacks piled atop the couch and chairs. Two more pairs of heels graced the cabinet that held the television and DVD player, and the empty hangers hooked over a floor lamp now held long black skirts and white blouses with ruffles around the neck and cuffs. It was as if the twins had come home from some dressy occasion, changed into play clothes, and gone off again.

On the dining table was a note: *Deborah — Sorry about the mess. We'll be back around 12. M & J.*

Twelve? It was now only eight-thirty.

In my bedroom, a red light on the answering machine blinked for attention. "Would whoever gets this tell May or June to call Carla?"

I finished unpacking, took a long shower, then got into bed with a book, intending to read until they returned.

I think I lasted all of three pages.

The sound of the front door closing woke me. There was a moment of disorientation, and before I could clear my head, the bed was full of arms and legs, bear hugs and bounces.

"Welcome to the High Country!"

"You should've let us know."

"We'd've straightened the place up."

"Mom said —"

"We heard —"

"Are you really?"

One of them grabbed my left hand.

"Oh my God! It's true!"

"Look at the size of that rock!"

"Mom said Christmas?"

"Can we be in the wedding?"

"Please?"

Laughing, I disentangled myself and sat up. And did an immediate double take.

All their lives, the twins had been so identical that even their own brother had trouble telling them apart. When they were five, though, May fell on a piece of broken glass and wound up with a tiny half-moon scar in front of her right earlobe that was so faint outsiders almost never noticed it. Family members were immensely grateful.

Their faces were still photocopies of each other, but their shoulder-length dark hair had undergone radical changes since last I saw them. Both heads were now covered in short curls. One was the color of a new penny, the other was a deep dark purple, almost the same shade as an eggplant.

They looked at each other and laughed at my reaction.

"We'll dye it back if you let us be in the wedding," Eggplant said with a grin.

"I wouldn't dream of it." I was having too much fun picturing Doris or Nadine's reaction to vaguely punk bridesmaids. On a one-to-ten scale for mild acts of rebellion, with green or fuchsia Mohawks, three facial piercings, and two visible tattoos as a ten, this barely qualified as a one, but my prissy sisters-in-law would see it as the first banana peel down that slippery slope to depravity.

"You look darling," I said, thinking again how the word "cute" must have been coined with these two in mind: small, compact bodies, upturned noses, the bubbly personality of cheerleaders, which indeed they'd been throughout high school. "Has y'all's mother seen you yet?"

"No, and don't tell her. Please? We want to surprise them when she and Dad come up next month."

"Oh, they'll be surprised, all right." I looked at Copper Top. "May, right?"

She smiled and nodded.

"Although," said June, "we're not really sure. I could be May for all we know."

"Huh?"

"Right before we came back here in August, we put Band-Aids on our faces so they couldn't see May's scar —"

"— and we challenged Mom and Dad and Phil to say which was which —"

"— and they couldn't," both girls chorused, reminding me all over again how attuned to each other's thoughts they were.

"There was wine," said June.

"Mom got a little tipsy," said May.

"And she confessed that she used to mix us up when we were babies."

"Then Dad said he had, too."

"And even Phil said he used to switch us

in our high chairs just to see if Mom would notice. Sometimes he forgot to switch us back."

"So for all we know," said May, "I might really be June."

They didn't seem to be very upset about the possibility.

"Oh, well," I said. " 'What's in a name?' "

"Credit cards?"

"Driver's license?"

I had forgotten how literal-minded they could be.

" 'That which we call a rose, by any other name would smell as sweet,' " I quoted.

They looked at each other blankly.

"Dickens?" May ventured.

"Don't tell me you never read *Romeo and Juliet*," I said.

June's face brightened. "Shakespeare!"

May shrugged. "I think we were sick that day."

I laughed. I had never been a scholar, but compared to these two?

"So why are y'all up here goofing off instead of studying in the library down at Tanser-MacLeod?" I asked, getting serious for a moment.

"We're not goofing off," June said indignantly. "Mom and Dad are paying us to paint the place."

"I hope they're not paying by the hour," I said. "Those brushes have been in that bucket so long that at least an inch of water has evaporated since the last time they were touched."

"We've been really, really busy."

"Studying."

"Midterm exams."

"Yeah, and papers were due."

"But we were going to get on it this weekend —"

"— only something came up."

"Some *thing* or some *one?*" I asked.

"Um, well . . . see, we're earning extra money by waiting tables up here."

"But we don't want Mom and Dad to know because they think we should spend every minute hitting the books," June explained.

I held up my hands. "Hey, I'm not up here to rat you out."

"So why *are* you here?" asked May.

I told them about the judges trying to swap courts for a week and how I'd been asked to substitute for the one who was subbing for the Beaufort judge, only he —

They started to look blank again.

"Never mind," I said glancing at the

clock. "It's late. I want to be down at the courthouse by nine and you need to get to bed, too, if you're going to make your first class."

"It's not until ten," May said hastily, "but you're probably tired. We'll be quiet tonight if you'll be quiet in the morning."

"You're spending the night here?"

"Yeah, late as it is, we'd just wake up everybody in the dorm if we went back now."

"Oh, I almost forgot," I said. "Somebody named Carla left a message for y'all to call her."

"The phone's fixed?" asked June.

"Cool," said May. "It hasn't been working since Friday night."

I decided there was no point in telling them it always helps to put the receiver back on the hook rather than on the floor.

"See you in the morning," I said, lying back on the pillow.

June switched off the lamp and they tiptoed from the room as if I were already asleep.

Minutes later, I was.

Chapter
5

Neither twin made it up before time for me to leave next morning. I rapped on the door of one bedroom and stuck my head in.

The face beneath purple hair blinked at me groggily, rolled over to tilt the bedside clock so she could read it, then moaned, "Just another half-hour, okay?" and pulled the quilt back over her bare shoulders.

"Will I see y'all again before the end of the week?" I asked.

"Mmmff," was my only answer.

Happily it was none of my business whether or not they got to class on time.

With my judicial robe slung over one arm and the strap of my laptop looped over the other shoulder, I let myself out into a fall morning so picture perfect it had probably been ordered up by the Cedar Gap Chamber of Commerce: turquoise blue sky, one puffy white cloud, and a bit of a breeze so that brown, gold, and orange leaves floated down and swirled around my feet as I crossed the drive. The air smelled fresher and cleaner than the fusty humid air I'd left in Colleton County and its slight nip of fall encouraged me to walk briskly down the steps to Main Street. I was feeling virtuous as hell by the time I reached the courthouse.

The Lafayette County Clerk of Court wasn't around at the moment, but someone in her office had been watching for me.

"Judge Knott? I'm Mary Kay Kare," said the woman, who looked to be about ten or twelve years older than me. "I'll be clerking for you this week." Short and blond, she wore a bright yellow cardigan over black slacks and a white shirt, with a string of purple beads around her neck.

"Is it Mrs. Kare or Ms.?"

"Well, it's Mrs., but you can just call me Mary Kay." She was as cheerful as sunshine as she handed me the day's calendar. "Is there anything else you need?"

"A cup of coffee?" I said hopefully.

"Already waiting for you," she said, beaming as she led me downstairs.

Most courthouses are built up. Lafayette

71

County's was built down. Entering at street level got you the usual Register of Deeds, Board of Elections, Clerk of Court, and so on, then the building literally went downhill from there. The lobby outside the two courtrooms on the level below had floor-to-ceiling glass walls that overlooked breathtaking vistas.

The bottom level housed the sheriff's department and county jail, Mrs. Kare told me.

I followed her through a door marked "Official Personnel Only" and down a hallway to an office behind the courtroom I'd be using. An insulated carafe sat on the desk with a business-size mug. "Judge Rawlings drinks coffee all day long, so we're in the habit of keeping it full for him."

She pointed to a tiny refrigerator built into a low bookcase. "There's half-and-half, if you use it."

"I don't, but thanks." A photograph of a chubby middle-aged white man and an equally chubby woman and boy stood on the desk. I thought he looked familiar from various conferences we'd probably attended together, but he wasn't someone I could say I knew. "Is that Judge Rawlings?"

She nodded and her blue eyes misted

over. "Bless his heart, this is the first vacation he's taken since his wife and son died."

"Died?" Startled, I looked again at the photograph, my automatic condescension washed away by the tears in Mary Kay Kare's eyes. Yes, it was a picture of three Teletubbies, but from the way the two adults smiled at each other, the photographer had also captured an aura of love that seemed to wreathe them.

"She was broadsided by a drunk driver two years ago, taking their boy to Little League practice. Guy ran the stop sign. Both of 'em were wearing seat belts, but they were still killed instantly."

"What about the driver?"

"Barely scratched. He'd been cited before, though, so this time it was prosecuted as vehicular homicide and he'll be in prison another few years. What made it so bad for Judge Rawlings is that he's the one that turned the kid loose with community service the last time he was up for DWI. Felt sorry for him. Two weeks later —"

It's a judge's worst nightmare in these days of budget deficits that spawn overcrowded penal institutions and overextended substance abuse programs: balancing the need to protect the community with the need to believe that offenders can reform themselves before they hurt someone else. Rawlings must have spent the last two years replaying his courtroom decision a million times, begging God for just one do-over.

I've been there. I know. God doesn't bargain and He doesn't give do-overs.

According to Mary Kay, I was the only judge hearing cases here today. The calendar held the usual Monday morning assortment of DWIs, assaults, and simple possession of marijuana or drug paraphernalia. From the coast to the mountains, it's the same predictable catalog of minor sins, and when I looked out over the people sitting there on the benches in front of me, it was the same panoply of wary, embarrassed, defiant, or defeated faces, although . . . ?

There was something different about this group, something I couldn't quite put my finger on.

Was it the assistant DA? Most ADAs are young men or women at the beginning of their careers. William Deeck had to be at least fifty and his rumpled blue suit was that of a man who didn't care about looks or labels. He sounded cranky and his facial expression struck me as dour when he stood to call the first case, but I soon realized that there was a twinkle behind his rimless glasses and that he had an exceedingly dry wit. More to the point, he was efficient and single-minded, presenting the state's cases so concisely that we had cleared more than half the day's calendar before the morning break.

I was congratulating myself on probably getting through before three o'clock, when I noticed that the courtroom was starting to fill back up again.

I leaned over and got Mary Kay's attention. "Are there add-ons I don't know about?"

She frowned and hastily rechecked the calendar. "Oh, gosh, yes! A probable cause hearing's scheduled for this morning. I'm so sorry, I don't know how I could have left that off. Oh, gosh!"

"It's okay," I soothed and turned my attention back to the DA, who said, "Call Dava Edwards Triplett."

An elderly attorney stood up and gestured to someone at the back of the courtroom. "Come on up, Dava."

A rabbity-looking white woman with lank blond hair and a gray pallor to her skin came forward and stood beside the attorney at the defense table, and that's when I finally realized that not a single person in this court today was black. Nor did I remember seeing any people of color on Cedar Gap's crowded sidewalks yesterday.

I'd heard that there were very few African-Americans in this part of the Blue Ridge Mountains, and here was confirmation. Although Latinos and Asians are filtering in, the population is still mostly white, still mostly Protestant, and the perception, deserved or not, is that bigotry is alive and well up in the hollows. The mountains have a history of harboring white supremacists and paramilitary separatists — look how bomber Eric Rudolph hid himself from FBI agents and bounty hunters alike for five years down in Cherokee County. More than one fundamentalist, conservative cult flourishes throughout Appalachia, although up in Watauga County there's a seven-thousand-acre transcendental meditation center founded by the Maharishi Mahesh Yogi, so maybe that particular stereotype is breaking down?

"Your Honor," said the DA, "Mrs. Triplett is charged with carrying a concealed weapon."

"How do you plead?" I asked the woman.

"Not guilty, ma'am."

"Proceed," I told the DA.

"Call Detective Fletcher."

The detective was of medium height and weight. Sandy brown hair thinning at the temples; neatly dressed in dark sports jacket, khaki pants, shirt, and blue tie. He came to the witness stand, placed his hand on the Bible, and swore to tell the truth.

"State your name and occupation."

"Glenn Fletcher. I've been a detective with the Lafayette Sheriff's Department for eight years now."

"And where were you on the afternoon of September twenty-fourth?"

"At the home of Mrs. Dava Triplett up near the end of Little Carlton Road."

"Why were you there?"

"We had been told that Mrs. Triplett was running a meth lab and we went up to ask her about it."

"Objection, Your Honor. Hearsay," said defense counsel.

Evidently, he was one of those who thought that every repeated conversation needed an objection, whether or not it pertained to the charges.

"Overruled," I said.

"Did anyone else go there with you?" asked the DA.

"Yes, sir. Sheriff Horton, Officers Mc-Kinley and Adams, and Agent Forrester of the SBI."

"Describe what happened when you got there."

"We knocked on the door, but the house appeared to be empty and there were no cars in the yard. While we were deciding how to proceed, we saw Mrs. Triplett's car slow down like she was going to turn in and then she must've seen us and changed her mind —"

"Objection," said defense counsel. "Calls for an unwarranted conclusion by the witness."

"Sustained," I said.

"What did you see Mrs. Triplett do?" the DA asked.

"I observed her as she drove past her driveway, up to the end of the road, where she turned around and started back down, so I went out and waved to her to stop."

"And did she?"

"Yes, sir. I identified myself and asked her if she was Dava Triplett. She replied that she was and asked if I wanted to see her driver's license. She started to reach over for her purse —"

"Objection. Conclusion."

"Overruled."

"— and I told her to keep her hands on the steering wheel."

"Then what happened?"

"I asked her if she had any weapons in the car?"

"What was her response?"

"She said she had a handgun, so I asked her to step out of the car and put her hands on the roof."

"Then what happened?"

"I asked her where the gun was and she said it was on the seat. I found it down in the crack between the seat and the back, completely covered by her purse. It was a nine-millimeter semiautomatic pistol with a fully loaded magazine."

"You then placed her under arrest?"

"Yes, sir."

"No further questions."

Defense counsel stood. His hair was white, his shoulders slightly stooped, but his voice was strong and confident. "Detective Fletcher, you said that the sheriff's department had been told that Mrs. Triplett was running a meth lab. Was it her ex-boyfriend that told y'all that?"

"I wasn't the one who spoke to the informant, sir, so I don't know."

"You do know, do you not, that he was arrested for possession of drug paraphernalia the day before you went out to Mrs. Triplett's house?"

"Objection," said the DA. "Irrelevant."

"Sustained," I said.

"What was Mrs. Triplett's behavior when you stopped her car? Was she defiant? Uncooperative?"

"No, sir. She was very cooperative."

"You said you went up there to search her house. Did you in fact carry out that search?"

"We did."

"What did you find?"

"We found four one-gallon jugs of anti-freeze and three cans of lantern fuel in the garage and two brand-new Igloo coolers in the trunk of her car."

"Those are items you might find in any garage in Lafayette County. What about all the essential items that go into furnishing a meth lab, Detective? Did you find a case of over-the-counter cold remedies in the house?"

"No, sir."

"Plastic tubing? Clear glass containers? Excessive amounts of drain cleaners? Coffee filters stained red?"

"No, sir."

"In short, all you found were jugs of antifreeze my client bought for her car because it has a leaky radiator and lantern fuel she keeps on hand for when the power goes out. Is that correct?"

"And the two new coolers," the detective said doggedly.

We're all educated these days on what it takes to cook up a batch of methamphetamine, and this woman might well have planned to start her own kitchen lab, a serious problem out here in these hills; but if she'd been at it before, the house would have smelled like the worst litterbox in the world and fumes would have so permeated curtains, carpets, and furniture that air fresheners and window fans would barely dent it. The point was moot though since Mrs. Triplett had not been charged with making meth. She was charged with concealing a weapon.

"Is it not a fact, Detective Fletcher, that when you first stopped Mrs. Triplett and looked through the open window, you actually saw her gun on the seat beside her in plain sight?"

"No, sir."

"Didn't the so-called concealment occur when she tried to extract her driver's license from her pocketbook and inadvertently covered the gun with her pocketbook at that point?"

"No, sir. It was over the gun and the gun was pushed down in the crack of the seat so that only the edge of the handle was visible when I lifted the purse."

"Sheriff Horton, two other officers of your department and an SBI agent were standing in Mrs. Triplett's yard. Is that correct?"

"Yes, sir."

"Were any of them with you at the car when you found the gun?"

"Sheriff Horton came over when he saw her step out of the car, but I had already found the gun by the time he got there."

"So none of your colleagues can corroborate your story?"

"No, sir, not really."

"When did you officially place my client under arrest? As soon as you found the gun or after you *didn't* find a meth lab?"

"Objection," said the DA. "Irrelevant."

"Overruled," I said. "The witness will answer."

"My colleagues were still searching the premises," he said, which was probably technically truthful.

"And just for the record, was Mrs. Triplett's gun properly registered and licensed?"

"Yessir."

"No further questions."

When Mrs. Triplett took the stand, she naturally testified to the same scenario her attorney had laid out: the gun was in plain view on the seat of the car until she unwittingly covered it with her pocketbook. "I never tried to hide it and I told him soon as he asked that I had it." She looked up at me. "It's a real rough neighborhood up there, ma'am. That's why I keep my gun close at hand, right there beside me where anybody can see it and know I'm not afraid to use it if I have to."

In the end, despite the physical signs on her body that she was a likely user, I was left with her word against that of a detective who was probably frustrated that they hadn't found enough evidence to arrest her for the more serious charge.

Unfortunately for Detective Fletcher, wishing doesn't make it so and there wasn't enough evidence nor even simple corroboration. Had I heard this case two weeks ago, I might have given him the benefit of the doubt, but now that I'm engaged to a sheriff's deputy, I know I'm going to have to lean over backward to keep my judgments fair and unbiased.

I nodded to the defense attorney and he and Mrs. Triplett stood to hear my decision.

"I find the defendant not guilty."

"Thank you, ma'am," she said, finally smiling.

"But in the future, Mrs. Triplett, I'd suggest that you keep your purse on the floor and your gun on the dashboard."

"I surely will, ma'am."

"At this time," I said, "the court will recess for fifteen minutes."

"All rise," said the bailiff.

Chapter
6

 I finished drying my hands and had just stepped out of Judge Rawlings's lavatory when Mary Kay stuck her head in the doorway and said, "Could you speak to Mr. Burke and Ms. Delorey?"

"Sure," I said, clueless as to who they might be.

"Judge Knott? I'm Gail Delorey," said the woman, who entered first. She was small and olive-skinned with dark brown hair that she had pulled back and tied with a maroon scarf that matched the thin maroon lines running through her black trouser suit. Her crisp white shirt was man-tailored and her hand was firm when she shook mine. I guessed her age to be mid-forties.

"Lucius Burke," said the man, who followed. "District Attorney here."

A slender man in a charcoal suit and a

blue-and-green tie, Burke's hair was now more salt than pepper, prematurely so, no doubt, since his face was almost wrinkle-free except for nice laugh lines at the corners of the greenest eyes I've ever seen. His handshake was utterly professional, yet I saw those eyes flicker up and down in quick, discreet assessment and I was glad I'd worn my favorite dark red knit dress.

"Welcome to Lafayette County."

"Thank you," I said, automatically noticing that his ring finger was bare.

(*"Yours isn't,"* the preacher reminded me sternly.)

I sat down behind the desk and laid my hands on its shining top, as if Dwight's ring were a shield against speculations and possibilities that were now off-limits to me.

"What can I do for you?" I asked Ms. Delorey.

(*"No ring on her finger either,"* the pragmatist said innocently.)

(*"Oh please,"* said the preacher, who has a built-in shit detector.)

Ms. Delorey exchanged a glance with the DA, then said, "When you go back into court, Mr. Burke will be asking you to find probable cause against my client, who's accused of voluntary manslaughter."

"And?"

"Ms. Delorey thought we ought to warn you that this is a rather high-profile case for this area," said Mr. Burke. (Really, his eyes were the most astonishing green.) "Lots of local interest. There will definitely be reporters and the station down in Howards Ford has sent a cameraman up to cover today's hearing."

I frowned at that.

"You don't allow cameras in your courtrooms?"

"Under no circumstances," I said firmly. I'd allowed it once and watched everyone immediately start playing to the cameras despite my instructions to ignore them. After that, I swore never again.

"What about tape recorders?" asked Ms. Delorey, showing me a tiny voice-activated model.

"Tape recorders are fine," I said, "as long as you don't delay us if the tape runs out or the batteries die."

After instructing the bailiff to announce that I would hold in contempt anyone who tried to use a camera of any description, I returned to the courtroom. As had been predicted, almost every bench was filled.

I took my seat and Mr. Burke rose to state that Daniel Wayne Freeman had been charged with voluntary manslaughter in the death of Dr. Carlyle Grayson Ledwig and that he was asking me to find probable cause to bind Mr. Freeman over for trial in superior court.

Maybe I'm just slow, but until that moment I hadn't connected "high profile" to Dr. Ledwig, yet here was the same young man whose picture I'd seen in the *High Country Courier.*

I opened the folder on the case and read through the rulings made last week at Daniel Freeman's first appearance. An accused's first appearance is the first court day after his arrest on charges that will carry serious prison time or worse if he's convicted. It's when the judge, in this case Judge Rawlings, reviews the warrant for arrest; determines what bond, if any, is appropriate; assures the defendant of his right to counsel if he can't afford to hire one; and sets a date for a probable cause hearing five to fifteen days later so that both the State and the defense will have enough time to prepare.

A probable cause hearing is more formal and more adversarial than the first appearance hearing because it's the proceeding that transfers a case to superior court unless district court — me — finds that there is insufficient cause to continue with the prosecution.

All the paperwork seemed to be in order. I nodded to Ms. Delorey and she and the defendant rose.

"Defense is ready to proceed, Your Honor," she said.

"How is your client pleading?" I asked.

"Not guilty," the young man said firmly, looking me straight in the eye.

He reminded me of some of my younger nephews. A lanky kid barely out of his teens, he had sandy brown hair that curled around his ears, a thin nose between wide-spaced hazel eyes, a deep summer tan, and a teenager's build that hadn't yet thickened into a man's frame. He was well-scrubbed and neatly dressed in a coat and tie, but then he would be, wouldn't he? Even for something as minor as a DWI, very few attorneys let their clients come to court looking like a mud turtle fished out of a drunk tank. First impressions are too important and you don't want to make a judge automatically unsympathetic to your client because he's wearing a kiss-my-ass T-shirt. On the other hand, his clean-cut Mom-and-apple-pie appearance probably wasn't a total sham because his short hair had not been cut short for this occasion.

For some reason, that's something I always notice, especially in summer and fall. I can usually tell when a neck hasn't seen sunshine in months, and this kid's tan went right up under his hairline all around.

His eyes fell as I continued to study him. He might be a killer, but I doubt if he was much of a con artist. Consummate liars can look you straight in the eye till hell freezes over.

I motioned for him to be seated and told Mr. Burke to proceed.

"Call Officer Brian McKinley to the stand."

Officer McKinley came forward, placed his hand on the Bible, and assured Mary Kay he intended to tell the truth, the whole truth, and nothing but the truth.

Both the DA and Ms. Delorey placed their tape recorders on the chest-level rail in front of the witness seat.

In his own words and referring occasionally to his notes, McKinley described how he'd been on regular patrol Thursday afternoon when a call came in at 4:35 that assistance was needed at 7482 Old Needham Road. He was only a mile from that location and he and the ambulance made it at approximately the same time.

Upon arrival, they were met by the defendant, who told them that the owner, Dr. Carlyle Ledwig, had fallen from the deck he was rebuilding. Freeman then led them around the house to a large, multilevel deck that was built out from the rockface to overlook Pritchard Cove. They could see a gap in the deck's temporary railing and Dr. Ledwig's body some thirty feet below, but to get to him, they had to wait another fifteen minutes for the fire and rescue truck to come with ropes and ladders.

"Was there anyone else there? Any family members? Neighbors?"

"No, sir, not on the deck itself. The houses aren't close together up there, but two men who lived next door did come to see what was happening. We advised them to stay clear of the deck. Dr. Ledwig's wife and daughters came home just as they were bringing him up."

"Where was the defendant through all this?" asked Burke.

"He was there on the deck with us."

"Did you observe anything unusual about him?"

"Objection," murmured Ms. Delorey. "Leading."

"Sustained," I said.

"Describe his appearance, please," Burke said.

"He seemed agitated and upset and he kept saying, 'Oh God, what's Carla going to think?' "

"Did you ascertain who Carla was?"

"His girlfriend — Dr. Ledwig's daughter."

"What else did you observe?"

"We had to restrain him from trying to climb down the side of the cliff. He didn't want us to wait for the fire truck. He said he thought there were ropes in Dr. Ledwig's garage and he wanted us to lower one of the ambulance team down to try and save the doctor's life."

"Why didn't you?"

"From the way the decedent was lying, they could tell that he didn't survive the fall. There was really nothing they could do for him at that point, even if they could've climbed down."

"Did the defendant say anything else?"

"He said he knew Dr. Ledwig was replacing some of the decking and the railings and that he'd come up from Howards Ford to help."

"Did he say how long he was there before he saw Dr. Ledwig's body?"

"He said it was only a few minutes. That he rang the bell, and when no one answered he walked around to the deck to see what was being done, looked over the railing and there he was. He said he knelt down and called to the doctor, then ran in the house and called us."

"No further questions."

Ms. Delorey looked over the small wire-rimmed glasses perched on the end of her nose. "Officer McKinley, you said that Mr. Freeman came onto the deck with you to show you where Dr. Ledwig had fallen?"

"Yes, ma'am."

"Does this mean you did not originally consider this a crime scene?"

"I didn't know what it was, ma'am."

"So you did *not* rope off the deck and keep everyone out except yourself and the rescue team?"

"Well, Mr. Freeman had already been there, but I didn't let nobody else come on that part of the deck, no, ma'am."

"No further questions," said Ms. Delorey.

I recessed for lunch at that point and, feeling in the mood for a quick order of chicken fingers, asked Mary Kay for directions to the nearest Hardee's or Chick-fil-A.

"You're kidding, right?"

I looked at her blankly.

"There aren't any fast-food chains in Cedar Gap. Not allowed. Nearest one's down in Howards Ford."

"Not allowed? How can you not allow McDonald's or Burger King?"

She laughed. "There used to be a Tastee-Freez, but it went bust and the town council voted not to allow any more chains in. Generates too much trash and they tend to drive out local cafés. They're not real happy with the Trading Post or Roxie's either because their customers aren't as careful as they ought to be about where they drop their napkins."

"So where do people go for a quick lunch?"

"Well, there's a new place next to the Trading Post. The Three Sisters Tea Room."

"A Russian tea room?" I asked, amused.

She smiled. "No, it's American and it's really good — salads and sandwiches made from bread baked right there in the kitchen every morning, but it's only open from twelve to four and there's always a line, so you might be better off at the High Country Café. It's just on the other side of the monument, about two doors off Main. Their chicken salad's not as good as the Tea Room, but it's not bad and you can usually get a seat."

Her assessment of the chicken salad was

an understatement. It was delicious. If that other place was better, I was going to have to check it out before I left Cedar Gap, long line or not.

I was back in the courtroom at one o'clock sharp.

"Call Detective Glenn Fletcher to the stand," said Burke.

As I watched Detective Fletcher come forward and once more take the oath to tell only the truth, I reminded myself to keep an open mind and not to let my earlier speculations about his willingness to bend the facts color my opinion of his testimony in this case.

What he had to say was fairly straightforward. As is routine in cases of violent or accidental death, he and members of the sheriff's department crime scene team had proceeded to Dr. Ledwig's residence, arriving there shortly after five.

"Mrs. Tina Ledwig and her daughter drove in right behind us."

"Miss Carla Ledwig?"

"No, sir, this was the younger sister, Patricia Ledwig."

Carla Ledwig? The quarter finally dropped. The same Carla that had left a message for the twins to call her?

"What did you do when you arrived?" asked Burke.

"We immediately secured the scene. Mrs. Ledwig was upset and wanted to go over to see what the recovery team was doing."

"You did not let them onto the deck?"

"No, sir."

"But Mr. Freeman continued to be there?"

"No, sir. We moved him outside our tape barrier, too, and our photographer took pictures of the entire scene before recovery began."

"Permission to approach?" asked Burke.

I nodded.

He handed a packet of four-by-six color photographs to Fletcher. "Are these the pictures that were taken on the deck?"

Fletcher did a pro forma flip-through. "Yes, sir."

Burke then handed copies to Ms. Delorey and to me.

Long framing shots captured the whole deck, from a handful of mailers carelessly heaped on a table beside the French doors that opened into the stone house to pots of bronze-colored chrysanthemums ranged along the steps. I saw exposed joists where the old decking had been removed, as well as a section of the railing. New planks were stacked next to a pair of sawhorses, and a circular power saw lay on a piece of wood across the sawhorses. From another angle and well behind the yellow police tape, Freeman stood near an older woman and an adolescent girl — the same older woman who now sat on the front row behind Lucius Burke.

I glanced across the aisle. The two young women seated there in support of Freeman were probably Patricia Ledwig and her sister, Carla. I wasn't sure which was which, though, because they were very similar in looks — same long brown hair, same thin faces.

Two pictures were of a body crumpled on a rocky ledge amid vivid orange and red underbrush. The close-up of Ledwig showed the head at an unnatural angle.

"Explain the photographs numbered five, six, and seven, please."

These were close-ups of the foundation joists, which seemed to run perpendicularly from the house out to the edge of the deck where part of the railing was missing.

"As you see, there is a large patch of blood here on the edge of the joist."

"Did you form a hypothesis as to how the doctor died?"

"Yes, sir."

Looking up at me, Fletcher pointed to the line of new planks that had been nailed to the joists. "It would appear that he had been working near the edge here, probably on his hands and knees. See this can of nails?"

I nodded.

"We think he was struck from the front and fell backward, hitting his head on this first joist and opening the wound that was subsequently found in the autopsy."

The next picture was a close-up of the joist. "This is where we found hair from the doctor's head. Whoever did it then pulled him to the edge and shoved him over, getting smears of blood on the edge of the planks."

Burke directed our attention to photograph number ten. "You are speaking of these smears here on the joist and at the edge of the deck?"

"Yes, sir. If you'll notice, there's also a fingerprint."

"Has the source of that blood been identified?"

"It was the decedent's."

"What about the fingerprint?"

"It was from the defendant's right middle finger."

"Photograph twelve?"

"Those are fibers caught in some splinters at the edge of the deck."

"Did you subsequently identify the source of those fibers?"

"Yes, sir. They came from the decedent's trousers."

"Were these photographs taken before or after Dr. Ledwig's body was retrieved?"

"Before."

"You're quite clear on that?"

"Yes, sir. As you can see, the photographs are time-dated. I believe you have photographs taken when the body was being lifted up and you can see that the time is several minutes later. The fibers and blood were photographed before we brought the body up."

"Describe photograph eighteen, if you would. What are we looking at there?"

Fletcher dutifully shuffled through the pile while Ms. Delorey and I did the same. It showed the reddish brown imprint of a diamond and two indistinct lines on the decking. I'd looked at enough shoe tracks in the last month to realize these were the tread marks of someone's sneaker. And guess who was the only one on that deck wearing sneakers with those marks?

You got it.

Further questioning revealed that it was

the blood on the joist that made them question whether the doctor had fallen accidentally. Dr. Ledwig had spoken by phone to a colleague at the clinic at 2:15. Freeman's 911 call was logged at 4:37. The autopsy confirmed that Ledwig had indeed died during that time period, but when the autopsy also showed that the fatal head wound had probably been administered with a hammer, deputies had gone back to the ravine and searched until they found it. Blood and hair from the doctor's head were still on the hammer.

Finally, in addition to the traces on the soles of his sneakers and his fingerprint on the edge of the deck, a smear of the doctor's blood was also found on the young man's jeans.

Each separate thing could be explained away by a skillful attorney, and when it was her turn, Ms. Delorey proved to be just that. She suggested that the young man's actions were the natural actions of a close friend of the family. Of course there was blood on the soles of his shoes. He had come to help his girlfriend's father work on the deck. When the doctor didn't answer the door, he'd walked around to the back, and yes, he'd crossed the deck to see how the repairs were coming. He hadn't noticed the blood on the edge of the planks and walked right through it. And when he saw the body and knelt down to call to the doctor, he'd knelt in blood and accidentally got some on his fingers.

"Couldn't all that be true, Detective Fletcher?"

"Yes, ma'am," he agreed.

"The blood on my client's pantleg. Was it a smear or a spatter?"

"It appeared to be a smear."

"But if he'd hit the doctor with a hammer, wouldn't he have been spattered with some of the blood?"

"Not necessarily, ma'am."

"When the hammer was found, was it tested for fingerprints?"

"Yes, ma'am."

"Were any found?"

"Only the decedent's, ma'am."

"He hit himself?"

"No, ma'am. The handle is made of a spongy black rubber with so many tiny holes that it didn't yield fingerprints. The prints we found were on the shaft and head."

"So no fingerprints of my client on the hammer, no spatters on my client's clothes, which would have happened if he'd been the one to use that hammer —"

"Objection," said Burke. "Is counsel asserting that she's an expert in blood spatters?"

"Withdrawn," said Delorey.

She had made a plausible explanation for the blood, but what couldn't be explained away was the rest of Fletcher's testimony. The statements he had taken from the various participants that evening and the next morning made it quite clear that Daniel Freeman had not gone to the Ledwig home to help repair the deck. He had gone to try and change the ultimatum the doctor had laid down to Freeman and his daughter when they told him she was pregnant and that they wanted to marry immediately.

Over his dead body, Ledwig had reportedly said. He told them he would arrange for an abortion and ordered her never to see the baby's father again. If she refused to comply, he would see to it that Freeman's scholarship at Fletcher-MacLeod was revoked. He would also cut her allowance immediately, stop paying her tuition, and would forbid her to come to the house or to see her younger sister for so long as the younger daughter expected his support.

Now, young women have been getting

pregnant without benefit of clergy for as long as the world has been turning, and fathers have been angry and threatened to kill the man or kick out the daughter for just as long, but in this day and age? When illegitimacy carries few social stigmas in most circles beyond a shrug and a sheepish smile? It puzzled me that a man of Dr. Ledwig's presumed intelligence and education would try to employ heavy-handed patriarchal power instead of psychology and common sense.

All of the statements Fletcher had taken were evasive about the reasons for the doctor's opposition to Freeman until he read aloud Freeman's statement taken Friday afternoon. " 'I told Dr. Ledwig that if my racial designation bothered him so much, I'd change it to white and the baby could go down as white, too, and he said that there'd never been a drop of nigger blood in his family and he'd be damned if it was going to start with his first grandchild.' "

I wasn't the only one whose eyes automatically swung to Daniel Freeman in fresh appraisal of his brown hair, his hazel eyes, his summer tan as Fletcher continued reading from the young man's statement.

" 'Yes, it made me mad, and yes, I wanted to punch him out, but I didn't.

103

And I didn't go out there yesterday to pick a fight. I thought maybe if he'd had time to calm down, I could make him see how stupid this whole race thing is. But when I got there, he was already down on the rocks, and no, I did not hit him with the hammer or push him off the deck.' "

I understood now why Burke had decided to go for voluntary manslaughter instead of murder. Murder, especially murder in the first degree, requires strong elements of hatred and premeditation — the classic "malice aforethought" so dear to television cop shows. Voluntary manslaughter places partial blame on the victim, who inflames the passions of his killer, who then kills in the heat of the moment.

Ms. Delorey did not put her client on the stand, but in her closing argument to me, she insisted that Dr. Ledwig's words were not enough to goad her client into killing.

Mr. Burke made a more convincing argument that they were.

"The State is not insisting that Mr. Freeman is a cold-blooded murderer, Your Honor. He's a good student, has never before been arrested, never even had a speeding ticket, but when Dr. Ledwig demanded that his daughter abort their child, effectively murdering their baby, when Dr. Ledwig taunted him and called him a *nigger,* the worst insult a white man can hurl at a man of African descent, Mr. Freeman lost it. He grabbed up that hammer and he struck his tormentor down; then, no doubt appalled by what he'd done, he pushed Dr. Ledwig over the edge of the deck, hoping that the fall would cover up the wound."

I found that there was indeed probable cause to bind Mr. Freeman over for trial in superior court and continued his bail at the twenty-five thousand Judge Rawlings had thought sufficient.

It was almost four o'clock, but with ADA William Deeck back at the prosecutor's table, we got through all the rest of the items on the calendar before I adjourned for the day.

Chapter 7

The twins had left me a note — *Back between 11 and 12 and we'll bring supper. XXX*
I guess they thought a greasy late-night snack would make up for the dirty coffee mugs and sticky smears I found on the dining table when I let myself into the condo and eased the strap of my laptop off my weary shoulder onto the only clean corner of the table.

As a Luddite friend keeps reminding me, a pad and pencil only weigh about six ounces; my laptop weighs seven pounds and felt like seventy that last flight of steps. Yeah, yeah, I could have left it locked in Rawlings's office at the courthouse, but I wanted to check my e-mail, something I hadn't had a chance to do all day and something that can't be done with a pad and pencil.

I put the dirty mugs and sugar-encrusted spoons in the dishwasher, wiped down the table, and plugged my modem cord into the kitchen phone jack. One of these days I'm going to look into wireless communication, but for now, I keep a twenty-five-foot phone cord in my laptop case.

Along with offers of Viagra, penile implants, breast enlargement, pornographic photographs, free septic tank inspections, and the opportunity to help a general's son fleece the Nigerian government of several million dollars, I found messages from Portland, my sole attendant if the wedding actually came off ("The way this baby's kicking I don't think I'm going to last till December. What about Halloween?"), from my cousin Beverly ("Forgot to tell you that there's no garbage pickup. You'll have to use the county's waste site on Ridge Road."), and a one-liner from Dwight ("You get there okay?").

I had my finger poised over the delete button for a message entitled "Want to party?" when I noticed that the unfamiliar sender had an *NC.rr.com* in the server tag. It was a woman Will had brought to one of the weekly family music sessions we hold at a cousin's barbecue house out near the farm. So many of us play the fiddle, guitar, banjo, or harmonica that even though none of us go every single week, there're usually at least six or eight who show up after Wednesday night choir practice or prayer meeting to eat barbecue, play and sing the old songs, or, as Haywood puts it, just fellowship together.

Your brother Will says you're up here alone this week? I know this isn't much notice, but we're having a party tonight and would love to have you join us. You probably don't remember us, but Will invited us to sit in with y'all when we were down in the Raleigh area last winter. (My husband Bobby has a big walrus mustache and plays guitar and harmonica. I don't have a mustache, but I do play the fiddle.)

Joyce Ashe

As soon as I read her description of her husband, I remembered who they were — early fifties, pleasant. They laughed at our jokes and slid right into the music with no fuss. I did notice that they were better dressed than we were, though. Nothing flashy. Their jeans and loafers were almost as worn as ours, but theirs had come with designer names and upscale brands; and their instruments were quality models, not the pawnshop finds that most of ours were. Will said they were down for one of his estate sales in Raleigh and I'd wondered at the time what his motive was in bringing them out to the country.

With Will, there's usually a motive.

He's three brothers up from me, the oldest of my mother's four children, and he's usually got a spare ace or three tucked in his sock or up his sleeve. A fast talker in both senses, Will earns a decent living as an auctioneer and appraiser, two callings that allow him to set his own hours; and although he knows how houses are put together and taken apart, which is why I let him supervise the building of my house, he's much more interested in the market value of a house's contents. He has Mother's charm and Daddy's streak of lawlessness. Everybody likes Will as long as they're not the ones he's messing over. It was not like him to be concerned about whether or not I had a social life while I was up here in the mountains, so he probably had an ulterior motive for strengthening the ties between the Ashes and himself.

Nevertheless, I *was* at loose ends this evening and I've always been up for a party.

"Wonderful!" said Joyce Ashe when I called the number she'd included in her e-mail. "We're up so many twisty roads you'd never find us. Why don't I have somebody pick you up? Say seven-thirty?"

"That'll be fine," I agreed and told her where I was staying.

"Casual dress and — hey! You didn't happen to bring your guitar, did you?"

"Actually, I did." There was a tricky chord change on a song I was learning and I'd stuck it in the trunk of my car thinking I'd get a chance to work it out. "Does this mean there'll be playing tonight?"

She laughed. "Always. Unless you want to sing for your supper?"

Dogs don't exactly howl when I open my mouth, but I'd as soon play Beethoven sonatas on the spoons as sing alone in front of strangers.

"Miss Deborah?" asked the man who knocked on my door an hour later. "I'm William Edward Johnson. Miss Joyce said you could use a lift out to their place?"

My driver proved to be a tubby little man pushing seventy-five like it was fifty. With his gray tie and black pants and a black vest buttoned over a long-sleeved maroon shirt, he looked like management.

But his cowhide work boots and the tufts of gray hair that curled up around the edges of a grease-stained Ford Motors ball cap suggested he might be the help.

A classic BMW convertible idled in the drive. The top was down and the creamy leather seats gleamed beneath the streetlight. Cool ride, right? Did I mention that the fenders were dented, the paint was chipped, the upholstery was in tatters, and the motor roared like a Mack truck?

"This is very kind of you, Mr. Johnson," I said and handed him my guitar case while he held the car door for me.

"Aw, call me Billy Ed," he said, slinging my guitar into the backseat. "And I guess you're Miss Debbie, right?"

"Wrong. Sorry. It's either Deborah or hey you."

Before I could get my seat belt fastened, he was peeling rubber, headed down that steep drive like a downhill skier trying to make time to the first slalom. The rear end fishtailed slightly as he braked and then made an immediate left turn to head up Main Street away from the center of town. He seemed totally oblivious to the people he'd cut off, just gunned on up the hill for about three miles, before making another left.

My hair kept whipping all around my face in the cool night air and Billy Ed glanced over. "Want me to stop and put up the top, Miss Deborah?"

"No," I said. "I love it."

"Good, 'cause the top's so tore, wouldn't do us much good anyhow." He reached under the seat and handed me a slightly cleaner ball cap.

With one hand on the steering wheel, the other fumbled to extract a cigarette from a crumpled pack.

I held my breath as he touched the glowing lighter to the tip of his cigarette, then returned the lighter to its hole, all the while negotiating a road that twisted worse than a black snake climbing a light pole. Every time we met a car from the opposite direction, I was uncomfortably aware that the road had no guardrails and that the narrow shoulders seemed to drop off into a dark abyss, despite the moon that was trying to break through some thin clouds.

"Dim your Gee-dee lights!" Billy Ed shouted when he brushed by a large vehicle with its headlights on high.

The other car was barely moving and its brake lights lit up the night.

"Turons!" he said derisively as he shifted

gears. "Know how you can tell tourists from the natives?"

"No."

"By the smell of their burnt-out brakes. Ought not to be allowed out at night, scared as they are."

I was glad he couldn't see my white knuckles.

"So how you know Miss Joyce and Bobby?" he asked above the roar of the motor.

"My brother introduced them to me, but I don't really know them," I said, leaning toward him to counterbalance the centrifugal force that wanted to sling me out of the car as he cornered sharply. "What about you?"

"I took on their old house up on the other side of the ridge about four or five years ago."

"Oh?"

"Yeah, their kids were grown and they wanted something smaller, closer to their work."

"What sort of work do they do?"

"Real estate. Property management. They have exclusive rights to Pritchard Cove."

"Pritchard Cove? Isn't that where Dr. Ledwig lived?"

"Ledwig?" He snorted. "Nope. I did hear tell he wanted to dynamite it off the face of the mountain, though."

"Why?" Not that I cared, but anything to distract me from this headlong hurtle into hell. "What *is* Pritchard Cove anyhow?"

"Well, some folks would say it's the best-planned community in the Blue Ridge Mountains. Others like Ledwig'll tell you it's a desecration of unspoiled land. Pritchard Cove was a mote in his eye. And not a teeny-tiny little mote either — it was a Gee-dee two-by-four beam. Wrecked his view."

I thought back to the pictures I'd seen in court today. Admittedly, the focus was on the deck and on the victim's body, not the view from that deck, but I couldn't remember seeing anything except a long vista of colorful treetops and I said as much.

"Well-planned," Billy Ed said again. "The houses were designed to blend into the shape of the land. Most of the trees weren't touched, and even when the leaves drop off it's hard to see 'em 'cause their covenant prohibits big grassy lawns. 'Course now, the houses *are* there and if you look hard enough —"

"I take it Dr. Ledwig looked?"

"With a magnifying glass."

By now we had made so many turns, there was no way I could have found my way back to Cedar Gap. All the turns ran together, except that each was onto a narrower road, until we finally pulled into a long graveled driveway that ran up a steep grade between trees that met overhead. We circled a thicket of hemlocks, then the ground abruptly leveled and the drive broadened into a huge circle of gravel in front of a long low house built of rough gray stones. From Jeeps and pickups to a couple of Land Rovers and one bright yellow Hummer, at least forty vehicles were parked beneath the trees.

The gravel drive turned to flagstones that led directly to a massive wooden door that stood ajar so that anyone could walk in. We passed through a large reception room, where the entire opposite wall was nothing but glass that looked out into the dark night. To one side was a three-foot-tall pottery jar filled with long branches of bright orange bittersweet berries. Overstuffed couches and chairs were clumped in conversational groupings before a stone wall with a fireplace spacious enough to roast an ox. A log fire snapped and crackled on the hearth. Above it hung a big

115

oil painting that looked like it could be a Bob Timberlake original. It pictured an old-fashioned kitchen table during jam-making — gleaming jars of jellied fruit capped with squares of colorful calico, a copper kettle and ladle, and an earthen-ware bowl of luscious blackberries awaiting their turn in the kettle.

An oversize quilting frame and several chairs stood in front of the windows and a brilliant king-size patchwork quilt was a work in progress. Beautiful hand-thrown mountain pottery glowed beneath individual baby spotlights in the ceiling.

More patchwork quilts were draped over the backs of the couches, and I had an impression of space and rustic luxury. If this was the "smaller place" the Ashes had bought when they downsized, how big was their previous house that Billy Ed "took on"?

There was no time to speculate, though. This level was empty, and Billy Ed was already disappearing with my guitar case down a flight of iron and stone steps at the end of the room, so I hurried after him.

Like the courthouse back in town, the Ashes' house was built down the side of a mountain. I saw another large room almost identical to the one above, complete with stone fireplace and a cheerful fire, except that here the wall of glass was punctuated with French doors that opened onto a wide stone terrace, and the painting over the fireplace was a romantic mountain vista. Unlike the first, this level buzzed with laughter, talk, the clink of silverware against plates, and the tinkle of ice in a variety of glasses. I smelled hot yeast rolls and the aroma of something savory that probably came from the copper chafing dishes on the loaded buffet table in the middle of the room. A bar backed onto the staircase and seemed to be better stocked than some I'd seen in restaurants. Two white-jacketed Latinos were busily filling drink orders.

As I paused near the bottom of the steps, my hostess detached herself from a group and came over with outstretched hands and a welcoming smile. "*So* pleased you could come, Judge Knott! Love your hat!"

"Call me Deborah," I said, belatedly remembering that I was still wearing the grimy cap Billy Ed had handed me in the car. I pulled it off, laughed at the raunchy logo, which I hadn't noticed before, and stuffed it into my shoulder bag. At least my jeans, white broadcloth shirt, and red wool cardigan were in sync with what everyone else here was wearing. "Thank you for inviting me."

"Not at all. Let's get you a drink and then come meet some of your colleagues."

Joyce Ashe was as I'd remembered her: an easygoing, big-boned woman carrying about twenty-five extra pounds and comfortable with it. She had one of the bartenders build me a Bloody Mary (I hadn't eaten anything since my chicken salad at noon and Bloody Marys always feel like food), refreshed her own bourbon and branch, then led me over to a group warming themselves by the fireplace.

"I hear you already know Lucius Burke," she said as the circle opened to admit us.

"Yes," I said, taking the hand the district attorney offered and trying not to fall into those incredible green eyes. The names of the two attorneys and someone who owned a ski lodge just on the other side of the Tennessee border went in one ear and out the other. To cover my lapse, I moved closer to the hearth to examine the picture. According to the little brass plate attached to the simple wood frame, it had been painted in 1903 by an artist named Genevieve Carlton. I read the title out loud: "*In Nature's Realm.*"

Joyce Ashe laughed. "Well, that's what

the artist called it. Bobby and I call it *The Mountains of Florida*."

I looked at the painting with renewed interest. "I didn't know Florida had any mountains," I said, stepping right into it.

"Oh, Lord, yes! Florida's got beautiful mountains." She paused two beats. "They just happen to lie in North Carolina."

I still didn't get it.

"Floridians think they own our mountains," the fortyish attorney — Liz Peters? — explained with a kindly smile.

"*Think?*" said a jovial silver-haired man who'd come up behind me. He was accompanied by a tall, heavyset man who sported a thick bushy mustache — Bobby Ashe. "There's no think about it, Liz darlin'. Joyce and Bobby and me, we've personally sold about half of Lafayette County to 'em, so damn straight they own our mountains, right, Bobby?"

Bobby Ashe hoisted his glass to the man and grinned broadly. "I never argue with a partner."

"Partner?" asked Ms. Peters, raising her eyebrows in surprise.

"Yep," said Bobby Ashe. He put one arm around Joyce, the other around the man. "It took us two months to hammer out the details, but we signed the last of the papers last week. You're looking at all three partners of the newly formed Osborne-Ashe High Country Realty."

"Wow!" said the young male attorney whose name hadn't registered on me.

"Wow is right," said Liz Peters, looking impressed.

"Congratulations," said Lucius Burke. He turned to me with a smile. "I may have to get you to refresh my memory on the statutes governing monopolies, though. Between 'em, they probably account for seventy percent of the property sales in this county."

"More like eighty," said the silver-haired man, giving me a puzzled look. "Have we met? You a new attorney here?"

"This is Judge Knott," said Bobby Ashe, flashing me a welcome smile. "She's sitting in for Tim Rawlings while he's down east on a fishing trip."

"Norman Osborne," said the man. "Nice to meet you, Judge."

"My pleasure. And please. Tonight, I'm just Deborah."

"Lucius tells us you found the kid that killed Carlyle Ledwig guilty today," said Joyce.

"Not guilty," Burke and I said together. I smiled at him and explained to the rest that all I'd done was find probable cause to bind that young man over for trial in superior court.

"Same thing, isn't it?" asked Norman Osborne.

"I hope so," said Burke.

I shook my head. "Not necessarily. He's still innocent until declared guilty by a jury of his peers."

"Gonna be hard to find one of those up here," Liz Peters said tartly.

Chapter
8

 "Oh, come on, Liz," said Joyce Ashe. "You'll have Deborah thinking we're nothing but a bunch of hillbilly ridge runners with a Klan robe in every closet."

"Just stating the obvious," said the unrepentant attorney.

As a district court judge who will never sit on a murder trial, and a flatlander to boot, I didn't have a dog in this fight. From here on, Freeman's guilt or innocence would play out in superior court. Nevertheless, I couldn't resist asking as innocently as possible, "What's the problem? Aren't there plenty of educated young people in your jury pool?"

"I'm not talking age or education," she said. "I'm talking race. You find me twelve black people in Cedar Gap and I'll send a donation to the Lafayette County Republican Party in your name."

I held up my hands in mock horror. "Not in *my* name you won't."

The others rolled their eyes and Bobby Ashe grinned at his wife. "Where'd you stash Liz's soapbox, honey?"

"I'm with Judge Knott on this," said the younger male attorney. Dotson? Dodson? "What's the problem? Hell, Freeman's just about as white as anybody around."

I couldn't quite place his accent but clearly it hadn't been formed in North Carolina.

"Speak for yourself, Matt Dodson," said the woman who had joined us a moment earlier. Mid-forties, tall and tan, with sunbleached blond hair, she had the healthy outdoor look of someone who ate six servings of fruits and vegetables a day and played at least two sets of tennis or nine holes of golf every morning. From the proprietary way she tucked her arm through Norman Osborne's, I gathered that she was Mrs. Osborne.

"I *am* speaking for myself," said Dodson. "Look at me."

We did. Black curly hair, warm brown eyes, deep olive skin.

Mrs. Osborne waved her hand impatiently. "Don't be silly, Matt. Your skin

123

may be a little dark, but you know you're Caucasian."

"I'm also Spanish. At least my mother is. Matt isn't short for Matthew. I was christened Matteo. And the Moors of North Africa were all over Spain. You think for one minute my family didn't mix it up with a few blackamoors along the way?"

"Well, now, if you're gonna go back hundreds of years," said Joyce Ashe, "we're all out of Africa originally, right?"

"Not if you believe the Bible, darlin'." Norman Osborne's grin implied that he didn't necessarily. "The Garden of Eden was in Iraq. Mesopotamia, not Africa."

I gave a mental groan. Surely I hadn't risked my life with a maniac driver just to spend yet another evening debating evolution and creationism?

Fortunately, Liz Peters wasn't that easily sidetracked. "Whether he's mostly white, Chinese, or Mesopotamian, the fact remains that Daniel Freeman calls himself an African-American, and there are precious few in Lafayette County."

"Not my fault if they don't want to live here," Bobby Ashe said. "Joyce and me, we don't care about the color of any client's skin, long as their money's green."

"Have you sold a single house in Pritchard Cove to any blacks?"

"As a matter of fact, we did. Remember the Gibsons?"

"Oh right." Her voice dripped with sarcasm. "One season fighting those damn flamingos, then they gave up and bought a place outside Asheville."

"Flamingos?" I asked.

Joyce Ashe shrugged her ample shoulders. "Someone kept planting plastic flamingos along their drive and —"

"Every lawn jockey isn't in the shape of a pickaninny," said Liz Peters.

"It was a joke, Liz. Not a good joke, but not racist."

"Some things aren't funny if you're on the receiving end," she snapped. Turning to me, she explained: "The implication was that the Gibsons were black Florida trash and didn't belong in Pritchard Cove with white Floridians."

"Floridiots!" said a short bald man, who'd been listening silently. "They can all go to hell."

"Bite your tongue, Tysinger," said Osborne. "They're our bread and butter."

"Yours maybe, not mine," he growled.

"What do you have against Floridians?" I asked.

"I'm sorry," said Joyce. "Deborah, this is

Sam Tysinger. And you didn't meet Sunny Osborne either."

Mrs. Osborne and I nodded to each other and murmured politely, but I was curious about Sam Tysinger's attitude. "What's wrong with Floridians?"

"Depends on whether they're seasonal or tourists," he said.

"Isn't that the same thing?"

"Lord, no, child!" said Sunny Osborne. "Seasonal people have wealth and education. They buy expensive second homes here and that gives them a vested interest in preserving and maintaining our community. Tourists merely come to have fun and don't care how much they trash up the place because they'll be gone in a week."

Sam Tysinger snorted. "At least the tourists spend money. Seasonal people just drive up everybody's property taxes, and don't add a damn thing to the local economy except for real estate commissions and cluttering up the ridges."

"Of course they contribute," said Bobby Ashe, stroking his outsize mustache. "We wouldn't have such a large office staff without them."

"That's right," his wife chimed in. "We hire people to clean their houses, take care of the yards —"

"Minimum-wage crap," the little man said scornfully. "And even that dries up during the off-season." He took a swallow of the drink in his hand and said to me, "Seasonal people want to pull up the drawbridge as soon as they've got their piece of a mountain. They want to live in a quaint little old-timey setting. Stop development. Turn back the clock. They'd like it if the roads weren't paved so the tourists would be discouraged from coming."

"Quilt and jelly. Quilt and jelly," said a stylish older woman who'd turned to us from a nearby conversation. "They think that's all we mountain women do. Quilt and jelly. I was having my nails done back in the summer and some woman at the next station wanted to know where I went to pick blackberries because she wanted to make herself some authentic mountain jam. I was the only local in the shop at the time and I guess she heard my accent." Her exasperation gave way to a nostalgic smile. "I sent her down to Potter's Bottom, where the chiggers and the mosquitoes are thick as fleas on a hound dog. Gave her a *real* sample of authentic mountain life."

"Now wait a minute," Sunny Osborne objected. "There're always going to be those who think we're dumb because we speak with a twang, but most of them want second homes here because they love it. And a lot of them give as much as they take. They contribute to the library and to the hospital and —"

"Things they use," Tysinger said with a cynical snort. "They don't want any kind of industry here. There's almost nothing for the young people. And —"

"And I say it's time we stopped boring Deborah to death," said Joyce. "She doesn't want to hear this."

Matt Dodson shrugged. "All I'm saying is, Freeman probably has less Negro blood than me, so why did Dr. Ledwig get so bent out of shape over it?"

"Probably because you don't want to marry his daughter," Sunny Osborne said.

"And you're not carrying a flag," said Lucius Burke. "Freeman could just as easily call himself Native American or white — according to his statement, he's descended from them on both sides, but by calling himself black he hopes to make people question what it really means to be black. He says he wants to make all racial designations irrelevant."

"Sounds like a good idea to me," said Liz Peters. "I don't know why we still have them anyhow. Whenever I have to check off my race, I always check 'other.' "

I laughed. "Me too."

Bobby Ashe frowned. "But aren't there legitimate reasons for people to know what race you are? Entitlement programs? Or what about medical reasons? Sickle-cell anemia, for instance?"

Sam Tysinger gave him a sardonic look. "And every Jew should write down his religion in case he develops Tay-Sachs?"

"I don't think Dr. Ledwig was worried about sickle-cell anemia, or Tay-Sachs either," said Liz Peters. "He was a bigot, pure and simple."

"You're bad-mouthing a good man who's not here tonight to defend himself," Norman Osborne protested. "Look at all the good he's done for Cedar Gap. The hospital. The geriatrics clinic. He's building a new senior center, too."

"Another one?" asked Tysinger with a puzzled look on his face.

"He's building *onto* the new senior center," said Mrs. Osborne. "At least that's what we hear that his will provides, but maybe we're speaking out of turn till everything's probated, right, honey?"

She squeezed his arm and he patted her hand affectionately.

"Right you are, darlin'." He gave a rueful

smile. "Always opening my mouth at the wrong time."

"Ah, Sam's still mad because Carlyle got the planning board to rule against his sign," said Lucius Burke.

"Oh, for heaven's sake," said Joyce Ashe. "Come on, Deborah. If they're going to start rehashing that, let me introduce you to some people with more interesting things on their minds."

"What was that about a sign?" I asked as we filled our plates at the buffet table a few minutes later.

"Sam owns several gem mine attractions around the county."

"Really?" I couldn't help smiling. I still have the little half-carat ruby I'd found in my bucket of mine tailings when Mother and Aunt Zell and I tried our luck at "mining" for gemstones. It cost Daddy more than it was worth to have it cut and set in a silver ring that we gave Mother for her birthday and which came back to me at her death, but I treasure its associations and said so.

"They're popular with the tourists," Joyce agreed, "but some of the seasonal people think they're tacky. They were grandfathered in when the new land use rules took effect, but Sam had a big ol' ramshackle billboard right where this one Florida man had to look at it every time he drove out of his driveway. Sam couldn't prove the man helped that sign fall down during a thunderstorm this summer, but it's a fact that the man did make a big donation to the hospital's building fund, and permission to put a big one back was denied. Now, you be sure and get you some of this chopped broccoli and raisin salad. I don't know what the caterer puts in her dressing, but it's delicious."

I followed in Joyce's wake as she worked the room, introducing me to several people along the way. It could have been a meeting of the Cedar Gap Chamber of Commerce. By the time we got out to the terrace, I had exchanged names with the owners or managers of most of the stores along Main Street. I had also met a dean from Tanser-MacLeod College who vaguely remembered the twins, the owner of an independent bluegrass label, and a heart surgeon from Long Island who was considering a second home that was listed by the newly formed Osborne-Ashe High Country Realty.

"See?" said Joyce, as we moved on. "Not all the seasonal people are from Florida."

As we approached the edge of the terrace, she was called back inside by one of the white-jacketed servers to attend to a minor domestic crisis. Most of the nearby tables were taken by people who were already in deep conversation with one another, so I set my plate on the wide wooden railing and looked out over the tops of descending trees that were a hazy blue in the moonlight.

"Enjoyin' the view?" drawled a voice behind me.

"It's lovely," I said, smiling up at Norman Osborne, who joined me with a drink in his hand. "Do you ever get tired of it?"

"Never. It's not just about buying and selling either."

"There's gold in them thar hills?"

"There is. No denying that, but these hills are like the seashores. They belong to everybody in the United States and it's up to us to develop smartly so we can preserve it for the generations to come."

I must have given an unladylike snort because he grinned and said, "We don't talk about it, Ledwig and me, but for every acre we've developed, we've put an equal parcel into the land conservancy."

"You must really miss him," I said.

"Who?"

"Dr. Ledwig. His death must have been a huge blow."

He looked out over the vista for a long silent minute while the party went on noisily around us, then glanced at me with a rueful smile. "Sorry, but I didn't quite catch your name."

"Judge Knott," I said. "Deborah Knott."

"From?"

"Over in Colleton County."

"Knott? Colleton County? You wouldn't happen to be kin to a man down there named Kezzie Knott, would you?"

"My father," I said, already knowing where this was going.

"Really? I'll be damned!" He chuckled. "And you a judge!"

He wasn't the first one to find it amusing that the man who'd once run the biggest bootlegging operation in eastern North Carolina had sired a judge for a daughter.

"Don't worry, darlin', your secret's safe with me."

I shrugged. It wasn't something to brag about, but nothing I'd ever tried to hide either. Waste of time anyhow. Be like trying to hide a mule in a petunia patch.

"Naw, it's okay," Osborne insisted. "See, my daddy used to have his own little 'still on a hill.' " A grin split his face as he softly sang the rest of the verse:

". . . where he runs him a gallon or two.
The crows in the sky
Git so drunk they cain't fly
From that good ol' mountain dew."

"Norman?" Sunny Osborne suddenly appeared at his side and laid a suntanned hand heavy with gold and diamond rings on his arm. "I wondered where you'd got to."

"Darlin', meet Judge Deborah Knott. She's Kezzie Knott's daughter."

She pushed back a strand of straw-colored hair and smiled at me. "I'm sorry. Who's Kezzie Knott?"

"You don't mind if I tell her, do you?" he asked.

"Not at all," I murmured.

"He was like my daddy," said Osborne. "Bad for making his own whiskey. Only my daddy kept it local and hers ran it from Florida to Canada. Or so they say."

"Or so they say," I agreed.

"How interesting," she said, eyeing my plate on the railing. "That looks delicious. I came to see if you were ready to eat, too, honey?"

"Sure," he said. "Good talking to you, ma'am."

As they walked away, I saw Osborne pull a small notebook from an inner pocket of his jacket and pause to scribble something.

Billy Ed came over to me then. "See any lights?" he asked.

I pointed with the forkful of broccoli salad that had been on its way to my mouth. "You mean that's Pritchard Cove down there?"

"Yep."

I looked closely and, sure enough, a scattering of lights could be seen through the trees.

"Where is the Ledwig house?"

He pointed off to the left. "You can't really see it from here. See that outcropping of rock? It's just on the other side."

"On the same road as this house?"

"Old Needham? Yep. Old Needham, new money. They oughta rename it Millionaire Row. Miss Joyce and Bobby here. The Ledwigs up there. The Osbornes a quarter mile on above them."

"And your house?"

"Oh, I'm on the other side of the ridge heading down toward Bedford."

He lit a fresh cigarette from the tip of the old one and inhaled deeply. "Yep, Ledwig did everything except move heaven and earth to keep the cove from being developed, but the developer got his permits in under the wire before Ledwig could get to the county commissioners."

I sampled a bit of the risotto Joyce had spooned onto my plate and looked at the tubby little man in the grimy ball cap, tie, and vest. "You wouldn't happen to be that developer, would you?"

"Yep." He grinned and handed me his card. "Be proud to show you around anytime you like."

Chapter
9

 By the time folks finished with food and were ready for music, I had circulated enough to have a fairly good sense of the late Carlyle Ledwig's standing in the community.

At least his standing in the local business community.

Everyone seemed to know that I'd conducted his killer's preliminary hearing, and they wanted to tell me how much they applauded my finding.

"I do feel sorry for his daughter, though," said one older woman, who recalled selling me the topaz necklace I'd fallen for the afternoon before. "To have your boyfriend kill your daddy? Poor Dr. Ledwig. He was such a fine Christian man."

"And so good with old folks." Her elderly tablemate nodded in agreement.

"When my Henry got Alzheimer's, Dr. Ledwig spotted it right away. Told us what to expect during every stage and helped us get him into a decent nursing home when the time came. I do hope they find someone who'll continue his ministry in geriatrics, because my time's surely coming."

"He was always looking what was good for the county," said the owner of a lumberyard between Cedar Gap and Howards Ford. "A lot of tree-huggers care more about woodpeckers or snail-darters than the families who've been trying to scrabble out a living in these hills for two hundred years. He was real open-minded about development, 'specially if it was clean and meant jobs for blue-collar workmen. Look at how he fought for KinderKuntry's easement."

"KinderKuntry?" I remembered the cutesy name from a week I'd spent in High Point during the spring furniture market last year.

Misunderstanding my interest, the lumberyard owner explained that the company made wooden tables and chairs for schools and day care centers. "They ship all over the country and employ about thirty workers full-time."

"I did hear Dr. Ledwig wasn't happy

about Pritchard Cove," I said.

"Well, maybe not at first. Not with it coming in right under his nose, but once it was finished and he saw how unintrusive smart growth could be when it was done right, he stopped automatically saying no the minute something new was proposed."

"Yeah?" someone else said cynically. "Try getting a testimonial about his open mind from Ten Star."

"Come on, now, bo. You're not going to say an asphalt company's as environmentally friendly as a gated community, are you?"

"Gives more year-round jobs," the other said stubbornly.

"Yeah, but look at what it does to our air and water. You want to live next to something spitting out more than twenty known toxic pollutants?"

When they moved into EPA guidelines and federal restrictions, I moved on.

I heard a couple of covert racist slurs against Daniel Freeman and blacks in general, but overall, people acted surprised that a basically decent man like Ledwig should be such a bigot as to goad a black man into killing him. To most of them, he'd seemed to treat all his elderly patients equally whether they were rich or poor, indigenous mountaineers or seasonal trans-

139

plants, white-collar professionals or Latino day laborers; and they were finding it hard to reconcile his bigotry to the man they thought they knew.

In the end, though, I was left with no reason to change my mind from the first impression I'd gathered when I read about him in the *High Country Courier* yesterday: a flawed man who tried to do good.

(*"Long as it was his conscience and his values that defined what 'good' actually meant,"* said the pragmatic voice in my head.)

(*"And how's that any different from the rest of us?"* the preacher asked quietly.)

A little after nine, those who'd brought instruments started drifting over to the big stone fireplace to begin tuning up. I knew I must have eaten off all my lipstick, and my fingers were sticky. I looked around for a lavatory but the one on this level was occupied and Joyce Ashe invited me to go downstairs. "Second door on the left."

Like the other staircases, this one was also built of black wrought iron and slabs of granite, and it curved down into a smaller space than the one I'd just left. Although this room too opened onto a terrace directly beneath the one overhead, its indirect lighting and cheerful patchwork accents gave it the look and feel of an intimate family den. There was no fireplace per se, but a waist-high rough oak shelf ran from one side of the rock wall to the other. It was at least eight inches thick, more than two feet wide, and looked as if it had been hewn with a hand ax out of the heart of a huge, majestic tree.

The shelf held a collection of wrought-iron candleholders of every shape and size, from a four-foot column suitable for a medieval cathedral to dainty slender sticks. Each was fitted with an appropriate white candle, whether thick and squat or tall and tapered. There had to be at least fifty clustered along the length of the shelf.

On the wall above the candles hung a large assortment of family snapshots, each in a different black wire frame. The central photograph was an eighteen-by-twenty-four of Joyce and Bobby Ashe surrounded by at least a dozen young children.

"Our grandchildren," said Joyce as she came down the steps behind me. "They're what it's all about. Do you have children, Deborah?"

"No," I answered. "But lots of nieces and nephews."

"Not the same," she said cheerfully.

"You'll see. Bobby fusses at me all the time for spoiling them, but he's just as bad and it's hard not to want to give them everything."

"Do they all live around here?"

"I wish! Bob Junior and his family are down in Asheville, but the rest are scattered from Manteo to Murphy."

"What about the Osbornes?" I asked. "Do they have children here?"

"No. Their one daughter's the assistant choral director for a big church up in Washington. Lives in Georgetown now."

There was a music stand over by the terrace doors and several instruments propped against the wall. Joyce picked up a guitar and a fiddle. "I'm so pleased you could make it tonight. You'll have to come back with your brother sometime."

"You mean Will?"

"Didn't he tell you? We heard him auction off some furniture in Raleigh the last time we were down. He's funny and sharp and really knows how to work a crowd, doesn't he?"

"He does that," I agreed.

"So we've asked him to come do next year's auction. We have a huge one for charity every September."

"Oh?"

"Oh yes. See, that's when a lot of our older seasonal people decide to move into retirement homes or assisted living. Instead of carting everything back to Florida or wherever, half the time they'll just give it to us and take the tax deduction." She touched the most massive of her iron candlesticks. "This originally came out of a twelfth-century castle near Madrid. You can't believe the quality of the goods. Brings people in from all over the Southeast. We cleared close to forty thousand this year."

A man emerged from the lavatory down the hall in time to hear Joyce's last remarks.

"You really ought not to miss it," he said enthusiastically. "I bought a tilt-top piecrust table last fall for a thousand less than I'd have paid at Sotheby's."

A thousand *less?* No wonder Will was anxious to cultivate this connection. If he made a good impression at next year's auction, he could be called back as a private appraiser. Old people always seem to find him charming, and old people with tilt-top piecrust tables?

I congratulated the man, told Joyce I'd see her upstairs, and slipped inside the lavatory for a quick check in the mirror. No lipstick and my hair could definitely use a comb.

When I emerged, random chords and snatches of melody floated down the stairwell and made me hurry back upstairs to join in.

Billy Ed had left my guitar propped by the hearth, and I reclaimed it, then took a nearby stool. I soon learned that while most had played together before (indeed, two were professional entertainers), several were newcomers like me whom the Ashes had invited to help celebrate their new partnership with Norman Osborne.

We played a rollicking version of "Arkansas Traveler" just to make sure everybody was on the same page, followed by "New River Train," with Bobby Ashe mimicking the haunting whistles on his harmonica. After that, different ones took the spotlight to play or sing.

I was surprised to see that Sunny Osborne played the dulcimer, and in response to calls from the audience, Norman Osborne stepped up with his guitar.

"This one's always been special to me," he said. "My mama taught me how to chord it when I was seven years old, but it wasn't till I married little Sunshine Monroe here that I understood what the words really mean."

With that, the two of them launched into that corny old standard, "You Are My Sunshine." At least, it should have been corny. For the most part, they sang it straight. And yet they'd somehow altered the tune and the tempo enough to make it their own. When his baritone and her strong soprano wound in and out of the familiar melody their instruments were playing, they created new harmonies that made the old song fresh again. I later learned they'd been married for twenty-seven years, yet there was such tenderness in his voice they could have been newly-weds; and when she looked up at him during the final singing of ". . . *you'll never know, dear, how much I love you,*" I was touched to see that her eyes were moist with unshed tears.

For a moment, I thought of Mother and Daddy, how they smiled at each other like this when they sang together, and once more I was wracked with doubt about Dwight's reasons for marrying me, about settling for sex and friendship instead of waiting for the true love of someone who would look at me the way Norman was looking at Sunny.

The Osbornes were followed by the

Ashes, who were urged on by their guests to perform a crowd-pleasing call-and-response full of bawdy double entendres that made everyone laugh.

At least a dozen guests had brought their instruments with them, and over the next hour different musicians shuttled in and out. Sunny Osborne, Joyce, and I settled into a groove, and we were content to play backup while others with more need to shine took front and center to sing or demonstrate some fancy picking or bowing. Among them was a white-haired old-timer in jeans and a plaid flannel shirt who played the banjo as if he'd been teethed on one. He was a big flirt and teased me into a short duel, which he let me win for a minute before leaving me in the dust helpless with laughter.

At ten we took a break and Lucius Burke brought over a bourbon and branch for Joyce and a frozen margarita for me that he'd mixed himself since the bartenders had left with the caterers after supper was over.

"You're staying for the second set, aren't you?" Joyce asked him.

"Sure," said Burke, who had surprised me a little earlier by knowing all the words to "Muhlenberg County." "I'm here till Bobby sings 'Amazing Grace.' "

"That's what we always close with," Joyce explained to me.

Bobby was standing over by the bar in deep conversation with several people and seemed in no hurry to emulate the fat lady.

"Can I get you a glass of something?" Burke asked Sunny as she flexed her fingers after playing so long.

"Thanks, but I need to find Norman. See where he's got to." She set her dulcimer on the stool and made her way through the crowd.

I took another sip of my margarita and complimented Burke on his choice of drink. We exchanged mini-bios — where we went to law school, when we first ran for office — and I kept it strictly casual. No flirting on my part. I even made sure I held my glass with my left hand so that there was no missing Dwight's ring. Eventually he turned back to Joyce, who had passed from solicitous hostess to relaxed guest at her own party.

"Congratulations again on the new partnership, Joyce. Bobby really seems hyped about it. Not that you guys were doing so poor before."

Joyce beamed. "No, but Norman Osborne's a real rainmaker. He does three times our business. We had Pritchard Cove and Arnetago, but he had exclusives in Beeton Ridge, Rabbit Hollow, Manitelya, *and* High Windy. He and Bobby have been out making the rounds all week and it's even better than we thought."

Those names meant nothing to me, but Lucius Burke was clearly impressed. "You have to hand it to Norman. He could sell gas logs to the Devil if he set his mind to it. Remember that guy from Pensacola who told Norman he only wanted a three-bedroom house and Norman —"

He broke off as the three of us registered that something was happening over by the bar. We heard Sunny Osborne's voice raised in exasperation: "— and I'm telling you he wouldn't do that."

"What's wrong?" asked Joyce as Sunny hurried toward us.

"I can't find Norman."

"Really?"

"I've looked all over the house and he's not here."

"Are you sure? Maybe he saw you were having fun playing and he hitched a ride home with someone."

I couldn't see that the crowd had

148

thinned much, but then I didn't know these people.

"He wouldn't go without telling me," Sunny insisted. Her purse lay on the floor beside her stool and she picked it up, took out a cell phone, and began punching numbers.

A young man came up to her. "I checked out by the cars, Sunny. He's not there."

"He's not answering his cell phone either," said Sunny. She hit a speed-dial number. "Nellie? It's me. Has Mr. Osborne come home? . . . Well, if he does, tell him to call me at once."

"Try Billy Ed," said Joyce. "He lives up your way, and I saw him leave over a half-hour ago."

Sunny shook her head, but she called the number Joyce gave her.

"Billy Ed? Sunny Osborne. Did you give Norman a ride home just now? . . . Well, did you see him when you were leaving?"

Clearly the answers were no, and when Sunny had hung up, Joyce asked, "Did you check all five bedrooms? Maybe he had too much to drink and decided to lie down for a minute."

"I looked, but you come with me and we'll look again."

Puzzled by Sunny's agitation, Joyce put

out her hand. "He's not sick, is he, Sunny? Is it his heart?"

"Of course not!" the other woman snapped. "He's never been sick a day in his life, not even a bad cold, and everything was fine his last physical. But this isn't like him. Are you coming or not?"

The two women went off together and I was left with my own problem. I must have been frowning because Lucius Burke said, "What's wrong?"

"I just realized I don't know how I'm getting back to Cedar Gap. Billy Ed brought me up and now he's gone."

"Oh, didn't Joyce tell you? I'm your designated driver. Your condo's on my way home." His eyes seemed to get greener with every sip of my margarita. "Did you want to go right now?"

(*"This is not a good idea,"* said the preacher.)

(*"Hey, don't look at me,"* said the pragmatist. *"I didn't arrange this."*)

"I didn't hear Bobby sing 'Amazing Grace' yet," I said demurely.

The search for Norman Osborne was unsuccessful, even though we all had a go at it. It reminded me of playing sardines at some of the big weekend house parties my mother used to throw when I was a child, with people bumping into one another coming and going, jostling pictures, opening closet doors, nudging chairs out of the way. I found myself smoothing down a coverlet in a guest-room where someone ahead of me had rucked it up to look under the bed. In the family room, three or four of the many iron candlesticks had been knocked over and I paused to right them. There was one fat candle left over, and I stood it in the back, then passed through to look around the terrace. Others were there before me, with flash-lights that they aimed down into the ravine in case he'd somehow taken a tumble.

The moon was bright but cast dark shadows under the trees and amid the granite outcroppings.

When it appeared that he was nowhere in the house, several of the men brought flashlights from their cars and patrolled as much of the grounds as they could, consid-ering the sharp dropoff behind the house. Others drove all the way up to the Osborne house and back down again, shining their lights in both ditches. On the whole, though, I got the impression that they were merely humoring Sunny.

Nevertheless, her anxiety affected everyone else and the party broke up early.

"Ol' Norman's probably sitting in a lounge somewhere, closing a million-dollar deal," said Lucius Burke as we drove back down the mountain. I was pleased to see that his car was a Chevy Blazer and that he wasn't a lead foot on the accelerator.

"He's done this before?" I was surprised. "Then why was Sunny so stressed by his disappearance?"

"You won't take this the wrong way?"

"Take what the wrong way?"

"If I say that some wives get more dependent on their husbands when they're going through the change?"

I laughed. "And how would you know that?"

"Actually, Sunny told it on herself. At least that's what I've heard. She was always playing tennis or volunteering at the hospital, but ever since she started the change, she says it's like she doesn't want to let Norman out of her sight. He's pretty patient with her, but even though he's his own boss, he still works. They say he's glad to get a breather. I guess even a good marriage can get a little claustrophobic."

"You been there?" I asked.

"In a good marriage? Nope. You?"

"Me neither," I said. "Fortunately it

didn't last long enough to get claustro-phobic."

"Didn't turn you off from trying again, though, did it? How long you been wearing that ring?"

"About a week."

"Didn't think it'd been long."

"What do you mean?"

He just smiled and I wondered if I'd given off vibes. Unattached woman vibes.

"Good guy?"

"Very."

"He an attorney, too?"

"No, a deputy sheriff."

Burke's smile grew broader. "He catches 'em and you send 'em to prison?"

"Sometimes."

"Won't that be a conflict of interest?"

"If it is, the district's big enough that other judges can handle it when he needs to testify in district court. A lot of his work is homicide and major felonies, though, so he winds up in superior court most of the time. What about you? Your ring on any-body's finger?"

"Nope."

Whether it was because we were going down instead of up or because Burke's driving didn't make me nervous, the trip back from the Ashe party felt shorter than going. The bright moon helped. Even the steep driveway up to Beverly's unit seemed less intimidating. I pointed to my doorway, and Burke left the motor running as he got out to open the back for my guitar case.

"That was a good party tonight," I said. "Thanks for the ride. Will I see you in court this week?"

"Probably."

Our hands brushed as I reached for the handle he was holding, and my ring gleamed in the moonlight.

"Do you ever take it off?" he asked, continuing his hold on the handle.

"Never," I said firmly.

"Too bad."

I don't know how much longer he would have gone on holding my guitar case if the twins hadn't swept up about then in their Jeep.

Chapter 10

"You were out with the luscious Lucius?" asked May as the tail-lights of Burke's Blazer disappeared down the drive.

"Luscious Lucius?" I laughed at the appropriateness of the tag. "Is that what the women here call him?"

"I thought you were engaged," said June. Both of them were staring at me in disapproval.

"Hey, wait a minute here," I said. "I wasn't *out* with him. He gave me a ride home from a party we both attended."

"A lift?" May's eyebrows shot right up to her copper curls.

"From the way you were holding hands," said June, "it looked like he was about to take his taxi fare out in trade."

"We weren't holding hands. He was giving me back my guitar." I walked over to my car and put it in the trunk while

June unlocked the door to the condo and held it open for May, who carried a large plastic cake box.

"That looks interesting," I said, but they weren't ready to climb down quite yet.

She dumped the box onto the kitchen table. "It's just leftovers. Didn't the luscious Lucius feed you?"

"Would you please stop that? What's wrong with you two?"

"We heard what went on at the courthouse today," said June.

"Huh?"

"Lucius Burke told you that Danny Freeman killed Dr. Ledwig and you believed him."

"You should have seen how stupid that was and turned Danny loose."

"Wait a minute. You know Daniel Freeman?" Before they could speak, I answered my own question. "Of course. Carla. It was his girlfriend that left a message for you to call, wasn't it?"

"She's having his baby. They're going to get married. You think she'd be stupid enough to hook up with a killer?"

"Look," I said. "Nobody knows they're going to be a killer till they actually do it. The man called him a *nigger* and —"

"Oh, shit, Deborah! If Dwight Bryant's

156

mother called you a piece of juking redneck trailer trash, would you smash her over the head?"

"Of course not. But —"

"No buts!" June said hotly. "You wouldn't and neither would Danny. He's one of the most grounded guys we know. He doesn't run from labels."

"He invites them," said May.

"They just validate the point he's trying to make."

"Strangers think he's white."

"Then when he says he's black —"

"— it makes people question their own prejudices."

"Messes with their minds."

They were falling back into twinspeak again, finishing each other's thoughts.

"All well and good," I said. "But the doctor was messing with their lives. He wanted the baby aborted and he wanted Freeman out of his daughter's life. Or else."

"Or else what?" they asked scornfully. "He was going to cut off Carla's allowance? Big whoop."

"*And* have Freeman's scholarship revoked," I said. "He was also going to forbid her to see her sister."

"Oh please," said June, and May rolled

her eyes as she opened the cake box. "Do you really think he could get a foundation to revoke a scholarship because his daughter got pregnant?"

"Or keep Carla and Trish from seeing each other?" May took what looked like a slab of homemade bread from the box, sliced off several thick pieces, and popped them into the four-slot toaster.

June set a small tub of some sort of chopped salad on the table and brought out lettuce and a jar of Duke's mayonnaise from the refrigerator. "She inherited fifty thousand from her grandmother when she turned eighteen, and they're both working part-time at a business they helped start."

"If her dad had followed through, though, she was going to drop out of school and work full-time till Danny fin-ishes, then go back after he has his degree and the baby's in day care," said May, smearing mayo on the first round of toast and passing them on to June, who added lettuce and salad, cut the sandwiches into triangles, and passed a couple to me.

Ambrosia! The texture and flavor of the toasted bread, the teasing familiarity of something not quite identifiable in the meat —

"Cedar Gap must be the chicken salad

capital of the state," I said. "I had a good one for lunch at the High Country Café and I was told there's a tea room in town that's even better, but this is the best I've ever eaten. Even the bread's almost as good as something y'all would make. Which restaurant are you working at?"

"The Mountain Laurel," said June.

"Are they open for lunch?"

"Sure are," May said, "and I don't know who told you the Tea Room was good, 'cause we've eaten there and the chicken salad stinks."

"Yeah," said June, nodding. "Not worth wasting your money. The Laurel's better."

"Do I need a reservation?"

"During leaf season? Oh yes."

"Enough about food," May said sternly. "Tell us why you let Burke talk you into finding Danny guilty."

I sighed and once more explained the difference between a probable cause hearing and a true trial. "If I'd actually found him guilty, he wouldn't be out on bond right now, and for what it's worth, he's only charged with voluntary manslaughter, not first-degree murder."

"How long could he get for that?" she asked.

"It doesn't matter," June said impa-

159

tiently. "He didn't do it."

"Then who did?" I asked, taking another bite of that delicious sandwich. "Carla? Her sister? Their mother?"

I was immediately shouted down with "No, no, *no!*" but I turned a deaf ear to their objections.

"You may not like it, but this was not a drive-by shooting. This is where someone was able to walk right up to him while he was practically hanging over the edge of a cliff and he didn't feel threatened. That means he knew his killer. So what about Carla's mother? Did she and the doctor have a good marriage?"

Both of them shrugged. "What difference does it make? She wasn't even there. She played tennis at the country club with some friends that afternoon and then picked Trish up at school. The police were there before she was."

"I still think it could've been someone after drugs," May said stubbornly.

"Was he known to keep drugs in the house?"

"No, but —"

"Maybe it was one of his crazy patients," June suggested.

"I thought he specialized in geriatrics?"

"He did, but some of them are gaga, so

senile they don't know what year it is."

"Yeah, remember the time Carla said that old man thought she was his big sister?"

"And that weird woman who threatened to run him over with her car because he testified for her son when her son was trying to get her power of attorney."

They looked at me with hope in their eyes. "It could be somebody like that, couldn't it?"

"If he'd been killed at the hospital, maybe, but people that gone wouldn't be running around the mountains loose, would they?" I thought of the comments dropped at the party tonight and said, "It could also be some of the businesspeople he pissed off around the area. People mentioned the gem mines, the Trading Post —"

"Not Simon!" they chorused.

"Who's Simon?"

"Simon Proffitt. Owns the Trading Post. Dr. Ledwig wanted to close him down."

"Thinks it's too trashy."

"Of course, Simon *did* almost shoot him," May reminded her twin.

"No, he didn't," said June. "That was just to scare him. Besides, Dr. Ledwig wasn't shot, remember?"

I licked the last of the chicken salad off

my fingers and shook my head when May offered me more. "Seriously, though, if Danny Freeman really didn't do it, what about your friend Carla? She had the same set of motives and she could have walked right up to him out on the deck. What's her alibi?"

"She was with us," June said. "We were studying for a test —"

"— in the library," said May, as usual, finishing the other's sentence, except this time June finished her own sentence at the same moment: "— in her room."

"So which was it?" I asked.

"Both," June said promptly. "We started out in the library, then finished up in her room."

"All afternoon," said May.

They were lying, of course. The question is, how deep were they in? "Is that what you told the police?"

They nodded.

"Did they ask you to sign a statement to that effect?"

"Um, yes," said May.

"Not smart to lie to the police in writing," I told them.

"We didn't lie to them," June said indignantly. "She really was with us all afternoon."

162

Her indignation sounded real, but I was too tired to pursue it. "Have it your way. I'm off to bed. I suppose you two are staying over again?"

Another nod.

"At this rate, your parents ought to ask the college for a rebate on your room and board."

May looked at me with guilt all over her pretty young face. "We're not in your way, are we?"

"Cramping your style?" asked June, going on the offensive. "Would you have asked the luscious Lucius in for a drink if we weren't here?"

"Dwight's an awfully nice man," May observed solemnly.

"Yeah, I really like him, too," said June.

"Too trusting, though."

"Lucky for him that we *are* here."

"Chaperons."

"Defenders of chastity."

With two sets of twin brothers, I know when I'm being double-teamed, but I was too sleepy to stay and hope to figure out what it was they were trying to keep me from noticing.

Instead, I yawned and headed down the hall to my bedroom. "Don't forget to put the cat out," I called back over my shoulder.

"Cat?" I heard May ask.

"She's got a cat here?" asked June.

I've really got to start remembering how literal-minded they are.

Chapter
11

I awoke Tuesday morning to the smell of coffee, sausage, and something sweetly fragrant. Wearing nothing except an oversize Carolina T-shirt that's been through the wash so many times it's almost handkerchief thin, I stumbled sleepily down the short hallway, stubbed my bare toes on a lamp base that protruded from the midden of furniture and clothes piled in the living room, and was fumbling in the cabinet for a coffee mug when someone rapped on the front door.

Without thinking the situation through, June went and opened it and I heard male voices, voices followed by the presence of three large male bodies in the kitchen. Two immediately eyed my T-shirt with unseemly interest; the third was Danny Freeman, who did a second take, realized who I was, and suddenly looked as startled as I felt.

"Paint crew's here," May chirped as she lifted a large casserole from the oven and turned to greet them. Her welcome died in mid-chirp as soon as she saw Freeman, and she darted a guilty glance toward me.

I was already heading down the hall with my coffee. She followed me into the bedroom and I glared at her. "You couldn't have mentioned this last night?"

"God, Deborah, I am so, so sorry. We didn't know Danny was coming with them. When we told Carla to send some guys up from school, we never dreamed she'd send Danny, too. I guess she thought it would help for him to do something physical instead of stewing about what's happening. Want me to tell him to leave?"

Before I could answer, she climbed back on the same hobbyhorse she and June were riding last night — "He's not a killer, though, Deborah. And you can't really think so either if you let him out on bond."

She had a point. But while I wasn't afraid he would suddenly attack someone with a paintbrush, it was still awkward as hell and nothing Miss Manners had prepared me for.

"Do as you like," I snapped. "I'm leaving for the courthouse as soon as I dress."

"Without eating anything? We made Granny Knott's baked toast."

So that was the source of the familiar aroma. When chickens almost stopped laying in the winter and breakfast rations for her hungry brood were scanty except for milk and butter from their cow, Daddy's mother created the dish as a way to stretch the eggs and to use up the bread ends before they got too stale and hard. She'd never heard of French toast, but this was a close version: thick slabs of bread are laid on a base of butter and brown sugar in a deep casserole dish, then left to sit in the refrigerator overnight in a batter of milk, eggs, and vanilla, and finally baked in a medium-hot oven till the edges crisp and the brown sugar caramelizes on the bottom.

Although she died long years before I was born and none of us keeps a milk cow anymore, her recipe was passed down and it's still comfort food in our family. Mother used to make it at least once a week when several of the boys were still at home and that aroma drifting up to our bedrooms was enough to roust out the sleepiest head.

The twins must have put one together last night from the leftover bread they brought home from the restaurant.

By the time I was dressed and ready to leave, Danny Freeman was in the bedroom across the hall with his back to the door as he pulled furniture away from the wall. I went silently down the hall with my laptop in one hand and my judicial robe in the other.

At the dining table, there was one serving of baked toast left in the casserole and a link of cured sausage. June deftly transferred both to a plate and waved it under my weak-willed nose until I put down robe and laptop and took it from her hand.

The others had finished eating except for final cups of coffee, and they covered the strain of my presence by speaking of classes and professors and Parents' Day, which I gathered was upcoming in another week or so. For some reason, the two guys thought it was funny that Beverly and Fred were coming up, too, and kept needling the twins about it until June flat told them to knock it off. I had the impression that my cousins had drafted extra help so that Beverly wouldn't blast them for not getting the painting done by the time they arrived.

They introduced me to Gary, a blue-eyed, corn-fed, pre-law student from West Virginia, and to the dark-eyed psych major named Duc, although at first I thought they were saying "Duck." "And you already met Danny, right?"

I looked up in dismay. Not realizing I was there, that young man had returned for another cup of coffee, and he halted in the archway as if unsure whether to retreat or keep coming.

He opted for brazening it out. "I guess this is the first time you ever ate breakfast with a killer in the house."

"Danny!" May and June protested together.

"Aw, come on, man," said Duc, who was clearly of Asian descent despite his southern drawl.

"Then you'd guess wrong," I told Freeman, matching his cool. "Besides, you did plead 'Not guilty' yesterday."

"But you didn't believe me."

"What I believed was irrelevant," I said stiffly. "My job yesterday was to look at the evidence, listen to the arguments, and rule on whether or not the State had enough cause to take you to trial. They showed me that you were there at the right time, you had the doctor's blood on your clothes, he was trying to end your relationship with his daughter, *and* you'd fought with him."

"Hell, half the people in Lafayette

169

County have fought with him!"

"Then your attorney will undoubtedly depose them and present that as part of her argument when it goes to trial," I said, sipping my coffee with more calmness than I felt.

Tension was building in the room, and the others looked uneasy.

"If you were still a lawyer," said June, "could you have gotten him off?"

I considered everything I'd heard yesterday. "Given the circumstantial evidence and lack of a more viable suspect, he would have still had to stand trial, but yes, I can see all sorts of issues that could raise enough reasonable doubt to ensure a not-guilty verdict."

"Then you *don't* think Danny did it!" May exclaimed.

I shrugged. "Doesn't matter what I think."

"See?" Freeman said, looking around the table with a fatalistic air. "The baby's going to grow up thinking I killed its grandfather."

"Oh, it is not!" snapped June.

"No, he's right," said Duc, already sounding like a psychologist. "It's human nature. They don't find out who really used that hammer, then even if Danny's lawyer gets him off, people are always going to wonder."

Freeman nodded. "I don't want my kids looking at me the way O.J.'s kids must look at him."

"It's a mess," Gary agreed. "The police think they have their man, so they're not going to look for anybody else unless you do get off. And even then . . ."

"You mean they're not still investigating?" May asked indignantly.

She and June fixed me with accusing eyes, as I lifted the last forkful of Granny K's baked toast to my lips.

"Don't look at me," I said. "I have absolutely no connection with the sheriff's department here."

"You couldn't get Dwight to give 'em a nudge?" asked June.

"Sorry. He wasn't even sure who the sheriff of Lafayette County is."

"But somebody should be working on this," May protested.

"Ms. Delorey said I ought to hire a private detective," said Freeman, "but my mom's already taken out a second mortgage for her retainer and —"

"You reckon *we* could do it?" asked June.

"Chip in for a detective?" May said.

"No, I mean do some investigating ourselves."

I about strangled on my coffee. *"What?"*

"Well, why not?" she asked stubbornly. "Between us all, we know a lot of people here in town."

"We might could ask around," May said, falling in with her twin's suggestion.

"— get Carla and Trish to tell us who had it in for their dad —"

"— check their alibis —"

"Duc volunteers at his geriatrics clinic once a week —"

"Well, yeah," said that young man, "but —"

By now the twins were picking up steam and they rolled right over his objections.

"Hey, wait a minute," I said. "This is too serious for you guys to start playing Nancy Drew and the Hardy Boys."

"We wouldn't be playing," said June.

"And if we did hear anything, we'd tell Danny's lawyer right away. Let her handle it."

Gary looked interested and said to me, "I think it's cool you're a judge. Most killers that show up in your court, what did they kill for?"

"I'm not that kind of a judge," I said. "The only time an accused killer comes to

172

district court here in North Carolina is for a first appearance or probable cause hearing. The actual trials are in superior court. Mostly, though, it's either a drug deal gone bad or a domestic situation that gets out of hand or when somebody gets dissed and loses his temper."

"But what about something like Dr. Ledwig? When it isn't domestic or drugs?"

"In law, we usually ask *cui bono?* Who benefits?"

Gary had heard the term. "Like Carla's mother?"

"Or Carla and Trish?" asked May.

"That too," I told them. "But there are benefits other than inheritance. Was he gouging somebody for a lot of money, for instance? Was he planning to block someone from *making* a lot of money? Did he know something that someone didn't want made public? In other words, whose life is going to be easier with him out of the way?"

"Not Carla's," Freeman said promptly, "and not mine either. Once I get my degree next spring, we can make it on our own. Besides, Carla loved him and I think he really loved her. Yeah, he was freaked about us once he heard I had black blood,

173

but she says he would have come around. She never saw any sign that he was a bigot when she was growing up."

He saw my skeptical look. "Yeah, yeah, I know. A lot of people can talk the talk till it affects them personally. But this was a guy who always voted a straight Democratic ticket and didn't care who knew it."

Since Lafayette County has gone Republican every election since Eisenhower, he had a point. It takes a committed liberal to swim against the strong tide of conservatism out here.

"Listen," I said to the twins, "if it makes y'all feel like you're doing something constructive to ask questions while you're out and about between your classes and your jobs, fine. But would you please remember that it's not as clear-cut as television cop shows make it seem? People aren't going to roll over for you just because you ask nicely, and you could be putting yourselves in danger. Whoever hit Ledwig probably didn't mean to and probably regretted it the instant it was done, but all the same, it's somebody who gets violent on impulse, so no one-on-one confrontations in lonely places, okay?"

"Okay," they promised.

As I went out the door, June said, "See,

Danny? I told you she doesn't think you did it."

If only it were that simple, I thought. Clearly the twins and those other two boys thought Freeman was innocent, and he was certainly giving off innocent vibes. But I've seen too many people who, in the heat of the moment, have done things so bad that they've gone into instant denial — *Only a monster could do this. I am not a monster. Ergo, I did not do this.*

Was that Danny Freeman?

Thank God I don't have to make life-and-death judgments. Give me the speeders, the shoplifters, the druggies, the check kiters, the shoving matches, the DWIs any day of the week.

Chapter 12

 Riding up to the Ashes' party with Billy Ed Johnson last night must have inoculated me — that or realizing that I was later getting out of the condo than I'd planned and would have to jog down those steps if I wanted to get to court on time. Whatever, I threw my robe onto the front seat of my car, slid my laptop in on top of it, and brushed a handful of bright yellow leaves from my windshield. Then, gearing the engine to its lowest setting so that I wouldn't have to stand on the brakes, I eased my car down that long steep drive.

As is often the case when I make myself do something I dread, the reality wasn't anywhere near what my imagination had painted. I did not pass out with vertigo, I did not flip ass-over-teakettle, I did not burn out my brakes. A few prosaic minutes later, I successfully turned into the courthouse drive-through. Someone else had parked in Judge Rawlings's space, though, and I had to drive on down a ramp to the visitors' lot and enter through the lower level, where the sheriff's office and jail were.

"Judge Knott, is it?" asked the lawman in plain clothes who held the door for me as I approached.

I looked at him more closely. Late thirties, slim build, about five-ten, brown hair, a gray corduroy sports jacket that didn't quite hide the gun on his belt. "Have we met?"

"No, ma'am. I'm with the detective squad here. George Underwood. Major Bryant told me to keep an eye out for you."

An unexpected spurt of happiness suddenly bubbled up inside. "You know Dwight?"

"Well, I can't say as I really *know* him. I think we might've met at one of the training sessions down in the Raleigh area. He and a good buddy of mine are friends, though, and Jack must've told him I work up here. Anyhow, he called to say hey and to tell me you were holding court in Cedar Gap this week. Guess he wanted some boots on the ground in case you needed anything." He grinned. "Or something like that."

"Or something like that," I agreed, smiling back.

"Anything I can do for you, you just let me know."

I assured Detective Underwood — "Call me George" — that I certainly would, and for starters had him point me toward the elevator.

Mary Kay was just bringing a fresh carafe of coffee when I got to Judge Rawlings's office. I still had about fifteen minutes before court convened, and I used it to call Dwight.

There was a time when learning he'd phoned someone like Underwood would have annoyed the hell out of me. Today, for some reason, it only amused me. Amused me, but also gave me an strange sensation I couldn't quite identify. It wasn't like feeling protected, exactly . . . more like cherished.

Cherished?

I've been loved a time or two, and guys have brought me flowers and candy and even an occasional piece of jewelry, but cherished? I found myself remembering something Minnie once told me when we were talking about romantic gestures.

"Your brother Seth's not one for mushy talk," she said, "and he might forget my birthday or our anniversary, but I've never once left the yard to drive somewhere overnight that he hasn't checked the oil and fluid levels in my car. In all these years we've been married, I've never had a radiator belt break on me or had to change the wipers or pushed the washer lever and found it empty. And you know something, Deborah? I must not be very romantic either, because that means more to me than any big bunch of roses."

The phone rang twice.

"Bryant here."

"Hey," I said.

"Deb'rah? Well, hey yourself, shug. I got your e-mail and just sat down to write you back. How's it going?"

"I met your friend George a few minutes ago."

"Oh?" From the wary tone of that one syllable, I knew he thought I was fixing to chew his hide.

"You checking up on me?"

He heard the laughter in my voice and relaxed with a warm chuckle of his own. "The eyes of a lawman are everywhere."

"No escape?"

"No point in even trying."

"So how are things down in the flatlands?"

"Same as when you left. Let's see now . . . Mama and I had Sunday dinner with Rob and Kate, then your dad and I aggravated some bass right before dark. Let 'em all go, though. And yesterday we set a few roadblocks around Widdington."

"Because of the increased drug activity they've had lately?"

"Yeah. It was the usual DWIs and expired licenses, but we did pick up a few ounces of this and that. Caught one guy with eighty thousand dollars in his trunk."

"And of course he didn't have the least little clue as to how it got there, right?"

"And since he said it wasn't his, we took it off his hands," Dwight agreed. "Maybe it'll buy a new school bus or two on down the line. Everything going okay up yonder in the hills? Seen much of your cousins?"

"Late and soon," I said and told him about yesterday's probable cause hearing, the twins' partisan defense of Danny Freeman, his unexpected presence at breakfast this morning, and how they hoped to uncover other suspects.

"You're not getting involved, are you?" he asked with a touch of his old bossiness.

"Don't worry. It's absolutely nothing to do with me."

An attorney from yesterday's court appeared in the doorway with an order that needed a judge's signature, so I told Dwight I'd see him Saturday morning and reached for the document.

Lucius Burke was passing in the hallway and stopped to say hello.

"Norman Osborne get home okay last night?" I asked, sliding my arms into the sleeves of my long black robe.

He shook his head. "And Sunny's already called me twice because the sheriff doesn't want to put out a missing persons report on him yet. I'm going down now to talk to him about it."

I zipped up my robe. "Could I ask you something?"

"Sure."

"Do you have the whole file on the Ledwig investigation?"

He nodded.

"I was wondering about the older daughter's alibi."

"Carla Ledwig? What about it?"

"She has one, right?"

"I guess. I couldn't tell you what it is off the top of my head, but I'm sure someone checked or I'd remember since it was her boyfriend who did it. Why?"

"No real reason." I explained about the twins and how they'd said Carla Ledwig had been with them all afternoon. "I was wondering if I could read their statement since they're my cousins."

If my explanation sounded lame, he was kind enough not to call me on it.

"Sure," he said. "I'll have my secretary pull it for you."

" 'Preciate it," I told him and headed for the courtroom to try and dispense a little justice.

The first case was being called before I realized I hadn't noticed his green eyes at all.

Lucius Burke was as good as his word. A few minutes before the morning break, a woman handed the file to Mary Kay and I took it back to chambers with me to see if I could figure out why the twins had lied about where they were.

"In the library," May had said.

"In Carla Ledwig's dorm room," June had said.

I read it through twice and was even more puzzled. According to the officer who took their statement, Carla and the twins had worked in the same restaurant that afternoon. Carla was a hostess there, and her unbroken presence was confirmed not only by the twins but by several prominent-sounding customers.

Now why would they lie to me about that?

I was halfway through the pre-lunch session before the answer hit me square in the face.

Chapter
13

TUESDAY, 9:30 a.m.

 In the house at the top of Old Needham Road, Sunny Osborne paced the stone terrace outside her bedroom like a restless golden tiger.

A golden tiger tethered by a telephonic chain.

She wished that she could call Tina Ledwig or Carolyn Gimpel or any of the others whom she regularly met for tennis at the club. See if Tina was sober enough to play. Waiting had never been easy for her. She had always been a woman of impulsive physical action. She needed to be chasing after a ball, slamming it back across the net, working off the tension that had her keyed tighter than a guitar string.

From this height, she could see the tree-covered hills of three counties. All the colors of autumn blazed around her as far as any eye could see, but she had no thought for their beauty because her whole being was focused on Norman, willing him to call, willing him to come home safely. How could he have vanished so utterly and completely in the half-mile between the two houses? She had already called all the neighbors again this morning. Still nothing.

Anxiety kept her circling back and forth where the phone sat on a table just inside the open French doors. She knew she was spooking the hell out of Nellie but she couldn't help herself. Every few minutes the housekeeper would peer anxiously around the corner, and here she was again, asking if there were anything she could bring. Tea? Coffee? A big glass of cold milk?

"Maybe you should call Miss Laura?"

"No!" she exploded. "Dammit, Nellie, go do your work and leave me alone!"

Calling their daughter would mean accepting that something dreadful, something unthinkable, something *final* had happened to Norman. He had always been bad for not checking in immediately when business required him to wine and dine someone unexpectedly. It was part of his good ol' boy self-image.

"Now, darlin', no real man calls his wife

and gets permission to go out," he would say. "Clients don't wanna deal with a pussy-whipped jellyfish."

Normally she didn't mind. She loved being married to a man's man, and his cheerful machismo didn't bother her. Let him tell himself and the world that he was the good-timing man married to a good-hearted woman, and let them both believe it — she knew who held the narrow edge of power in this house. Besides, even on those late nights, he was usually home by midnight and he damn well did manage a discreet call every time.

Twice before in their marriage, however, there had been nights like the one she'd just endured. The first time began on a Saturday afternoon when Laura was a toddler, about a year before he finally hit it big. He had run out to pick up a gallon of milk and hadn't come home until after seven the next morning — without the milk, and sporting a massive hangover. At the dairy case, he had run into an old Army buddy and had gone back to the buddy's vacation condo, where they proceeded to empty every bottle in the house as they relived boot camp.

She had been terrified out of her mind and at two that morning had called the highway patrol and the local hospital to ask if there had been a wreck or if he'd been brought in half-dead.

He had acted embarrassed and repentant and swore on his mother's memory that it would never happen again. Except that twelve years later, it did.

That time she had forced herself to wait it out, and when he came dragging in at midmorning the next day, she didn't say a single angry word — nothing of how frightened she'd been, the tears she'd cried, the rage she'd felt when she saw his car pull into the drive and he emerged from it unscathed. She had smiled sweet acceptance of his explanation and shamefaced apology, had made him breakfast, then insisted he go sleep off his headache in an upstairs guestroom, well away from the sound of vacuum cleaners, telephones, and Laura's stereo.

When he awoke, she and Laura were gone, along with a sizable withdrawal from their joint savings. No note, no nothing.

He called her family and his; he called all their friends, all of Laura's friends; but she'd covered her tracks too well. She stayed away eight days, and when he came home from the office that ninth day, he found a drink waiting by his chair, their dinner in the oven, Laura upstairs talking to her friends on the phone, everything normal.

"Oh God, thank you, Jesus!" he'd said, holding her tightly as if he never meant to let her get beyond his fingertips ever again. "I was so damned scared you weren't coming back."

"Were you?" she'd asked. "How'd it feel, darlin'?"

From that night forward, despite his continued pronouncements about what a real man did or didn't do, if he was going to be more than an hour late, he always found a way to call her.

Yet here it was, almost fourteen hours since anyone had seen him and not a peep. Joyce Ashe had driven her home and offered to stay the night, but Sunny had sent her off to search the house one more time. Sometime before dawn, she changed clothes and lay down on the bed. She hadn't expected to sleep, yet she did eventually drift off for an hour or two.

Now she circled back to the portable phone there on the table and willed it to ring.

When it continued silent, she pulled the cellular from her pocket and hit the redial button.

"District Attorney's office," said a perky voice.

"It's me again, Suanna. Put me through to Lucius?"

"I'm sorry, Mrs. Osborne, but he's down talking to Sheriff Horton about doing something now instead of waiting the whole twenty-four hours."

"About fricking time," said Sunny.

"Yes, ma'am. I know you must be just about worried to death. How 'bout I have him call you soon as he comes back?"

"Thanks, Suanna."

When the house phone finally rang about twenty minutes later, she snatched it up eagerly. "Norman? Lucius?"

"Sorry, sweetie," said Joyce Ashe. "Just wanted to see if you'd heard anything since we talked."

"Nothing except that Lucius is trying to get Tom Horton off his fat ass and go do something. Are you at the office?"

"Yes. Norman and Bobby were supposed to show the Big Bear property this morning, so I came in to hold down the fort. You doing okay?"

"I guess so. Just going crazy with the waiting."

"You want to come wait down here at the office? I could order in. I bet you

189

haven't eaten a thing since last night."

"That's okay, thanks. I keep thinking maybe he did try to walk home with the moon so bright last night. He's always been a fool for moonlight. And maybe he took a tumble. He could come walking in any minute, all banged up and cussing the state for not having guardrails on this road. Right?"

"I'll bet that's it," Joyce said sturdily. "Probably twisted his ankle or something. The sooner they start really looking for him, the quicker they'll find him."

"Thanks, Joyce. I'll call you soon as I hear anything, okay?"

"Sure, sweetie."

Sunny was glad to ring off. She'd always liked Joyce, liked her, that is, in that slightly condescending way of someone higher up the pecking order. The Ashes had built a good business, but Norman's father had been buying and selling land in these hills before Bobby Ashe was a cinder in his daddy's eye. When the big boom started, Norman had seen the opportunities first and had jumped in fast enough to get a lock on the prime pieces of Lafayette real estate. No one else came close to matching his volume of sales, although the Ashes were head and shoulders above their lesser competitors. Until recently, it had been easy to socialize with Joyce. Since the merger, though, she felt so much apprehension that it was hard to act natural around her.

"Don't worry about it, darlin'," Norman kept telling her. "Bobby and Joyce, it's not like they're going to drown. He's a big boy, and anytime you want to swim in the big pond, you can't whine if you get a little wet."

TUESDAY, 10:05 a.m.

Joyce Ashe sighed as she hung up her phone. The longer Norman Osborne stayed missing, the harder it was not to expect the worst. With so many out looking for him last night, if he had indeed taken the tumble Sunny was now hoping for, he must have been knocked out pretty bad not to have heard them. She couldn't say that to Sunny, of course, not in the state she was in. Best to keep it positive and upbeat.

How he even got out of the room without Sunny noticing was the biggest mystery. It was like they were joined at the hip these last two or three months. Sunny had been Norman's secretary in the early years, even had her own real estate license, which she'd kept updated so she could step in when he was shorthanded; but ever since her hot flashes began, she'd started showing up with Norman every time he dropped by the office here in Cedar Gap, taking notes on her steno pad almost like she was suspicious that things were going too much her and Bobby's way during this transition period.

"Just getting my hand back in," she'd said. "You and Bobby seem to have so much fun working together, it makes me see what I've missed out there on the tennis courts and ski slopes."

Joyce sure hoped this was just a passing phase and that Sunny would go back to the tennis courts once her hormones settled down and Norman settled in here. Right now, she was such a distraction that Bobby was complaining that Norman couldn't seem to keep his mind on the business. "She's always butting in, running her mouth so hard we can't hear ourselves think."

Lord help Bobby and me both if menopause ever turns me into such a clinging vine, she told herself. *He'd probably lop me off at the root.*

She turned back to the architect's plans

for remodeling two of their properties a few doors down Main Street to make one large modern office interior that could house both aspects of their newly combined businesses. Their sales office would still front onto Main Street. The architect proposed a facelift that blended a recognition of old-fashioned virtues with modern efficiency yet kept within the guidelines drafted by the planning board. New windows would allow them to display pictures of their most enticing properties as if they were jewels. The management aspects would be handled from the adjoining rear building, which they wanted to raise so as to provide a well-designed and suitably camouflaged parking deck underneath.

Once the leaves had fallen and the seasonal people were gone back to Florida or wherever, finding men in the building trades was never a problem. With a little luck and the promise of a completion bonus, the work might actually be finished by the first of the year so that Norman could move his records and his staff up from his Howards Ford office. And damned if Sunny hadn't come along for every meeting with the architect as well, claiming she was too nervous to stay home alone, even though the Osbornes had a live-in housekeeper in their garage apartment.

She should take a page out of Tina Ledwig's book and get herself a dog. Tina had always joked that if Carlyle died before her, she'd buy a little yippy dog the next day and sell that big house on Old Needham Road the next week.

True to her word, Tina had been in last week with her new King Charles spaniel and had asked them to list the house.

Her speed had startled Joyce. Weird to realize that it was only two weeks ago Sunday that she and Bobby had stopped by for a quick drink. She remembered how they had rolled their eyes at each other as Carlyle stomped around snorting so much fire over little Carla getting herself knocked up by some colored boy — as if that was the worst thing a kid could do to her parents — that Bobby'd told him about the merger just to take his mind off the baby. Next day, she and Bobby had driven down to Asheville to see about Bob Junior, and when they got back and heard that Carlyle was dead, it was hard to take in.

Yet, a week later, there was Tina sitting in her office, telling Joyce to sell the house.

"You sure you want to do something this serious this fast?" Joyce had asked her.

"Most grief counselors advise waiting a year."

"A year? Hell, no! I've hated that damn house from the beginning. Like living in a stone barn. Carla's in a dorm at Tanser-Mac, Trish'll be there or someplace else next year. What am I going to do with five bedrooms? I want y'all to find me a cozy little three-bedroom condo right next to the fairway at Rabbit Hollow, not an inch over twenty-five hundred square feet, you hear?"

"I don't know if they come that small in Rabbit Hollow," Joyce had said dryly, "but we'll certainly find out."

Like Bobby, she had grown up on White Fox Creek in a cold-water cabin with an outhouse out back. Five kids in a house whose entire four rooms would fit in the one room she'd used for the party last night, with space to spare. Even with all they'd spent on their children, the two of them sometimes looked around at how far they'd come, how much they'd acquired, and could hardly believe it.

And now — *ta-da!* — Rabbit Hollow!

If Carlyle had died a week earlier, she'd have had to send Tina to Norman, who held the exclusive on it. With the partnership a six-day-old done deal, though, she could show Tina any house there, and she'd immediately made an appointment to stop by the Ledwig house to take pictures and write up the specs, although Bobby and Norman both thought it was hardly worth going to that much trouble when she told them.

"Hell, it won't stay on the market long enough to get the pictures developed unless you put them in the one-hour box," they'd said.

"New neighbors?" said Sunny, who of course was there that day. "Let's try to find a buyer that'll be here year-round."

With both Norman and Sunny facing her, only Joyce had seen Bobby make his gag-me face, but maybe Sunny was right to suggest it. Seasonal people weren't as involved in the community and they didn't care whether or not the roads ever got plowed. Some developments in the county were like ghost towns from the end of October to the first of May and the streets never saw a snowplow all winter long because no one was there.

Of the eight houses on the half-mile stretch of Old Needham Road between the Ashes' house at the bottom and the Osbornes' at the top, three had already been closed for the winter and the other two would be by the middle of October. Nice to have the caretaker accounts, but sometimes those empty houses made Joyce feel awfully isolated.

The bell on the outer door jingled, abruptly interrupting her musings on all that had happened these last two weeks. Joyce looked through the glass front of her office to see one of their staff get up to greet the arrival. Almost immediately, it registered who he was and she went out to him.

"Hey, Sheriff! You finally ready to put a bid on that house Shirley likes?"

"Wish I could, Miss Joyce. You get the county commissioners to vote me a raise and we'll sure talk about it."

"Then I reckon you're here about Norman Osborne?"

He nodded. "Me and some of my men are fixing to start an official search along Old Needham Road between your place and his, but I was wondering if we could search your house, too?"

"Well, sure," she said, "but there must've been thirty of us that already did that last night."

"I know. Mr. Burke told me about y'all's party, but for it to be official, I'd feel better doing it myself if that's all right with you?"

"Give me five minutes and I'll be right behind you."

She signaled to their office manager and looked around for her camera and measuring meter. As long as she was up there, she might as well keep her afternoon appointment with Tina.

TUESDAY, 11 a.m.

"You're going to do what?" asked Carla Ledwig as she changed into an apron and hairnet at the Three Sisters Tea Room. "That's crazy! You aren't detectives, for God's sake."

May looked at her twin and sighed.

"We already got this from our cousin," said June. "We don't need it from you. She's a judge. She has to be official, but you —"

"— you should jump on this like white on rice. It's Danny's hide we're trying to save," May reminded her.

"Yes, but —"

"Answer me this: can y'all afford a real detective?"

"You know we can't. And Mother won't even discuss it. She thinks Danny did it and she half blames me, too, and every

198

time I ask her to help me hire one, she throws it in my face that I blew my trust fund."

"So go with the flow. What can one professional detective do that a bunch of us can't?" May gently shaped the soft dough into long rectangles as she spoke. A smear of flour dusted her cheek. "Between us, we must know most of the people, and we certainly know Cedar Gap better than any strange detective you could bring up from Asheville or Charlotte."

Carla frowned as May sprinkled the dough with cinnamon and brown sugar and rolled it up. "But you don't own a gun and you don't have a license."

"What the hell do we need a gun for? And who needs a license just to ask some questions?" After rolling each rectangle, May passed them on to June, who sliced them into thick rounds and laid them into buttered baking trays.

Carla added the tray to the cart parked in the warmest part of the big kitchen, where more rolls were rising, and she checked on the loaves baking in the oven, loaves made from dough that had been mixed the afternoon before and set to rise overnight in the cooler. Today's pumpkin and deep-dish apple pies were already cooling on a second cart. Here at the Tea Room, the kitchen was aswirl with spicy aromas.

At a nearby counter a middle-aged Mexican woman separated cooked chickens from their skin and bones while a young Korean woman diced celery and apples. At the deep sink in the rear, a skinny little white woman was washing a huge pile of fresh mixed greens and spinning them dry. Except for Carla, who had two morning classes on Tuesdays and Thursdays, they had been working since nine-thirty, and bowls of watercress and thinly sliced cucumbers were chilling in the big cooler beside a container of whipped butter.

"Should I start the pecans?" Carla asked now.

"Just waiting for you," May said.

Carla dumped a bowl of pecan bits into a large iron skillet, added a chunk of unsalted butter, and began stirring immediately so that the nuts would brown without burning. One of the things that set their chicken salad apart from other cafés was a generous sprinkle of fried pecans. And that reminded June.

"Hey, Kim," she called. "Could you ask Maria to please be more careful about the gristle? Some woman really freaked over a piece in her sandwich Friday. I thought for a minute there we were going to have to comp her whole lunch."

"Sure," said the Korean and burst into colloquial Spanish. The other woman looked over at June.

"*Por favor?*" asked June. A purple curl had escaped from her hairnet and she pushed it away from her eyes with the back of her slender wrist.

The woman nodded and gave an apologetic shrug.

"I really wish we'd paid attention in that Spanish class last semester," May sighed for about the hundredth time since the Tea Room opened in September.

Carla echoed her sigh. "I wish I'd taken Spanish instead of French."

"And I wish you'd think who else could've killed your dad," said June.

"I have thought," Carla protested. "I don't know!" Her eyes brimmed in sudden tears. It had been more than two weeks, yet she still wasn't used to his loss. And yes, he could be autocratic and demanding as hell, but until Danny, he'd also been loving and supportive.

"Everybody liked him — other doctors and nurses at the hospital and the clinic, the volunteers at the senior center, everybody at church. They all loved and respected Dad."

"C'mon, Carla," May protested. "That's not what Duc told us. One of the therapists said he was impossible to please."

"I know who he means and she's a total slacker." Butter sizzled around the pecan pieces and she stirred them angrily. "The rest of the staff adored him."

"Well, what about the way he tried to bully Simon into selling him the Trading Post? We were there, for crissakes. You heard how mad Simon got."

"You don't think Simon — ?"

May gave an impatient wave of her sticky hand. "Of course not. Everybody knows he's an old sweetie underneath. I could see him punching somebody out in the store, but he wouldn't go charging up to y'all's house."

Except that even as she was saying it, May could indeed see Simon Proffitt getting an official notice about some pesky little violation and, with that firecracker temper of his, storming off to the source of the citation. She looked up and saw that Carla and June were picturing the same scenario.

The true reality of murder hit them at the same time.

Carla stirred the pecans slowly. "It could be somebody we know and like, couldn't it?"

"Not necessarily," said June.

"Maybe," said May, and repeated what Deborah had told them earlier this morning about looking for whose life would be easier with Dr. Ledwig gone.

"Who benefits? Besides Mom and Trish and me? Well, Mom controls everything till Trish's twenty-five. The baby will be in first grade before we're entitled to anything. And there was a lot of insurance — a regular policy for us and then one for his associates that covered the buyout of his share in the hospital and clinic if he died before retirement. It all goes into the estate. Guess it's a good thing for Mom that the bartender out at the club remembers serving her a gin collins at two o'clock in the afternoon before the others showed up for doubles."

Her young voice was bitter.

The twins looked at her compassionately, knowing how much Tina Ledwig's alcoholism hurt.

"Nobody thinks for a moment that your mother —"

"It's okay, you don't have to say it." Tears glistened again in Carla's hazel eyes.

"It wasn't the world's greatest marriage and they probably would've separated after Trish finished high school, but Dad would've been fair with her. He really was a good man. He didn't just give lip service. Ethics were important to him."

She blotted her eyes on the sleeve of her T-shirt and took a deep breath, trying to make herself stay objective. "But he did invest in real estate all over the High Country. For all I know, he could've pissed off a dozen Simon Proffitts. I guess I could ask Mr. Norman. He'll know." Then her shoulders slumped. "Or maybe not. He and Dad used to be really tight, but Trish said the funeral was the first time he'd been to the house since August."

"Really?"

"They have a fight?"

"Who knows? Trish didn't notice till he came, and that reminded her that she hadn't seen him in like forever, and when she asked Mom why, Mom shrugged her off."

"Betcha he's somebody that could've walked up on that deck without your dad feeling threatened," May said.

"I guess."

"Will you at least ask your mother why they stopped being friends?"

"I can ask, but she's so out of it half the time I don't see how she can hit a ball back over the net without falling on her face."

"All the same, maybe she or Trish heard him say something about troubles at the hospital or with patients at the geriatrics clinic."

"And maybe Simon's heard stuff." June finished slicing the last of the cinnamon rolls. "When you don't like somebody, you usually know who else has problems with him."

For a few minutes, there was nothing but the sound of food preparation in the kitchen: Carla's spatula as she kept the pecans moving in the skillet, the rhythmic beat of Kim's knife against the chopping block, baking pans shuttling in and out of the ovens.

They were really getting this routine down good, May thought. Then she glanced up at the clock over the kitchen door. "Omigod! Look at the time! Half an hour till showtime, people! Did anybody fill the urns yet?"

"I did it when I first got here," said Carla, turning the nuts into a bowl lined with paper towels to drain away any excess butter.

She hung her apron on a peg near the

door, pulled off her T-shirt and hairnet, and slipped into a white blouse with ruffles at the neck and cuffs. She straightened the old-fashioned cameo on the black velvet ribbon around her neck and smoothed her long black skirt, then picked up a stack of neatly folded pink napkins beside the door and headed out to the dining room for a last-minute inspection.

"And listen, guys, I'm sorry, but I'm going to have to cut out by two-fifteen today. I have a test at three and if I miss this one, I can't make it up."

"That's okay," said June. "We'll manage."

Chapter
14

While two of Sheriff Horton's detectives gave the Ashe home a final thorough search, several patrol officers spread out along Old Needham Road. The sheriff himself stood on the lower terrace with Lucius Burke and Captain George Underwood and looked down across the treetops into Pritchard Cove. The walkie-talkie in his hand occasionally emitted staticky bursts of speech. Somewhere down there, a couple of his men with binoculars were carefully scanning the mountainside for anything that might be a man. Already they had sent their colleagues scrambling to investigate two fallen trees and several rocks. It didn't help that their description of Norman Osborne included brown slacks and a russet-colored sweater over a dark plaid shirt.

"Too bad he wasn't wearing red," said Burke as they waited.

"Wouldn't make it any easier. Half the damn trees are red, too," Horton said, nodding sourly toward a particularly brilliant maple.

"Yeah," said George Underwood. As head of the detective squad, he had a pair of binoculars slung around his own neck and had already scoped out the area from here. "And even if they were all still green, you ever try to spot a cardinal singing in an oak tree?"

They agreed it was amazing the way bright-colored birds could melt into sunlit foliage.

"I keep telling the commissioners they need to let me have a bloodhound," Horton grumbled. "God knows enough tourons get lost every year to justify the cost."

Burke and Underwood maintained a discreet silence. Most tourists who wandered off the hiking trails usually wandered right back on again, and whenever someone did stay lost, as happened once or twice a season, they could always borrow a bloodhound and its handler from one of the larger neighboring counties. Cheaper to compensate the helpful authority than to fund a man and dog full-time, never mind that Sheriff Horton made it clear that he felt humiliated for the honor of Lafayette County each time he had to ask somebody else to send over a dog.

"Well, the hell with it," said Horton, as much to himself as to the others. He was sixty-three years old and he'd already decided he wasn't going to run again. Let his successor fight with those penny-pinching commissioners. Maybe some college-educated hotshot like Underwood here could take them on, pry loose a few more dollars. He was tired of going hat in hand every year to beg for enough money to do the job properly. From here on out, he'd do his job, but bedamned if he was going to exert himself too much. They'd get what they paid for and nothing more.

It no longer fretted him that he'd never have a house like this one. He'd done all right for someone who'd barely scraped through high school. A lot better than his brother, who'd gone all the way through college — first Horton ever to get a degree. Law enforcement might not pay much, but it sure paid more than teaching math to horny, dumbass teenagers. 'Course now, if he'd been willing to bend the law the way Bobby Ashe had when he was first starting in real estate . . . Not that anything had ever been proved, but look at the way his kids had turned out. Apples don't roll far from the tree, do they?

"Anybody thirsty?" asked Joyce Ashe from the doorway. She carried several bottles of water.

"Now, that's real kind of you," Lucius Burke said. He unscrewed the cap from the pale blue bottle and drank deeply. The others followed suit, although Horton shook his head in amazement as he first studied the label.

"Who'd ever think you could get people to pay good money for plain old water?" he asked.

Joyce grinned. "Don't you wish it was you and me?"

Horton grinned back. For all her big house and fancy car, Joyce Ashe was okay. Hadn't got above her raising. And she'd worked hard for everything she had. Too bad there were things money couldn't buy, because for all the money they'd made, they might as well have dug a big hole in the front yard and dumped half of it in. That's probably what it'd cost them in lawyers and rehab over the years. He still remembered how she'd cried the first time Bob Junior got picked up for dealing and —

The walkie-talkie gave a screech.

"Yeah?"

"Sorry, Sheriff. That dark shape Carmichael saw? It was just another rock."

Horton sighed and took a swallow of the water.

Underwood set his bottle on the dark wood railing and went back to scanning the hillside to the left of the terrace. Even though the morning had a light nip in the air, the water was cold enough to give off beads of condensation.

"Saw you talking with that substitute judge this morning," Horton told him. "She a friend of yours?"

"Friend of a friend. Or rather girlfriend of a friend of a friend."

"Lucky friend," Lucius Burke said lightly.

"Sorry 'bout that," Joyce said to him. "When I met her back in the summer, she didn't seem to be attached to anybody."

"She here with you last night?" asked Underwood.

"No, I just gave her a ride back to town."

"Thought you were still seeing some lady lawyer over in Boone," Horton said.

Burke shrugged. "Didn't work out."

Joyce Ashe glanced at her watch. "I need to make a few phone calls. Get anybody anything else?"

Burke and Horton shook their heads.

"Me either," said Underwood as he lifted the bottle and drank another swallow.

A drop of condensation dripped onto his binoculars and he pulled out his handkerchief to wipe it away, then frowned. The handkerchief had a small wet spot of brownish red.

He wiped the bottom of the bottle. More staining.

"What's that?" asked Horton.

Underwood put his nose close to the damp spot on the railing where his water bottle had sat and sniffed. "Smells like blood."

"The hell you say!"

"Tell them to take another look right under us."

Horton barked orders into his walkie-talkie and soon the officers converged directly below the damp place on the railing, where oaks and laurels grew thick and bushy.

They found Norman Osborne's body halfway up a tree, folded in half over a limb.

The ground dropped off so sharply there that Horton needed to hold on to a rope to work his way down through the laurel thicket.

"Damn it all," he said, glaring at the

men who'd first worked this spot. "How many times you gotta be told to look up when you're searching a wooded area? It ain't enough to cover the ground. You gotta look in the fuckin' trees, too."

Underwood agreed, and yet, with so many limbs and trunks and the bushes that crowded all the spaces between, even knowing the body was here, the eye didn't automatically home in on it.

Osborne hung across a limb like the first dead buck of hunting season. His head was nearly even with his feet and there was a deep laceration on the back of his head.

"Careful, Sheriff," said Underwood. He put his hand on Horton's arm to keep him from walking closer and pointed to the ground where ants and flies were busily feeding on the gore that had puddled on the brown leaves.

"Poor bastard must've bled out," Horton said.

Underwood nodded. "Just like Ledwig."

"Oh, shit!" said Horton as he and Lucius Burke shared a startled glance.

"Hey, now, wait just a damn minute here," said Burke.

Underwood shrugged. "Two men going off decks? Friends? Both with head wounds?"

213

"Doesn't necessarily mean they're related," Burke argued.

"Don't it?" Sheriff Horton gave a cynical, seen-it-all snort. "I wanna be there when you try telling that to the Freeman kid's lawyer."

Chapter
15

As Mary Kay had warned me, the Three Sisters Tea Room was jammed when I got there a little past noon, but I quietly worked my way through the vestibule, where at least six people waited to be seated in a room that could accommodate about three dozen.

When people glared at me, I smiled politely and murmured, "I have a reservation."

"They take reservations?" a woman asked indignantly. "I was told they didn't."

"I'm a relative," I said.

The young hostess who approached with a frown for my pushiness was wearing a long black skirt, white ruffled blouse, and a retro black velvet and cameo choker, a costume meant to conjure up a more gracious era, no doubt, and appropriate for a tea room decorated in pink and white with fresh flowers at every small table. I remembered her from my courtroom yesterday where she had sat immediately behind Danny Freeman.

"I'm sorry —" she began.

"Carla Ledwig?" I asked, eyeing her trim waistline. Her pregnancy wasn't yet showing.

"Yes?"

"I'm Judge Knott. I believe my cousins are here? May and June Pittman?"

Her annoyance turned to alarm as she recognized me.

"Well, yes, but they're really sort of busy right now."

I drew myself up to look as official as possible. "Nevertheless, I'd like to see them. Now."

"I'll tell them you're here."

"Why don't I tell them myself?" I said pleasantly and pointed to a set of double doors at the rear. "Through there?"

She nodded.

From my own waitressing days I knew to enter through the right door, so that I didn't collide with the young Asian woman who came through the left one carrying a large tray filled with luscious-looking open-faced cucumber and watercress sandwiches. Like Carla Ledwig, she also wore ruffles, long skirt, and a ribbon choker.

"I'm sorry," she said as we met in the short hallway. "This is the kitchen. Restrooms are around the corner."

I smiled, nodded, and continued through the door.

At the long central counter in the kitchen, the twins seemed to have an assembly line going, the same sort of assembly line as when they put together sandwiches for our midnight snack last night.

May spotted me first and groaned.

"What?" said June and looked up. "Oh, shit!"

"You guys are so busted," I said, shaking my head. "The food here stinks? You thought that would keep me away after my clerk keeps telling me how good it is? When were you planning to tell your mom and dad that you've dropped out of school? Oh, wait! Bet I know. Parents' Day, right?"

June shook her head. "Wrong."

"We were going to fake it that weekend," said May. "Keep it going till Christmas, when they won't get our grade cards."

"I thought Tanser-MacLeod was a small school. How're the professors not going to notice a pair of twins who aren't regis—

Ah! So that's why you cut and dyed your hair. To change your looks for Parents' Day."

"It would've worked, too," May said.

"It still can." June looked at me with pleading eyes. "They don't have to know yet."

"They don't? You're going to wait till they drop another bundle on tuition and board you aren't using?"

"They haven't dropped a bundle. We didn't register this semester."

"Your dad's a CPA. He didn't notice that the check was never cashed?"

"Well . . . actually it was."

They had gone back to work as two waitresses scurried in and out. The menu seemed to be limited to a couple of salads and three or four sandwiches, which were served on unmatched luncheon plates decorated in cabbage roses, daisies, or other floral patterns. Rather attractive little plates, now that I looked. Unasked, May slid one my way.

I started to tell them I couldn't be bribed, but egg salad on a bed of crisp watercress? With cracked grain toast points drenched in butter?

When it was lunchtime?

I perched on a nearby stool and said,

"So how did you manage about the check? Know someone in the bursar's office?"

"We'd never ask anyone to steal for us," June said reprovingly.

"We told Mom and Dad we wanted to manage the money ourselves —"

"— write our own checks for the various fees —"

"— get an appreciation for how much our education was costing them."

"And they bought it?"

"Yep. Deposited the money directly in our personal accounts."

"But why not just tell them you don't want to go to school anymore?" I asked.

"Look," said May. "Mom and Dad love us, but they don't think we're real bright."

"And we aren't," said June. "Not about book stuff anyhow."

"But we know food, right?"

Since my mouth was full of their delicious argument at the moment, I merely nodded.

"They knew we'd never make it through dental school like Phil or accounting like Dad, but they thought we could maybe teach kindergarten."

I watched a shared shudder run through both of them.

"And instead you talked your way in

here as chefs? Not bad." I looked at the two older women, who stayed busy in the back bringing them fresh supplies. "Which one's the owner?"

June giggled. "We are."

"*What?*"

"Well, we own fifty percent, and Carla, she's the third 'sister' here at Three Sisters. She owns the other fifty percent. Our tuition and her trust fund."

"We're not making enough yet to be totally self-supporting here, so we waitress evenings at the Laurel for extra cash to pay our living expenses for when the condo's rented and we can't crash there."

Now that their secret was blown, the twins seemed happy to be able to tell someone new exactly what they had accomplished: how they'd talked the owner into leasing them this space, the remodeling and how expensive it was to furnish a kitchen, how they'd talked some antique dealers into supplying them with tables and chairs, which their customers could then buy if they wanted — "you wouldn't believe how many do" — how they'd scoured flea markets for dishes and glasses and flatware, and how scared they'd been that no one would come back a second time since they didn't even serve soup yet.

"We vary the salads and sandwich fillings, still there're never more than four or five choices on our menu. We're only open for lunch and early tea — noon till four — but our breads and desserts seem to keep people coming through the door."

I learned that Carla was an accounting student. Since she was still going to school full-time, her sweat equity consisted of keeping the books and making sure the proper taxes were paid, both for the restaurant and for their workers and themselves.

"Finding reliable help's been the biggest problem," said June.

As if on cue, the door swung open and a pimply-faced college student skidded in.

"Sorry, sorry, sorry!" he said. "The leaf people held me up. I swear I'll leave earlier tomorrow."

No ribbon choker for him. No ruffles either. Instead, he grabbed a plain apron from a nearby hook, tied it around his waist, picked up a large empty tray, and went out to begin busing the tables.

"Please say you won't tell Mom and Dad," May begged.

I had a feeling that Beverly and Fred might not be as angry or disappointed as the twins feared. They probably wouldn't be thrilled to learn that they'd bankrolled a restaurant instead of a college education, but once they got over that, they might even be proud of this entrepreneurial venture.

I said as much, but they still urged me to keep their secret, and after a serving of warm apple pie topped with clotted cream, I finally agreed. But I didn't let them off that easily. I scored a couple of cinnamon rolls to take back to the courthouse to share with my clerk at the afternoon break.

There was still a line at the front door when I left, and the sidewalks were as full of tourists today as they'd been on Sunday. Who knew leaves were such a draw? I mean, our trees down in Colleton County turn colors every bit as glorious as these up here, but you don't see tons of out-of-state license plates parked at every vista, and our towns aren't overrun with leaf lovers. I guess the hills really do make a difference.

As I neared the courthouse, I saw a patrol car come screaming out of the exit, siren blaring, lights flashing. And further up the street I saw an ambulance, its emergency lights flashing, too. It waited for the patrol car to thread a way through the slow-moving traffic, then it turned onto

Main Street and both vehicles sped up the hill to disappear through the trees.

My first thought was that a couple of tourists had carelessly driven into each other. My second thought was of Norman Osborne, who had walked out of Joyce and Bobby Ashe's party and disappeared. I hoped that this meant they'd found him and that he wasn't too badly hurt.

Chapter
16

Afternoon court gave me a type of case I'd never had before when Gerald Tuzzolino, a retired Miami dentist, and his wife, Elizabeth, a tax attorney in a private Miami practice, took their seats at the defense table. Both wore beautifully tailored suits. I don't know Armani from Anderson, but his didn't look as if it'd been found on a rack at Sears, and hers was definitely high-end, too — a bronze raw silk that flattered her brunette coloring. They were charged with four separate counts of receiving stolen property. The actual thief was currently serving a sentence in the county jail, a short sentence because the Tuzzolinos might never have been caught had he not voluntarily come forward and informed on them.

Although the four counts could have been combined and tried in superior court,

I was guessing that Lucius Burke wanted to avoid letting a jury decide whether to believe a known felon or the respectable-looking Tuzzolinos.

As laid out by the prosecution, Mr. and Mrs. Tuzzolino, who were fifty-one and forty-four, respectively, had bought a $900,000 house last year in High Windy, one of the first gated communities built in Lafayette County when it was still legal to put houses on the very top of ridges. I remembered that it was one of the Osborne properties that Joyce Ashe had spoken of with awe, so I looked at the Tuzzolinos with renewed interest. Nine hundred thousand for a summer home?

As alleged by the State, Mrs. Tuzzolino had met Ross Watson, a convicted thief, when he was doing his community service at the public library in Howards Ford this past May. She had stopped to ask him about the flowers he was tending and, impressed by his knowledge of local horticulture, had hired him to jazz up the borders at her place in Windy Ridge.

"Did you tell her about your criminal record?" asked William Deeck, who was prosecuting that afternoon.

"Yes, sir," said the unsavory-looking Watson. His nose appeared to have been broken several times and two of his front teeth were missing. "She said it didn't matter. She just wanted nicer flowers than the management company provided."

Unfortunately, Mrs. Tuzzolino's taste for nicer things did not stop with summer flowers. She had seen a six-hundred-dollar raku vase at an art gallery here in Cedar Gap that would look wonderful on the hearth in her bedroom. There was an eight-hundred-dollar handstitched quilt in a crafts store over in Justin that would be the perfect accent to hang from the railing of an upper landing overlooking their great room. And on one of their bargain hunting forays, Dr. Tuzzolino's fancy had been caught by a bronze statuette of a black bear fishing for trout in a mountain stream. The antiques store called it a steal at seven hundred.

So Watson stole it for him.

He also stole the quilt and vase she wanted.

According to Watson, their falling-out had come when Mrs. Tuzzolino tried to jerk him around on paying him what they'd agreed to. When he balked, she threatened to put the items in her garage and tell the police that he'd stashed them there without her knowledge.

"She said, 'Who do you think they're going to believe? A convicted thief or an attorney with a platinum American Express card?'"

Despite many objections from Mrs. Tuzzolino, who was acting as attorney for herself and her husband, Watson testified that he'd been told that if he'd bring her the nicely weathered teak bench that sat in the garden at the Mountain Laurel Restaurant, a bench that originally retailed for over a thousand dollars, she would pay him in full and they'd call it quits.

"That's when I decided to talk to my parole officer, and she took me to talk to Mr. Burke and Captain Underwood."

"That's Captain George Underwood from the sheriff's department here?" asked Deeck.

"Yessir."

With the Mountain Laurel's cooperation, they had loaded the bench into Watson's pickup and the Tuzzolinos were arrested when they paid for the bench after Watson gleefully described to them how he and his good buddy George here had managed to get it out of the Mountain Laurel's garden without being seen.

"And I was right," Watson said, the empty spaces between his teeth flashing triumphantly. "They didn't give me but half what was owing."

"Your Honor," said the assistant DA, "it was my intention to call Captain George Underwood at this point, but I've been told —"

At that moment, Underwood entered the side door, so he was immediately called to the stand, sworn in, and his testimony confirmed Watson's. Underwood further testified that upon his securing a search warrant, the quilt, the vase, and the statuette had been identified as stolen goods by their respective owners, who had all filed reports earlier. "There were other suspicious items of value in the house that the Tuzzolinos couldn't provide receipts for, but since we couldn't identify the original owners, we had to leave them."

"Objection!" cried Mrs. Tuzzolino. "That's an unwarranted allegation."

"Sustained," I agreed.

She dragged out the cross-examination for ten more minutes, then, when the State rested its case, she took the stand herself and asserted that she hadn't known the goods were stolen. She had bought them in good faith and in utter trust, and no, she had no idea that Watson had ever served time for felony theft. As for the teak bench,

Underwood's actions amounted to entrapment.

I had heard enough.

I found the Tuzzolinos guilty as charged. "What is the State asking, Mr. Deeck?"

Deeck stood and looked at me over the top of those rimless glasses. In his dry monotone, he said, "Your Honor, these are people who could afford to buy everything that they asked Mr. Watson to steal for them. As Mrs. Tuzzolino herself was so quick to say, she carries platinum charge cards in her wallet. Given the ongoing nature of their criminal enterprise, the State would like to see a fine commensurate to the crime, over and above restitution, and it would not be overkill to require supervision beyond the presumptive period of incarceration."

Mrs. Tuzzolino was clearly appalled. "Your Honor — !"

I motioned for her to stand. "Before I pass sentence, Mrs. Tuzzolino, do you or your husband have anything you would like to say to this court?"

Throughout the entire proceedings, Dr. Tuzzolino had sat at the defense table looking interested but not terribly involved, so I was not surprised that he just gazed at me blankly and that it was his wife who rose to speak for both of them.

With tears in her eyes, she explained that her husband was suffering from Parkinson's, which is why he had been forced to take early retirement. "A dentist has to have steady hands."

I glanced over at Dr. Tuzzolino, and now that I looked more closely at his hands as they lay on the table in front of him, I could see that he did indeed seem to have a slight tremor.

"Medication is keeping it under control for now, but when he was diagnosed last year he went into a deep depression." Earnestly she explained that after buying a second home up here in these cool and beautiful hills, away from the heat and bustle of Miami, he was almost his old self.

"He'll never get better, but his downhill progress has slowed," she said. "I discovered that nice things lift his spirit, help him not feel so depressed. That's why I was so ready to buy from Mr. Watson without asking a lot of questions. Since my husband's retirement, it's gotten harder and harder to make ends meet, and Mr. Watson seemed to offer a solution."

"You have a home in Miami?"

She nodded.

"Palm Beach?" I hazarded.

"No." A suggestion of disdain passed across her face. "The Gables."

"The Gables?"

"Coral Gables," she admitted reluctantly. "That's where my practice is."

Images of wide, winding streets, royal palms, pools, and oak-shaded tennis courts floated through my mind. "That's quite a wealthy area, too, isn't it?"

"I guess. It's not Star Island, but it's much more historical. Our house isn't directly on the water, though." She could see where this was going and was clearly torn between begging poverty and enlightening the ignorant about life in "the Gables."

"When your husband retired, did he sell his dental practice?"

She nodded. "But he got nothing close to what it was worth. He was in a partnership with a younger dentist, who couldn't afford to buy him out. His key-man insurance —"

"His what?" I interrupted, not catching the term since she'd run the words together.

"Key, man," she repeated, enunciating each word separately.

Instantly, I thought of the insurance my cousin Reid and I had carried on my older cousin John Claude when we first restructured our law firm after Reid's dad retired. A "key-man" policy covers the death of someone who is key to the success of a business enterprise or professional partnership, as John Claude was to two young attorneys like Reid and me.

"It paid out to the partnership only if my husband died, not if he got sick."

Mrs. Tuzzolino's voice turned bitter as she described how his partner claimed that without that insurance money he couldn't afford to buy her husband's percentage of the business. He'd threatened to declare bankruptcy if they tried to hold him to the terms of the partnership's buy-sell agreement, another familiar term from my own partnership.

Even though he was our rainmaker at the start, John Claude had declared his faith in our potential by splitting the partnership into three equal shares. If he'd died, the key-man insurance would have paid us a third of the firm's worth, which wouldn't have made up for his loss. On the plus side however, if he'd become sick or incapacitated, Reid and I would only have had to come up with a third to buy him out under the terms of the partnership's buy-sell agreement, not the half John Claude was probably worth at the time.

"We had to dissolve the partnership and sell out," said Mrs. Tuzzolino, "but it was a bloody fire sale."

My heart bled. Poor lady. Two expensive homes to keep up? Having to scrape along on whatever few pennies they'd managed to save from two high-yield careers?

"I'm willing to pay restitution and a fine, Your Honor, but I'm begging you, woman to woman, to suspend any active sentence you were thinking of imposing." A tear trickled slowly down her smooth cheek. (Botox or plastic surgery?) "My husband needs me. If you separate us, he could sink back into depression. Maybe even harm himself."

"I'm sorry," I told her, "but life is full of choices and you made yours when you chose Mr. Watson to be your personal shopper."

I ordered a mental health evaluation for Dr. Tuzzolino and sentenced them both to a total of eight months, six of it suspended to five years of supervised probation. In addition to restitution, I added up the value of the stolen goods — three thousand dollars if I counted the teak bench as worth nine hundred — and fined them nine thousand dollars.

Her tears disappeared as quickly as they

had come. She coolly gave notice of appeal, and I set their bond at a hundred thousand.

After that, I needed a break and one of May's cinnamon rolls to get the taste of Mrs. Tuzzolino out of my mouth.

Chapter
17

Within moments of recessing, I heard some of the rumors swirling through the halls back of the courtroom. They said Norman Osborne had been found somewhere below Joyce and Bobby Ashe's house. He had tripped over the railing on the lower terrace and banged his head. He had been beaten to death. He had been knifed. He had collapsed from a heart attack. Take your pick. The only thing everyone agreed on was that he was dead.

Dead?

That big easygoing man who'd stood on the terrace beside me last night and teased me for being a bootlegger's daughter?

That successful, hard-nosed businessman, who hadn't been at all shy about singing his love for his wife in front of a crowd?

Even though I'd only met him last night,

I felt a touch of the shock and dismay that must be running through the people who'd known him better.

Poor Sunny. I had enjoyed making music with her and Joyce last night. What could she be feeling now? Still so much in love with her husband, so dependent on him for emotional support. She must be shattered.

And the Ashes. So pleased with the prospects of their brand-new partnership, a partnership now abruptly ended.

Mary Kay declined my offer of a cinnamon roll — "I'm doing the no-carbs thing this week" — and went off to see what she could find out.

In the end, I wound up sharing with George Underwood. We nodded to each other as he moved through the hall amid attorneys, parole officers, and assorted law personnel, and when he stopped inside my door, I saw him looking hungrily at the rolls.

"Have one," I said. "I'll bet you missed lunch."

He didn't have to be asked a second time.

There was an extra cup sitting on Rawlings's bookcase, and I gestured for Underwood to help himself from the coffee carafe as well.

"I didn't realize you were head of the detective squad."

"It's not a very big one," he said. "Probably half the men your Major Bryant supervises."

"But it's true what they're saying about Norman Osborne? That he died from a fall off the Ashes' terrace last night?"

" 'Fraid so. I heard you were there?"

"Well, I didn't actually see him fall, but yes, I was there when he went missing."

"The way they described it, you would've been facing the room, playing the guitar?"

"Yes, but if you're asking me who came and went before his wife missed him, I can't help you. Most of the faces were unfamiliar. The only ones I could say for sure were in the room the whole time before he disappeared were Mrs. Osborne and Mrs. Ashe."

"What about before the music started? Did he have any words with anybody?"

"Like a fight? No. It was all very pleasant. They were celebrating the new partnership. I guess you heard about that?"

He nodded.

"The only thing halfway argumentative was when someone called Dr. Ledwig a bigot and Osborne defended him and —

oh my God!" I said. "It's the same as Ledwig! He took a fall just like Osborne. Was Osborne hit over the head, too? They were friends. Are the two deaths related?"

"Whoa, slow down," he said, sounding for a moment just like Dwight. "It's early days for that. Yes, he was hit on the head, and yes, he seems to've been thrown over, but it could be a complete coincidence. We're still looking for the weapon. We found blood on the railing of the bottom terrace and along the edge of the tiles. Looks like someone hit him so hard, he fell across the railing, and then they probably grabbed his legs and swung them over and let gravity do the rest."

He had finished the bun in three bites, so I tore a small piece off mine and passed the rest of it over to him.

"You sure you don't want it?" he asked.

"I'm sure," I lied.

"Thanks. The others were going to pick up some hot dogs at the Trading Post, but I was afraid I'd miss court if I stopped to eat. Anyhow, the EMT who looked at his head said it was probably loss of blood that actually killed him, not the blow and not the fall. If he'd landed with his head up, he might have lived. We'll have to wait and see what the autopsy shows. The blow was to the back of the head, not front like Ledwig, and it was only one laceration." He held his thumb and index finger about two inches apart. "But the EMT thinks it was a full-thickness tear and being on the head and him hanging head down . . ."

"You don't have to elaborate," I said. "A medical examiner once told me that under the right circumstances you could bleed to death from a relatively small scalp wound in fifteen or twenty minutes, that the scalp is nothing but a mass of tiny blood vessels."

"Be good if we could find the weapon," said Underwood.

I had been visualizing the lower level of the Ashe home, the pottery, the photographs of their children and grandchildren, the long ledge crowded with candlesticks, the — Wait a minute! Candlesticks?

"Could it have been one of those candleholders?" I asked, describing the oak shelf where they stood.

He knew it and nodded. "We thought of that, but there must be forty-five or fifty on that shelf, and just eyeballing with a magnifying glass, we didn't see blood on any of them."

"Because it's not there anymore."

"Huh?"

"Last night, when everyone was looking

for Norman Osborne, I noticed that some of the candlesticks had been knocked over. I straightened them, but there was one extra candle left. I stood it up at the back, so maybe you didn't notice?"

"We didn't," he admitted. "*I* didn't."

"That many candles, why would you? But the missing holder has to be fairly massive because the leftover candle's one of those tall fat ones and I noticed that Joyce varied them in proportion to the holder. The base is probably six or eight inches in diameter. At least."

"That would certainly cut a two-inch gash," he said. He drained his coffee cup and stood to go. "I'll get the guys back out there. Whoever did this probably heaved the thing as far as they could. God knows where it could have rolled to. Maybe you could adjourn early this afternoon? Ride up with me and show me where the candlesticks were when you noticed them?"

"Sure," I said.

"That might trigger Mrs. Ashe's memory. She didn't think any were missing."

"My fault. When I set them up, I must have covered the gaps." I glanced at my watch. Break time was over. "Meet you at four o'clock?"

"I'll be downstairs," he said.

Chapter
18

I had told William Deeck that I wanted to adjourn at four, and he did his best, but the last case ran a few minutes past. As I gaveled the session adjourned and the handful of people who remained rose to leave, the door at the back of the courtroom opened a crack and May peeked in. Seeing that court was over, she pushed through the door and hurried up to the bench.

"I was afraid I wouldn't get to talk to you." She still had on her apron, and flour dusted her copper-colored hair.

"What's up?" I asked as I finished signing some forms for Mary Kay.

May waited till she turned to go, then whispered urgently, "We heard Norman Osborne's dead?"

"Yes. I'm sorry. Did y'all know him?"

"Not us, but Carla did." By now we were

alone in the courtroom, and her voice returned to its normal level. "He and her dad used to be really tight and now he's been killed the same way, right?"

"That's how it's looking," I said.

"So the same person must have killed them both, right?"

"Not necessarily."

"But two old guys? Friends? The same exact way? Isn't that enough to undo what you did to Danny yesterday?"

I shook my head. "Sorry, May. It doesn't work like that. It's up to the district attorney to decide whether to go forward on his case."

May drew her small frame up indignantly. "But if the same person —"

"*If.* That's the operative word here." I stepped down from the bench. "Come on back with me so I can get out of this robe."

She trailed along behind me, arguing as we went that since Danny Freeman could prove he'd been working down in Howards Ford last night, he couldn't have had anything to do with Norman Osborne's death. And if he was innocent of that, then anybody with a grain of sense should agree he was also innocent of Carlyle Ledwig's death, right?

"Well, it's certainly another argument his

attorney can present to the jury when it goes to trial," I assured her as I unzipped my robe and hung it on a hook behind the door.

When she started huffing in frustration again, I said, "Look, May, for what it's worth, I think you may be right."

She brightened. "Really?"

"Coincidences can and do happen, but this is way too similar."

"*Yes!*" Her fist punched the air. "I can't wait till Carla gets out of class."

"Don't get too excited," I warned. "That was a purely civilian opinion and it wouldn't carry an ounce of weight with the DA."

"You're no civilian. You're a judge." Her dark eyes flashed with sudden mischief. "And I bet it would too carry some weight with the luscious Lucius."

I laughed and made shooing motions with my hands. "Don't you have some bread to make? Go!"

"Time to make the doughnuts," she droned, mimicking a commercial that was popular when she was a kid. "See you around midnight."

Up since daybreak, on her feet at the Tea Room since ten, and now she would go mix up the dough for tomorrow's bread, then waitress at the Mountain Laurel Restaurant till eleven tonight; yet her steps were light as she darted down the hall. I'm still three years away from forty, but just thinking about her schedule made me feel tired.

When I got downstairs, the door to George Underwood's office was open and I could hear him on the phone as I got closer.

"Okay, honey, let's hear you spell black . . . That's right, it starts off just like blue. Bl-bl-ack . . . Hey! Good! Now what about yellow? . . . Green? . . . Okay, Miss Smartypants, spell chartreuse."

He was still laughing as I paused in his doorway, and he gave me a wave. "Gotta go now, sweetheart. Tell Mommy I'll try to be home for supper, okay? . . . Love you."

"Sorry," I said. "That last case ran a little long."

"It's all right." He grabbed his jacket from the coatrack. "We're not on any schedule."

"Was that your daughter?"

"Yeah. She aced her spelling test today. When you're in first grade, every day's a nice adventure." He pulled his office door to and we walked down the hall, past uniformed officers who nodded as we passed. "The nine-year-old still likes school, too, but the oldest's in sixth grade now and it's starting to be cool to gripe about it."

"All girls?"

"The older two are boys." He held the outer door for me and we stepped out into late-afternoon sunlight. "You have kids?"

"Just nieces and nephews."

"What about Major Bryant?"

"A son. He lives with his mother in Virginia, though."

"Rough," Underwood said sympathetically.

I nodded.

Another one of the reasons Dwight said he wanted to get married was so he could make a real home for Cal down here and maybe get the custody agreement modified. I like Cal and I think he likes me, but for the first time, I felt a touch of apprehension. If this wedding comes off, it won't be for weekend visits only. We'll probably have him for holidays, certainly for several weeks every summer. I'll be his stepmother. He'll be part of my daily life.

A stepmother?

Me?

I remember all the tales I've heard of how some of my brothers resented my mother when Daddy remarried so quickly after their own mother died. She eventually won them all over, but things must have been uncomfortable the first year or so.

Of course, Jonna's still alive and kicking — still bitching, too, according to Dwight's mother. (Dwight takes in stride her gripes about the size of his child-support payments, but Miss Emily's more outspoken.) Anyhow, it's not as if I'm going to usurp Jonna's place in Cal's affections. And he's still young enough to adapt, unlike my last lover's sixteen-year-old daughter, who never stopped scheming to get her parents back together.

And did.

But that's all spilt milk under the bridge now, as my brother Haywood would say, and no point crying over it, although I'd certainly done my share of crying last spring and kept a good pity party going for myself halfway through the summer.

Underwood waited while I unlocked the trunk of my car and stashed my laptop.

"You sure you don't want me to follow you in my car so you don't have to bring me back?" I asked.

"No problem." He held the door of a nearby unmarked car and helped me figure out the unfamiliar seat belt. "I have to come back this way to get home."

"You live here in town?"

"On *my* salary?" He gave an amused snort. "No, we live down in Howards Ford. No schools up here anyhow. And most of the subdivisions have rules against toys left on the driveway."

"No toys?"

"All bikes, trikes, and games have to be stowed in the backyard or out of sight. Goes with the rules about keeping the grass mowed and the hedges clipped. You'd be amazed how many calls we get about unmowed grass every summer."

I shuddered. "Even without all that regimentation, it'd probably still be dull for children here. No school activities, no Mc-Donald's, no movies."

"Hey, we have movies," Underwood said with mock indignation as we pulled out of the parking lot and onto the street. "There's a film festival every summer in the little park back of the library."

"Let me guess," I said. "Art films? Foreign imports with subtitles?"

"You got it."

"No popcorn?"

"Nope, but lots of white wine in plastic goblets."

"And little cubes of jalapeño cheese on those long jazzed-up toothpicks?"

"Hey, I *thought* I'd seen you somewhere before!"

Having established our proletarian bona fides, I settled back in my seat and said, "So tell me about Deeck. How come a man his age isn't in private practice?"

"Raking in the big bucks?"

"He seems competent enough for it."

"He did have a private practice at one time and was well on his way to his first million from what people say."

"What happened?"

"Well, it was before I joined the department, but the way I heard it, one week in superior court, three of his clients got acquitted — a rapist, a wife-beater, and a child molester. They say that when the final jury returned a not-guilty verdict on the child molester, he went straight back to his office and hung a 'Closed' sign on the door. Split every penny of the three fees he got among his staff and then applied to Mr. Burke's predecessor for a job as a prosecutor. He probably could've run for DA himself, but he's not political. They say he just wants to make sure he's never again responsible for helping guilty scum go free."

"I can relate to that," I said.

"That why you ran for judge?"

"Actually, it was for the opposite reason. I was tired of seeing basically decent people get stiffed by a bigoted judge."

"Sounds like the flip side of Mr. Deeck's coin. He's good people."

"What about Norman Osborne? Was he good, too?"

Underwood shrugged. "He might've bent the rules a little, but I never heard that he actually broke them."

"And Dr. Ledwig?"

"Same." He thought about that a moment as he made a left turn off the main highway, then emended, "Or maybe a little more straight-arrow. I think he pretty much played by the rules. And made damn sure others played by them, too."

"Yet, despite their different moral standards, he and Osborne were good friends and did business together?"

"So they say. You ask Major Bryant this many questions?"

"And he can be just as tight-mouthed as you when he wants to be."

Underwood laughed.

"Anyhow, I'm district court," I reminded him. "Not superior. So it's not like he taints things or I have to recuse myself.

Very few of his cases ever show up in my court."

"And those that do?"

"We've never discussed them beforehand and they're usually pretty solid."

"Not like yesterday's concealed weapon?"

For once, I held my tongue. Not for me to criticize his boss's decision to go to trial for the wrong reason.

"Dava Triplett really is involved with making meth, you know."

"Then charge her with it and show the evidence," I said. "Don't ask a judge to carry the water bucket for sloppy work."

"Major Bryant must be a brave man," Underwood said, his lips twitching.

"And not that I'm trying to second-guess you, but what about a search warrant for the Ashe house?"

"Right here." He patted the front of his jacket. "Had our magistrate sign it before we went up there this morning. Even though Sheriff Horton had the owner's verbal permission, I like to get the paper, too."

"Good," I said. "And as long as we're dotting all the i's, you're not scheduled to testify in district court again this week, are you?"

He shook his head. "If I was, I wouldn't have eaten your sweet rolls and somebody else would be driving you up here right now."

Which only confirmed my opinion that Underwood was another one who followed the rules and that it'd been Horton's decision to let the Triplett matter go to court, not his.

This was the third time I'd been driven over this route and by now I was starting to recognize most of the turns. The ditches next to the rockface were overgrown with wild asters whose deep blue echoed the sky above, and I discovered that I could look over the side of the road into sheer dropoffs without the dizziness I'd felt on Sunday. Part of it, of course, was that, unlike last night, we were moving at a moderate speed, slowed down by out-of-state drivers who clogged both lanes on this beautiful sunny afternoon.

"You ever get impatient with all the tourists?" I asked.

He shrugged. "Not really. The tourists are fine. They can get a little rowdy at times, drink too much, toss their trash out the car windows, even throw a few punches at each other. It's the seasonal people that can wear you down. People like the

Tuzzolinos, who think their money entitles them. Life can get pretty hardscrabble up some of these dirt roads, then you turn around and see people putting up million-dollar houses on land your granddad used to hunt over, see the county running water lines where your grandma used to tote buckets up from a spring, paving the dirt roads they never bothered to pave when the houses were four-room log cabins.

"Take Pritchard Cove. The last Pritchards sold out three years after the first concrete drive was poured. Couldn't afford the taxes on the homeplace. Took the money and moved on over into Tennessee. They keep on driving up the price of real estate and my kids'll never be able to live in these hills."

"It's not just here," I told him. "Same thing's happening down in Colleton County. Only it's not seasonal people, but people who've relocated."

"At least they support a year-round economy," said Underwood. "Half our businesses close down in the winter. Cedar Gap's normal population's about eleven hundred. From May to mid-October, it's closer to eight thousand on any given day."

"And on this given day, they all seem to be out here looking at leaves." No sooner had I spoken than the road swung out around a huge boulder and I caught my breath at the spectacular vista of hill after rolling hill set on fire by the afternoon sun as it drifted down the western sky. "What a fantastic view!"

"Can't fault people for wanting to live here," he agreed.

"Or real estate agents like Osborne and the Ashes for capitalizing on that want."

Abruptly, it hit me all over again why I was in this car.

"How did Sunny take it?" I asked.

" 'Bout like you'd think," he said somberly. "Mrs. Ashe went up with Mr. Burke and me to tell her."

It said something to me that the sheriff would send Underwood rather than go inform a new widow himself. Either he didn't want to be the bearer of bad news in case it became a matter of kill the messenger on election day, or he wanted his chief of detectives to see Sunny Osborne's reaction for himself.

"She took it hard," Underwood told me. "Mrs. Ledwig was there and the first thing she said after she heard was, 'Well, thank God my Carla's not sleeping with a killer.' "

"They have any idea who would have

253

wanted both men dead?"

"Nope." He made a final turn into the long drive that led up through the trees to the Ashe home. "Mrs. Osborne isn't buying the idea that the two are connected. In fact, she almost lost it when Mrs. Ledwig kept going on and on about it. But Mrs. Ledwig says they'd planned to buy out the Trading Post and redevelop that lot together. Wishful thinking according to Mrs. Ashe, and knowing ol' Simon —"

"Who?"

"Simon Proffitt. Owns the Trading Post. You know."

"Sorry," I said, shaking my head. "I know the name, but I never met him."

"Old guy? Plays a mean banjo? They say he was dueling with you at the party last night."

"That was Simon Proffitt?"

"Yeah. They also say he and Norman Osborne had a talk down in the den right before Osborne went missing, not a particularly friendly talk either. I plan to stop by and question him this evening."

I found myself remembering the twins' spirited defense of the old man when they were casting about for alternate killers. They said he'd waved a shotgun at Osborne and Ledwig.

If George Underwood had also heard about that incident, he didn't mention it now. He parked on the gravel landing behind several patrol cars. As we got out, he asked the uniformed officer who was keeping a two-man TV crew at bay, "They find it yet?"

"No, sir. Not that I heard."

Like last night, the massive oak door stood ajar again and we walked in.

Chapter
19

 Without their crackling fires, their clusters of chattering guests, or festive tables of glassware and party food, the two upper levels of the Ashe house looked more like beautifully decorated resort lobbies than a lived-in private home.

The third level down was where fantasy met reality. With one wall against the mountain itself, the only natural light came from the wall of glass opposite the stairs. Instead of feeling dark and cavelike, though, the den was as cheerful and friendly as I remembered from last night. The tray ceiling was brightened by concealed lighting, and baby spots enhanced the vibrant paintings on the walls and the brilliant patchwork that adorned the oversize squashy cushions tossed upon pale blond leather furniture. Handstitched quilts were used as both throws and wall hangings.

Beyond double French doors in the glass wall, Sheriff Horton and Lucius Burke stood on the shady terrace with Bobby Ashe and two uniforms. Yellow tape marked off a restricted section of the railing near the far end of the terrace, and all the men were leaning on an unmarked section to look down into the gorge.

As George Underwood and I came down the stone steps, Joyce and a woman I recognized as Mrs. Ledwig from court yesterday sat at opposite ends of one long leather couch. Each had a drink in hand, and not their first, judging from the way Mrs. Ledwig lounged back into the patchwork cushions. A nearby armoire stood open, revealing several bottles, an assortment of glasses, and an ice bucket. There were bowls of nuts and a cheese tray on a low table in front of the couch, but neither woman seemed to have touched them. At the moment, drinks were enough.

Joyce came to her feet the instant she realized who I was, and crossed the room to us, shaking her head mournfully.

"Isn't this just awful, Deborah? Who would have thought it last night?"

I made the appropriate commiserating noises as she led me over to the couch and introduced me to Mrs. Ledwig, who already seemed to know George Underwood from the investigation of her husband's death.

"Call me Tina," she said, extending a cool hand, as Underwood stepped onto the terrace to speak to the others.

A tangle of gold bracelets slid back along her slender wrist, but her clasp was surprisingly strong until I remembered that she and Sunny Osborne played tennis together. Superficially, she even looked a little like Sunny. Her tawny hair was shorter, but as expertly styled and colored and set off by the thin blue silk sweater she wore over black tights. Her eyes were an intense blue in an attractive, suntanned face. I couldn't decide if the slight puffiness around her eyes and mouth indicated a drinking problem or prolonged grief.

In a tailored russet jacket and matching plaid slacks, Joyce looked as if she'd just come from the office. With a tilt of her head toward the armoire, she asked if she could fix me a drink.

"Perhaps later," I told her as I sat down in a chair opposite them.

"This must be very painful for you," I said to Tina Ledwig, gesturing to the men out on the deck. "Bringing it all back."

"Because of Carl, you mean?"

I nodded.

She shrugged. "It's going to be worse for Sunny. She and Norm still loved each other."

"Oh, Tina," Joyce protested. "You and Carlyle —"

"— were headed for a divorce court as soon as Trish graduated from high school," Tina Ledwig said flatly, taking another swallow of her drink, which, from the smell and look of it, was scotch on the rocks.

She leaned back with both thin arms carelessly lying along the top of the colorful cushion that supported her shoulders, one hand dangling empty, the fingertips of the other lightly holding her old-fashioned glass by the rim. Any less tension and the glass would surely smash to the hardwood floor. She wasn't drunk or slurring her speech, but she'd certainly had enough to speak candidly.

"It's no big secret, Joyce. You and I both know some of our friends at the club couldn't decide whether to send wreaths or bouquets. I'm sorry he was killed like that before he and Carla could make up, but he could be a holier-than-thou pompous prick at times and I'd be a hypocrite to start shedding crocodile tears. Hell, before it's over, I'll probably wind up spending as much on shrinks for my daughters as you've spent on yours."

I risked a glance at Joyce, whose lips had tightened. Psychiatrists for her daughters?

"At least there'll be enough cash that's not tied up in real estate," said Tina Ledwig, swirling the amber liquid around the ice cubes in her drink. "Thank God for partnership insurance! Did y'all have one in place for Norm, too? Or will you and Bobby have to cough up the buyout?"

Joyce was clearly annoyed with Tina's indiscreet speech and turned back to me. "George Underwood says you noticed last night that one of my candlesticks is missing?"

I nodded.

"So that's why they're still out there," Tina said, as if finally connecting the dots. "I wondered what they were looking for."

I followed Joyce over to the end of the ledge near the windows. One of the French doors was ajar and Bobby Ashe pushed it open for the others.

"Judge," Lucius Burke said formally as he entered. "Did my secretary get you that deposition you wanted?"

"Yes, thank you. I'll give it back to you tomorrow."

His face was just as handsome as yesterday, his eyes were meltingly green, yet I still felt oddly immune. No time to wonder why, though, with the others crowding in.

"Hey, Deborah," Bobby said in a sober drawl. "Hell of a note, idn't it?"

I agreed.

"Get anybody anything?" he asked, heading for the well-stocked armoire. "Deborah? Sheriff? Burke?"

We all shook our heads.

Tina Ledwig held her now-empty glass out to him as he passed.

Since everyone else seemed to assume we'd already met, Sheriff Horton introduced himself to me. "Captain Underwood says you think Mr. Osborne was hit with one of these candlesticks, Judge Knott?"

"Only that it's a possibility," I said. "We all spread out to search the house last night, and when I came down here and walked over toward the terrace doors, I saw where some had been knocked over. This group here on the end."

With my hand, I circled the air above a cluster of the heavy iron candleholders.

"I thought someone had been careless, so I set them up, and when I put the candles back where I thought they went, I noticed that this one" — I pointed to where it stood against the stone wall — "was left over, so I stuck it there."

"Mrs. Ashe?" Underwood asked.

Joyce looked from the fat solitary candle back to the ironware grouped together at the end of the oak slab. "I'm sorry. I've been trying to decide ever since you told me what Deborah noticed, but I honestly don't remember. There are so many. If it held that candle, though, then it would probably look like this one or maybe that one down there."

As she spoke, she touched a couple of heavy holders. One was short and squat and looked like a black iron saucer welded to a cylinder that was the size and shape of a three-pound shortening can, not the easiest thing in the world to pick up.

Certainly wouldn't have been my choice of weapon.

The other was taller. Vaguely shaped like an abstract hourglass, it flared at the base and again at the top, but narrowed in the middle until it was about the diameter of a baseball bat handle.

Joyce appealed to her husband, who had rejoined us. "Honey, didn't we have five of these to start with?"

Bobby Ashe stroked his big brown walrus mustache and his brow wrinkled as he tried to visualize the way this candle-laden slab must have looked before the party started. "Them the ones we got at that forge up in Pennsylvania?"

"No, these came from that blacksmith over near Hillsborough."

"Oh, yeah. Yeah, you're right. I believe we did buy five. He said he'd give us a better price break if we took all six, but you didn't want an even number, remember?"

We were all counting with our eyes. Only four of that particular style remained on the ledge, and Joyce was becoming more positive that the evening had begun with five.

"If the men don't find it out there, could we maybe borrow one of these to show the ME?" asked Underwood.

"Sure," Joyce and Bobby said together.

Underwood carefully slid the lone candle into a plastic bag. "And in the meantime, we'll check this for fingerprints. If we get anything usable, we may have to ask y'all to come down and give us yours. You, too, Judge."

"But we live here," Bobby protested. "Me and Joyce, we got our fingerprints on everything in the house."

He was a big bulky man, and with his head reared back like that, he reminded me of a bull walrus defending his territory.

"Well, hell, Bobby," said Sheriff Horton, "we know that. It'd be for elimination purposes. And don't y'all have a woman comes in to help?"

"I'll need her name, too," said Underwood.

As if summoned by a bell, a plump middle-aged white woman came halfway down the stairs and paused to catch Joyce's eye. "Mrs. Ashe?"

Joyce excused herself to go see what was wanted upstairs in the kitchen and the men went back out on the terrace. Left to my own ends for the moment, I rejoined Tina Ledwig, who hadn't stirred from the couch.

"You must think I'm a coldhearted bitch," she said lazily as I helped myself to a slice of cheese.

"Not at all," I murmured inanely.

She sighed. "Half the people in this town will tell you Carl hung the moon. Hell, I don't know. Maybe he did. I'll have to check tonight. See if his name's on it."

"I heard he's responsible for the town's new senior center."

"The Carlyle Grayson Ledwig Senior Center. Oh yes. Lots of brownie points for that."

"They say it's quite a facility."

"State of the art," she agreed. "God knows it cost enough."

"What else do they plan to build on to it?"

"Build on?"

"I understand Dr. Ledwig left money to expand it?"

"Expand it? Where'd you get that idea? It's already three times bigger than this town'll ever need."

"Mrs. Osborne said that's what she'd heard. That your husband left money to expand the center."

"Don't know where she'd hear that."

"From Mr. Osborne, maybe?" Not that I gave a damn. I was just making conversation till Underwood came back and drove me to pick up my car at the courthouse.

"Not from Norm," Tina said firmly. "He's on the current board — *was* on the current board," she corrected herself. "Once it was built, Carl turned title, running, and maintenance over to the county. Saint Carl of Cedar Gap."

"Sounds like a good thing to have done," I said.

She gave a cynical snort. "Good for the clinic, too. Boosted the summer client base. Always kept his eye on the balance sheet, Carl did."

"Is that where your daughter gets her business flair?"

She looked at me blankly.

"Your daughter Carla." Did she not know her daughter had opened a café? Was she as in the dark as my cousin Beverly?

Comprehension dawned in her blue eyes. "Business flair? That little tea room thingy that her friends talked her into blowing her trust fund on? Thank God Carl never found out about *that!* He couldn't stand Simon Proffitt."

Before I could ask what Simon Proffitt had to do with the price of watercress sandwiches, Joyce came down the stairs, and from outside I heard a shout followed by a babble of voices.

"Oh," said Joyce. "Sounds like they found it."

Chapter
20

On our drive back to town, George Underwood wasn't optimistic about lifting fingerprints from the surface of the iron candleholder his men had found.

"Too rough and dimpled," he said.

"That's the price you pay for handmade craftsy stuff," I told him.

He gave a rueful smile. "I doubt if the Ashes were thinking murder weapon when they bought it."

"Lucky for the killer, though. He probably wasn't thinking about fingerprints either."

"Just snatched up the closest solid thing at hand," Underwood agreed.

"Which probably means he did intend to kill Osborne when he followed him out onto the terrace."

"He?" There was an amused note in his voice.

"Or she. I'm not a member of the PC language police. 'He' works for me till we know for sure. Especially since more men kill than women."

"More men get caught, anyhow," he conceded, a definite grin on his face.

I laughed. "And on behalf of women everywhere, we thank you for that dubious praise."

The sun had gone down shortly before we left the Ashe home, but the moon had already cleared the horizon. Nearly full now, it sheathed the hills in a silvery blue light. Leaf people come and go with the sun, and the narrow road was almost deserted on this Tuesday night.

Only Tuesday? It felt as if I'd been here a week.

Possibilities from last night played through my mind.

"Impulsive like Ledwig's killer," I mused, "but not in the heat of the moment."

"How you figure that?"

"Would you go out on a deserted terrace with someone you'd been fighting with?" I asked.

"If it was coming to blows, I might take it outside."

"With someone who was bringing along

an iron candlestick?"

"It was dark. The killer could have palmed it."

"Then why was he struck on the back of his head? If Osborne expected to fight, he'd be facing his attacker."

"Not if he walked out first."

"Then you'd have found blood on the terrace near the door, not over at the edge."

"True. On the other hand, maybe Osborne thought the fight — argument, whatever — was over and he walked out there to cool off, not realizing his killer had followed."

"When I went down to freshen up, that level was almost deserted," I said. "Osborne could've gone to use the lavatory, too, and the killer followed him. If others had been around, Osborne might still be alive. But if the killer got lucky and it was just the two of them, he might have suggested they step out for a breath of fresh air or to look at the moon or a half-dozen other things. Once Osborne was leaning on the railing, looking out over Pritchard Cove —"

"Then it's just one good blow to drape him over the railing, up with the legs, and 'Hasta la vista, baby!' " said Underwood, finishing my scenario.

"That's why I think it was pure impulse. Carpe diem."

"Seize the day? But why this particular day, I wonder? What was Osborne going to do or say last night or today that made the killer feel he had to do it then?"

"What I said before. It could've been sheer impulse and nothing more. He'd already decided Osborne had to go. What better time than at a large party where suspicion could be spread around? If it were me, I'd start with all the usual suspects — wives, children, beneficiaries, business associates, and enemies — then eliminate any of those who weren't at the party last night or who had alibis for when Dr. Ledwig was killed."

"You really think the two are linked?"

"Don't you?"

"Well, Danny Freeman didn't kill Osborne, that's for sure. And I'd hate like hell to think we've got two killers running around loose. So! Wives? You and Joyce alibi Sunny Osborne, and the bartender out at the country club alibis Tina Ledwig, who wasn't even at the party. Children? Ledwig's daughters are in the clear there, and the Osborne daughter's in DC."

"Beneficiaries?" I asked.

"Well, Ledwig's medical associates gain his share of the clinic and hospital. The insurance they carried on him pays for that. If the Ashes had the same sort of policy on Osborne, it'll buy out the share of the business Sunny would've inherited. She gets a bundle of cash, they get exclusives to the properties he controlled, and that's sure a motive for both of them, but there's no crossover to Ledwig that I can see. Sunny gains nothing by Ledwig's death and neither do the Ashes. Besides, they were down in Asheville that day for their son's hearing and —"

"Hearing?" I asked.

"Oh shit! Sorry. Forget I said that, okay?"

"I won't repeat it," I told him, "but I won't forget it, and I *am* a judge. I can get the details with a single phone call, so you might as well go ahead and tell me yourself."

He took a deep breath, clearly annoyed with himself for that slip of the tongue. "Their oldest son, Bob Junior. He and his wife are both hooked on meth. They were cooking a batch last spring and the house went up in flames. Killed one of the grandchildren. The other two are still in a burn unit at the hospital there. They're going to make it, but I guess Bobby and Joyce are paying all the bills on that, too."

"Oh, dear Lord," I whispered.

"Yeah." He paused at a stop sign to make another right turn. "Anyhow, the hearing was the same Monday Ledwig died, and Bobby and Joyce were there all day."

A heartbreaking way to collect an alibi. I thought of the photographs of children and grandchildren on the wall of the Ashe den and the love on Joyce's face when she spoke of them last night. Yet I'd heard nothing in her voice to betray the grief she must still be feeling.

Denial?

I know how much it hurts when one of my nephews or nieces messes up. The pain must be cubed when it's your child.

And to lose a grandchild like that?

Because your son thought he could cook up something as volatile as methamphetamine in the kitchen?

Joke: How do lawmen find a meth lab?

Answer: They follow the fire engines.

For a moment, the only break in the silence between us was when Underwood switched his headlights from bright to dim and back again.

"So you're left looking for enemies," I

said. "Tina Ledwig might not've loved her husband, but she seems to think everyone else did."

"Not everyone," said Underwood, dimming his lights as another car approached. Now that we were on the main road to Cedar Gap, traffic was picking up. "Simon Proffitt and Billy Ed Johnson both fought with Ledwig before he died."

"And you said Proffitt had words with Osborne last night?"

"According to our DA anyhow. Burke says it was low-volume but intense."

As the car passed by, a deer bounded across the highway in front of us. Underwood instinctively touched his brakes, but the deer was gone before we got close.

"Rutting season," he murmured before turning back to mull over the possibilities aloud. Ledwig may have quarreled with Proffitt and Johnson, but if Osborne and Johnson had clashed, Underwood didn't know of it. Indeed, he thought the two men had worked together on a couple of mutually profitable projects without any problems.

"I talked to Norman Osborne for a few minutes last night," I said. "He struck me as a good ol' boy who loved his wife and was loyal to his friends. I got the feeling that he might cut you off at the knees but that there wouldn't be any malice in it."

"That was Osborne all right." We were on Main Street now. Underwood paused at the red light and a knot of tourists passed in the crosswalk, heading for Roxie's ice-cream stand. "You never met Ledwig, did you?"

"No, and I can't quite get a feel for him. For some reason, though, despite all his good works, that prejudice he felt against Danny Freeman makes me wonder if there wasn't a coldness at his core."

Underwood shook his head. "I didn't know him either, but I do hear he made sure people heard about all those good works and about his fine upstanding moral character as well."

"He didn't hide his light under a bushel?"

"Not unless that bushel had his name carved in marble with a spotlight playing on it."

"You didn't like him," I said.

"I told you. I didn't know him."

"But?"

My persistence brought a rueful smile. "Okay. My wife's uncle was on the town council a few years back. I don't need to go into the details. Let's just say he did somebody a minor favor. Something that didn't hurt anybody or profit anyone monetarily and wasn't even technically against the rules. Ledwig found out and got all righteous about it. Made a big hoopla. Blew it all out of proportion. Uncle Artie lost his seat on the council and Ledwig got to parade around as a defender of public virtue.

"And before you ask if Uncle Artie has an alibi for the day Ledwig bought it," Underwood said as he made a left turn into the courthouse parking lot, "he died last spring."

He pulled up next to my car. "Oh well. At least we've got a fairly narrow window for when Osborne was killed. Just wish we had the same for Ledwig."

"What about the UPS guy?" I asked as I opened the door.

"What UPS guy?"

"UPS, FedEx, whichever. Whoever brought those brown envelopes that were on the deck that day."

"Huh?"

"In the crime scene photos Lucius Burke showed me at the hearing Monday," I said impatiently. "There were several brown mailers on a table by the door. Looked like books or stuff you'd order off the Internet.

There would be a time stamp for when they were delivered. Didn't anyone check?"

"Jesus!" he swore softly. "That god-damned Fletcher! Nobody mentioned any packages to me."

"You weren't there at all that day?"

"Nope. Fletcher caught it. It was his big case."

"Well, you ought to take another look at those pictures, because now that I think of it, the delivery guy usually leaves them at the front door if no one answers the bell, so why were they on the deck? If they arrived before Tina Ledwig left home, wouldn't she have brought them inside?"

"Maybe Ledwig was outside and just stuck them there himself."

"Whichever, it might could help you narrow the time," I said.

"I'll get Fletcher on it first thing in the morning," said Underwood. "Good thing you noticed."

Then he ruined the compliment by laughing.

"What?" I asked.

"I'm thinking Bryant's probably braver than I realized."

"How do you mean?"

"A man doesn't get away with much if

he's got a real noticing wife."

"I imagine he'll survive," I said dryly and closed the car door behind me.

The condo was deserted when I got back, although a strong odor of fresh paint permeated the place. The three bedrooms, both baths, the living room, and the kitchen ceiling, too, gleamed in the lamp-light. Not only that, but all the furniture had been put back in place. True, there were still piles of books and clothes on the couch, but at least it didn't sit in the middle of the floor any longer.

Happily, the pickup paint crew was gone, although, by the look of the buckets and brushes grouped on newspapers on the kitchen floor, they intended to come back tomorrow and do the cabinets.

My bedroom was disheveled and all my toiletries lay in the sink, but that was okay. The guys had made a surprisingly neat job of it. Beverly and Fred should be pleased when they came up for Parents' Day.

I plugged my modem into the phone jack and fired up my laptop. Amid the usual spam were judicial notices, a political cartoon from Minnie, and an inspirational tract that had been forwarded through a half-dozen mailboxes before landing up in

Naomi's and thus to every family member currently online. At least I assume she sends them to everybody else and doesn't single me out as the Devil's only playmate. Portland had sent a delicious bit of gossip about a pompous state supreme court justice we both dislike, and there was a funny note of congratulations from Terry Wilson. He's a special agent for the SBI and a onetime boyfriend who still goes fishing with Daddy and Dwight. He'd just heard about Dwight and me but claimed he'd seen it coming for at least a year.

Right.

And from Dwight himself?

Nothing.

Nada.

Zilch.

Chapter
21

 While George Underwood waited for Deborah Knott to start her car and drive away, he called Fletcher's pager and left a callback message. If that asshole had overlooked something that critical, he was due a serious butt-chewing.

Underwood's cell phone rang as he circled the monument and headed on down toward the Trading Post, but it wasn't Fletcher.

"Hey, hon," his wife said. "I'm putting the biscuits in the oven. You gonna be here when they get out?"

He'd planned to stop and talk to Simon Proffitt, but the judge's sweet rolls were all he'd had since breakfast and the thought of his wife's biscuits and smothered pork chops was too tempting.

"Be there in fifteen minutes," he promised.

For once, luck was with him. As he pulled up at the Trading Post, he spotted Simon at the door and waved the old man over.

"Get out and set a spell," Simon invited.

"Can't stop right now, but we need to talk, Mr. Proffitt."

"*Mister* Proffitt? What'd I do now?"

"Nothing, I hope, but I do have to ask you a few questions tomorrow. In my office."

" 'Cause Norman Osborne went and got hisself killed last night and somebody tattled that I told him to go to hell?"

"I hear you told Dr. Ledwig the same thing and offered to help him along with Lizzie."

A nostalgic smile started to spread across the wrinkled face, till a scowl abruptly replaced it as Proffitt realized the implications of what the sheriff's deputy was saying. "You ain't trying to hang them two on me, are you? Ledwig won't shot. Osborne neither."

"I know, I know," Underwood said in a soothing tone. "Be at my office at nine tomorrow. I'll take your statement. You'll tell me what you were doing when Ledwig died and who-all you talked to last night before Osborne went missing and then I can cross you off my list, okay?"

"Go to hell!" Proffitt said and turned to stomp back to his store.

"Nine o'clock," Underwood called. He knew he ought to collar that old hothead and get his alibi right then, but it had been a long and hungry day, so he headed on down the hill to Howards Ford, where his wife and children and hot biscuits waited.

He was just pulling into his own driveway when his phone rang again.

"Hey, Captain," Fletcher said. "What's up?"

TUESDAY EVENING, 10 p.m.

"Mom?"

Tina Ledwig dragged her eyes from the television screen to her younger daughter standing in the doorway of her bedroom. Her new spaniel scrambled off her lap and bounded over to dance around Trish's ankles, paws in air, till Trish bent down to pet it.

"Hey, honey. Homework all done?"

The girl gave the dumb question all the attention it deserved by ignoring it completely. "Have you seen a UPS package from Amazon?"

Tina looked at her blankly.

"I ordered some CDs from them, and with all the stuff about Dad and Carla, I forgot till just now. I checked it out on the computer, and according to the tracking number, it came the day Dad died. Have you seen it?"

Tina tried to focus. "CDs? UPS?"

"Oh shit!" Disgust and despair filled Trish's young voice as she turned away.

"No, wait!" Tina said. "There *were* some packages and stuff by the deck door that day. I thought they were all for your dad and I put them on the desk in his study."

If Trish heard, she didn't respond, just kept going, the little dog at her heels.

Tina turned back to the television. Something else that was going to need cleaning out before they could move. Carl's study. Where he holed up every night after dinner before coming up to bed. Not her bed, the bed in the room next to this one, through that connecting door.

Only they hadn't connected in — how long was it?

He'd blamed the vodka for his lack of interest, but they both knew it was his lack of interest that caused her to turn to vodka.

She lifted the skirt of the table next to her lounge chair and reached for the bottle hidden there.

Chapter
22

I was rooting around in the refrigerator and not finding much of interest when the phone rang.

To my surprise, it was Lucius Burke, who had left the Ashe home shortly before Underwood and me.

"Look," he said, "I know you're just ten minutes in front of a preacher away from being a married lady, but I'm down here at the Mountain Laurel and they're running a special on grilled brook trout and we both have to eat supper, right? And since I'm not arguing any cases before you the rest of the week and I do have a couple of questions about last night, why don't you come join me?"

I laughed. Not the most subtle invitation I'd ever had, but I love fish of any description and shared meals are always more fun than solitary sandwiches. And it was obvious that Dwight didn't give a damn about me or how I might be spending my evenings. Out of sight, out of mind.

"Order me a Bloody Mary, not too spicy, and I'll be there in five minutes," I told him.

According to the back of its menu, the Mountain Laurel Restaurant on Main Street began life as a summer residence for a robber baron's granddaughter. Built in the Queen Anne style so popular in the late 1800s, it dripped enough lacy gingerbread from every eave and angle to give a house painter nightmares and stop tourists dead in their tracks with dreams of romantic mountain summers spent lazing in one of the many wicker swings and rockers that dotted the wide wraparound porch.

Inside, most of the downstairs walls had been removed to create an airy open space. Instead of being tricked out like some Victorian fantasy, however, the dining room was almost plain, softened by the pale pink cloths that covered the sensible square tables and by baskets of ferns that hung in front of illuminated stained-glass windows. A few restrained botanical prints hung on the walls.

Here at seven-thirty, all the tables were

taken and several people without reservations waited out on the porch even though the night air was cool enough for fall jackets.

The hostess led me to Lucius Burke's table, and as I approached he stood and held my chair for me. A Bloody Mary awaited in a tall and elegant glass.

"Nice," I said.

"The restaurant, the drink, or the prospect of dinner?"

His green eyes twinkled in the glow of the tiny lamp on the tabletop between us.

"Everything. I'm glad you called me."

When I looked around the room, I saw that most of the men wore jackets and ties, although a few bold ones like Lucius wore crewneck sweaters under their jackets. The women were sleek in boiled wool Chanel-type suits and chunky gold or silver necklaces with matching earrings. I took a discreet glance at the prices on the right side of the menu and realized that this place catered to the wealthy seasonal people, not budget-minded day-trippers. Except for the waitresses, there couldn't have been more than three other women under the age of forty in the restaurant.

Except for the waitresses?

Too late I remembered that the twins

285

worked here, and, sure enough, there was June, deftly distributing plates to a table of six at the far side of the room. With a little luck —

"Did you wish a few more minutes to look over the menu?" inquired a familiar voice from behind me, and I looked up to meet May's startled eyes. "Deborah?"

"Hey, May," I said. "You know Mr. Burke, don't you? Lucius, this is my cousin May Pittman. Her parents own the condo I'm using this week."

Before they could do more than murmur polite acknowledgments, I said, "Lucius says you have a grilled trout special? That sounds good to me."

Barely hiding her disapproval, May took our orders and flounced away.

"She didn't even ask what kind of dressing I want on my salad," I said.

He smiled. "Does she think you're cheating on your deputy?"

"Probably." I sipped my Bloody Mary. It was perfectly seasoned. "You said you had questions about last night?"

"One of Sheriff Horton's detectives may ask you about this tomorrow. We were wondering about your relationship with Norman Osborne?"

"Relationship?" I was puzzled. "There

was no relationship between us. What gave you that idea?"

"Osborne carried a little notepad in his jacket pocket. Your name was there on a list with a question mark beside it."

"Really? What sort of list?"

"His home phone number. His wife's cell phone number. A note about the date Ledwig died, followed by several miscellaneous names. All of them were there last night. Some of them were recent customers of his. We were wondering if you were a customer, too?"

I shook my head.

"Not planning to buy a second home up here in the High Country?"

"Sorry. But now that you mention it . . ." I described to him how Norman Osborne had scribbled something on a notepad as Sunny led him away to the buffet tables. "Maybe that's when he wrote my name down, but I can't imagine why."

"We'll ask Sunny tomorrow," he said.

"She should know," I agreed, then, changing the subject, I asked, "Will Osborne's death make you revisit your decision about Danny Freeman?"

"Sure knocks it into a cocked hat," he said. "His attorney's already been in my office asking for a dismissal."

May returned with our salads, and she had taken it upon herself to drench mine in a heavy blue cheese dressing.

"I'm so sorry," I said sweetly, handing it back to her. "You seem to have brought me someone else's. I wanted olive oil on the side."

"I'll switch with you," Lucius said. "I like blue cheese."

"You sure?"

"Positive."

He passed me his virgin salad and the two little cruets that had accompanied it.

While we ate, we compared notes on mutual acquaintances, the type of crimes he prosecuted in an area whose population fluctuated with the seasons, and what the political climate was like out here — conservative in the small towns and hollows, liberal around the college down in Howards Ford.

Our trout arrived hot and crispy from the grill as our conversation wound back to the deaths of Ledwig and Osborne and whether there was indeed a connection.

"Captain Underwood seems to think there is," I said.

"Sound man," said Burke. "I'm hoping he'll run for sheriff when Horton retires.

Make my life a little easier. His cases are always solid."

"Speaking of which, did Fletcher say anything to you about interviewing your local UPS or FedEx delivery people?"

He shook his head. "In relation to what?"

I described what I had noticed in the photographs. Like Underwood, the mailers had skipped his attention, too, which was understandable since he hadn't gone out to the Ledwig home that day either. He agreed, though, that it might help pinpoint the time a little more precisely. "Too bad Fletcher and Horton missed them."

"It was a big deck," I said, "and they were naturally concentrating on the other side."

"All the same," he said.

"Yeah," I agreed.

We both passed on dessert but lingered over coffee, which seemed to annoy May even more, although she was careful to hide her annoyance from Burke. Every time I glanced past his head toward the service area, she and June had their heads together and were glaring at me. Their disapproval amused me. Here were a pair who'd lied to their parents, spent their tuition money on opening a café, and had suborned friends into supporting that lie. Now they were indignant because I was having a friendly dinner with a colleague?

Please!

Burke left May a generous tip and we walked out to our cars together. The moon cast lacy shadows through trees that were fast losing their leaves.

"It was a nice dinner," I said. "Thank you for asking me."

"Thank you for coming," he said, a quizzical look on his face.

I wasn't surprised when he drew me to him — the moonlight practically demanded it — and I didn't resist as our lips met.

It was a perfectly fine kiss, but neither of us was breathing heavily when it was over.

"Sorry," he said with a rueful smile, "but I wanted to know."

"That's okay," I told him. "I did, too."

Chapter
23

 I was asleep before the twins returned to the condo, nevertheless, they were up before me next morning. I think they deliberately dragged themselves out of bed early so they could rag on me the moment I stuck my head in the kitchen.

"You kissed him!" June said. "I saw you."

I shrugged. "And?"

May grabbed my left hand. "Doesn't this ring mean a thing to you?"

I reclaimed my hand and poured a mug of coffee. The diamond flashed in the sunlight streaming through the east window and I looked at it thoughtfully. "I think it's real pretty, don't you?"

"Deborah!"

"Be serious," said June. "How would you like it if you caught Dwight kissing someone else?"

"Dwight didn't catch me," I pointed out. "You were the ones spying. If you saw us kiss, then you also saw us get in our own cars and drive off in different directions, so drop it, okay?"

Truth to tell, the whole incident had kept me tossing and turning during the night. What did it mean that I couldn't respond to a man as smart and handsome as Lucius Burke? Lafayette County's district attorney was as luscious as his nickname, virile and sexy, with green eyes to die for. I've always been a sucker for green eyes. My bigamous first marriage was to a green-eyed man, and the first guy to really break my heart? He'd had green eyes, too. So what was going on here?

(*"Is it that promise you made your daddy?"* asked the preacher. *"How you were going to be true to Dwight?"*)

(The pragmatist sniffed. *"Get real. It's not just green-eyed men you've played the fool with over the years."*)

For a moment a snatch of my favorite Waylon Jennings CD played in my head: *". . . been a whole lot of good women shed a tear for a brown-eyed handsome man . . ."*

A knock on the door abruptly interrupted my uneasy thoughts.

When May opened it, the girl who entered looked vaguely familiar, but I didn't peg her till June said, "Hey, Trish. You're out early."

"School," she said, making a face as she looked at her watch. "I can only stay about ten minutes. Carla said you wanted to ask me about Dad and Mr. Norman?"

She registered who I was about the same time I made her.

"Aren't you the judge from Danny's hearing Monday?"

"She's our cousin," May explained as I nodded.

"And you're Trish Ledwig, right?" I said.

"It's okay," said June. "She's on our side. Sort of."

"Pretend I'm not here," I said. "In fact, I'll leave if you like."

"That's okay." She sat down at the table across from me, and when the twins offered her coffee, asked if she could have a Coke instead.

Caffeine's caffeine whether it fizzes or steams.

I studied her over the rim of my mug as she popped the top of the Coke can. Like her sister, she had long dark hair and hazel eyes, and a pretty heart-shaped face. She wore well-cut jeans, boots, and a brown leather jacket over a buttercup yellow jersey. There were tiny gold studs in her ears, and a small gold cross hung from a thin chain. No makeup except for a dash of lipstick.

"Do you know what's going to happen to Danny?" she asked.

I shook my head. "Sorry, I don't."

"There's a deputy up at the house right now asking about when some stuff was delivered. He even made me dig out the envelope my CDs came in."

"You still had it?" I asked, surprised.

She looked equally surprised. "You know about it?"

"Those pictures they showed me in court Monday," I reminded her. "I noticed some mailers lying on a table by the deck door."

Enlightenment crossed her young face. "So that's why they're just now asking."

"But those pictures were taken two weeks ago," I said.

"Longer." Her voice was sad. "Dad was killed sixteen days ago."

"And you still had the mailer your CD came in?"

"They're all still there." She explained how she'd forgotten about the order she'd placed till last night, when she'd thought to check the tracking number. "Mom just gathered them up that day and stuck them in Dad's study."

"Do you remember the time on the tracking page?" I asked.

"I printed it out for the deputy — two thirty-eight."

"Are packages routinely left on the deck?"

Trish shook her head. "They're usually leaning against the front door if nobody's home when they come."

The twins appreciated the significance of what Trish was saying, but they were more interested in learning why her dad's friendship with Norman Osborne seemed to have cooled in the month or so before his death.

"I really don't know," Trish told them, "but I've been thinking about it ever since Carla asked me. I did remember a phone call that Sunday, though. The day before he died."

"Osborne called him?" May asked.

"No, Dad called Mr. Norman. See, what happened was that Bobby and Joyce Ashe stopped by for drinks. Dad was still freaking about Carla and Danny so I stayed in my room till after they were gone, but when I went downstairs to ask Dad about my car — it was in the shop and I was having to get him or Mom to drive me places — he was on the phone in the living room and I heard him say, 'I'm sorry, Norman, but I can't stand by and let you do this to them.' And then he said, 'I don't care if it *is* legal, it's not ethical.' Then he saw me and told Mr. Norman he'd call him later and hung up."

"Legal but not ethical," June mused.

"You don't know what that was about?" asked May.

"No, but whatever it was might not've been why they hadn't seen much of each other before, because Dad sounded like he'd just found out about something he didn't want Mr. Norman to do, not like it was something he'd known all along."

"Who was the 'them'?" I said. "The Ashes?"

"I don't know. I'll try asking Mom again, but . . ." Her voice trailed off and the twins exchanged knowing glances.

Having seen Tina Ledwig's capacity for vodka last evening, I had a feeling I knew what Trish's "but" meant.

She checked her watch. "Time's up. Gotta go. If Mom says anything, I'll tell you. It sucks that she won't help Carla hire a real detective. I just hope you can figure it out because it's eating her and Danny up. Dad could be tight-assed about things, but he would've come around and Carla knows that."

She grabbed her Coke and left.

I followed her example and headed for my morning shower before the twins could get on my case again.

Wednesday seemed to be Lafayette County's day for assaults on females and domestic violence in general, but at lunchtime I didn't have to go out because George Underwood appeared at my chamber door with a thermos of hot homemade vegetable beef soup.

"What's this in aid of?" I asked, breathing in the hearty aroma as he opened the thermos and filled two mugs for both of us.

"A thank-you for noticing those packages," he said. "We talked to the UPS guy that made the delivery that afternoon. Looks like Mrs. Ledwig's alibi's not as tight as we thought it was. She matches the description of the woman he gave the packages to. He says she was walking out to her car when he got there, so he handed her the things and the computerized scanner automatically entered the time — thirty-eight minutes after the bartender says she came into the club."

"I take it you'll be speaking to the bartender again?"

Underwood nodded. "I called the club. He comes on duty at one."

Afternoon court was made interesting by the fact that I had caught on to the flow and rhythm of William Deeck's methods. Yesterday, for instance, I noticed that he would present me with a string of egregious check-bouncers, habitual shoplifters, or repeat thieves, then slide in someone who seemed basically decent or who had yielded to temptation for the first time. His prosecution would be just as rigorous, but the contrast between defendants was such that most judges would automatically be more inclined to listen sympathetically to whatever justifications a court-appointed attorney might offer.

If Deeck realized that I knew, he didn't let on by so much as a raised eyebrow.

It was late in the afternoon. We had just finished four trashy cases of domestic violence, men and women hammering on each other. The first, second, and fourth were men who had punched out their women. The third was a woman who'd thrown a kettle of boiling water on her man because he drank up all her bourbon — "And then damned if he didn't smoke my last cigarette, too!"

Not a marriage license among them and I've quit trying to decide whether or not this is a good thing.

Then Deeck presented me with something completely different: the State v. Richard Granger, a tall, lanky man who appeared to be in his mid-fifties. Granger was accused of hunting turkeys out of season up on Laudermilk Ridge, a rather wild and isolated area. Testifying against him with great relish was an equally raw-boned neighbor, Hank Smith, who differed in appearance mainly by the large, slightly soiled bandage over his left ear.

In exchange for Smith's testimony, the State had agreed not to prosecute him for hunting out of season himself.

I listened in bemusement as Deeck laid out the facts of the case. I've been told by one of my colleagues over in Hickory that the real mountain seasons aren't spring, summer, autumn, or winter, but rather deer, bear, quail, and turkey. Unfortunately for Granger, turkey season ended back in May.

"Nevertheless, we will show the court that Mr. Granger went up to Laudermilk last month to shoot one. Call Mr. Hank Smith to the stand."

Mr. Smith came forward, laid his hand on the Bible, and soon launched into his account of how he'd been up on the ridge himself that morning when he spied Granger coming up the trail with his shotgun.

"I knowed right away what he was after. If it was squirrels he was wanting, he could've bagged hisself one without never leaving his yard. And he'd be carrying his twenty-two, not his twelve-gauge."

Smith was such a natural-born story-teller that for a moment he seemed to forget that he was sitting in a witness box instead of on somebody's front porch. Caught up in the telling of the tale, he let his admiration of Granger's talent almost outweigh his grudge over the personal cost to himself.

"Dick's a champion turkey caller. You a tom, you'd swear it was the J. Lo of turkey hens a-promising you the best night of your life. Ain't never seen the day he couldn't call one up. And sure enough, one come a-walking right out into the clearing up above me, heading on down to where Dick was hiding. 'Bout the time I raised up to shoot, he let fire himself. Winged me right on the ear here."

In other words, he'd planned to poach from the poacher and lost part of an ear for his sins.

"Mr. Granger's not being charged with assault?" I asked Deeck.

"No, Your Honor. It was clearly an accident." He paused, then added dryly, "The State feels that had Mr. Granger been aiming at Mr. Smith, Mr. Smith would probably be missing a head now, not merely an ear."

"I thought I was up there all by myself," Granger volunteered, nodding vigorous agreement. "Right when I was pulling the trigger, Hank here popped up like a full-blown rhododendron. I do purely hate it happened like that, ma'am."

I suppressed a smile and told Granger he'd have a chance to speak his piece later.

As Deeck continued questioning Smith, Granger leaned over and spoke into his court-appointed attorney's ear. They conferred for a moment, then the attorney rose and said, "Your Honor, at this time, my client would like to change his plea to guilty with mitigating circumstances and throw himself on the mercy of the court."

"Very well," I said. "You may step down, Mr. Smith. Mr. Granger?"

The man stood to address me with simple dignity. He wore a denim jacket over a flannel shirt and jeans. Jacket, shirt, and jeans had been washed so often that they were thin and faded, but they were immaculate and had a just-ironed look to them. Seated on the bench behind him was a woman with a worried face. Her hair was almost completely white and her black slacks were as faded as his jeans, but her soft blue cardigan looked brand-new. It had mock pearl buttons and pearl beaded flowers around the yoke. If asked, I'd have to say it was probably a gift from a dutiful relative who didn't see her very often. It reminded me of the sort of sweater some of my older brothers would give Aunt Zell for her birthday or Christmas.

"Your Honor, ma'am, my wife's got a bad heart and I ain't been able to work myself since I hurt my back at the chip mill three years ago. They didn't have no insurance on anybody there and the government says I ain't entitled to workman's compensation, so the onliest way we got to feed ourselves is from our little garden patch and with what I can catch or kill. Now I know it's against the law to shoot turkeys in September, but, ma'am, it's got to where it ain't legal to shoot nothing but crows from May to October and I ain't never been real partial to eating crow."

"Me either," I told him sympathetically.

I thought of the Tuzzolinos from yesterday's court. A Coral Gables dentist and a Lafayette County mill worker. Both men disabled, but what a difference in the way they tried to provide for their wives. No key-man insurance for the Grangers of the world. No health insurance, precious few safety nets.

Okay, so maybe Deeck was trying to manipulate my emotions, but he didn't really need to. I'm a softy for self-reliant throwbacks like Granger. Squirrels and rabbits kept my daddy's family alive when he was a boy, and he still fumes about the foolishness of slapping a season on what he calls "tree rats."

"The law is the law," my internal preacher sternly reminded me. *"You don't get to choose which laws to enforce and you can't let him off scot-free."*

"No, but you can come pretty damn close," said the pragmatist.

Instead of a fine or jail time such as I'd given the Tuzzolinos, I gave him a PJC — prayer for judgment continued — on condition he not kill turkeys out of season and that he pay the hundred-dollar court costs.

"Thank you, Your Honor," said the attorney.

Deeck didn't thank me but a small satisfied smile lurked in the corner of his mouth as he called his next case.

Chapter
24

When I passed the dispatcher's station on my way through to the lower-level parking area, George Underwood was there and he walked out into the late-afternoon sunshine with me.

"Any luck with that bartender?" I asked.

"Not really. He's ready to swear on any Bible I want to hand him that Tina Ledwig was definitely there by five minutes past two the day her husband was killed. Says he remembers because he ran out of her favorite brand of vodka the day before and they didn't get in another shipment till the next morning. He even showed me the invoices. *And* gave me the names of a foursome who were waiting for a two-fifteen tee time."

"Sounds pretty conclusive," I said.

"Yeah. He had to comp her a couple of free Smirnoffs to stop her bitching, which is another reason he remembers. Unless he's a real good actor, he was still pissed about it, too, if you'll excuse my French."

"So when will you talk to the UPS guy again?" I asked.

"He's not due back up here till sometime after lunch tomorrow. I left word down in Asheville for him to come by."

"Do you suppose that automatic dater on his computer was off?"

Underwood shrugged. "Who knows? One thing's for sure, though — somebody's screwed up somewhere, 'cause if Mrs. Ledwig was sitting at the bar in the Rabbit Hollow Country Club at two-thirty-eight, then she certainly couldn't have been taking delivery from a UPS driver."

"Let me know how it comes out," I told him as I went on over to my car.

Once I had my key in the ignition, though, I hesitated about where to go. I'd already damaged my credit card too much to embark on another round of Cedar Gap shopping, yet it was only five-thirty and much too early for dinner.

Dwight's always telling me not to get involved in things that don't concern me, and had he been waiting for me at the condo, maybe I'd have gone straight there.

(*"Only maybe?"* leered the pragmatist.)

(*"Please!"* said the preacher, averting his eyes as erotic images suddenly flooded my senses.)

But Dwight wasn't there, and okay, I'll admit it: curiosity has always been an itch I have to scratch. Like chigger bites.

Five-thirty is smack in the middle of Dobbs's moderate rush hour back home, but here in Cedar Gap it seemed to bring a temporary lull. Most of the leaf lovers had dwindled with the setting sun; the rest were sitting around the monument, licking ice-cream cones and soaking up the last rays of sunshine, while the seasonal people hadn't yet come out for dinner.

The front part of the real estate office was dark, but I could see Joyce Ashe at the back when I rapped on the glass door. She looked up with a frown that immediately changed into a professional smile of welcome even before she recognized who it was.

"Hey, Deborah!" she said, holding the door wide for me. "Looking to buy a vacation place?"

"Sorry," I said. "What I'm actually looking for is someone to come have a drink with me. You free?"

"Now that's the best offer I've had all day! Give me ten minutes to finish up this new house and I'm your gal."

While her fingers flew across the keyboard of her computer, I looked through a photo album of properties they had listed. A prominent bulletin board labeled "Osborne-Ashe High Country Realty" was covered with various architectural renderings for the ambitious facelift they planned to give this building.

It was closer to fifteen minutes before Joyce gave a sigh of satisfaction and the laser printer came to life and began cranking out copies of the new material, complete with color photos and all specifications.

"Done!" she said. "I've earned that drink."

"I'm surprised you're so hands-on," I said. "I should think you'd have a secretary to do all this."

"I do have a secretary. Two secretaries, actually, and Bobby nags me to delegate more, but I like the detail work, keeping tabs on what's happening where. I know I'll have to change now that we're getting so much bigger, but I also know I'm going to miss being down in the trenches."

"You'll still be taking on all of Norman

Osborne's properties, then?"

"Oh, yes. Bobby's down in Howards Ford right now, going over stuff with the lawyers and the insurance people. You wouldn't believe —" She broke off with a wry smile. "Well, yes, I guess you would believe, being a lawyer yourself once, right?"

"Right," I said, smiling back. "Why draw up just one document when ten will impress the clients?"

She laughed and reached for the red jacket that went with her tailored navy blue dress. "Drinks. Let me think . . . you been to the Rock yet?"

I shook my head and she picked up the nearest phone, punched in some numbers, and said, "Kevin? Joyce Ashe. A friend and I are headed your way. Any chance you could clear us a table out on the terrace? . . . Great! Be there in five minutes."

She hung up and said, "It's right outside of town on the main road. Follow me."

I trailed her white Plymouth four-by-four up Main Street, past the condo, and on out of town. As promised, in less than five minutes we were pulling into the busy parking lot of what looked like a rustic hunting lodge built on the side of the mountain. Joyce zoomed right over to a spot on the very edge of the downsloping lot, and although there was a space next to her and although I've never had any reason to doubt my emergency brakes, I waited till someone pulled out of a level space nearer the front, next to a huge granite boulder that probably gave the place its name.

"Flatlander!" Joyce gibed.

"Hey, what can I tell you?" I said sheepishly.

A middle-aged man came through the crowded room and Joyce introduced me to the owner, who led us outside. The night air was chilly and my jacket wasn't very heavy, but I needn't have worried. Out on the terrace, each table had an umbrella, and each umbrella shaft contained a heating element that beamed down enough warmth to keep us comfortable.

The view seemed to stretch east for a million miles, with row after row of blue mountaintops blending one into the other. It was that magical hour when the sun had sunk behind the ridge and a haze rose from the valley below. Night had not completely captured the sky, yet a couple of bright stars dotted the dark blue above us. Our drinks arrived just when the moon began to edge itself up from the horizon, like a golden swimmer pulling himself up from a dark pool.

"This is so beautiful," I sighed.

Our drinks came — a Bloody Mary for me, a martini for her — and we raised our glasses to the harvest moon as it cleared the horizon, big and yellow.

"Is it full tonight, I wonder?" Joyce asked, draining half her glass with one thirsty swallow.

"Not till Friday," I said.

She was amused. "You carry an almanac around with you or are you just romantic?"

"Some of both, probably," I admitted.

She glanced at my ring. "He romantic, too?"

Dwight? Romantic?

" 'Fraid not," I said. "What about Bobby?"

"Only when he's romancing a prospective client," she said with a broad smile.

I told her how I'd known Dwight since infancy, then asked how she and Bobby met.

"He was the boy next door, if you can call a hollow beyond the nearest ridge next door."

She pronounced it "holler," an endearing holdover of her native mountain speech, much the way my daddy and older brothers still say "chimbly" for chimney or "tar arn" for tire iron, or the way our down easters say "hoi toide" for high tide. I treasure these remnants of dialects. When television finally finishes smoothing out all the regional differences, we will have lost a special part of our heritage.

"We both grew up poorer than Job's turkey, but Bobby always had big dreams. We were thirteen years old, standing barefooted in White Fox Creek, when he told me he was going to marry me and give me diamonds and pearls." She glanced at the diamonds on her sturdy fingers, as if pinching herself that they were really there. "It was a rough and rocky road in the beginning." Her eyes grew dreamy as she sipped her martini.

"And now you're the biggest real estate and management firm in Lafayette County," I said softly.

"Bobby's doing, not mine. I was happy where we were, but he always felt we got Norman's crumbs. Talk about romancing! Not that he sucked up to Norman. He's too proud for that. But he laid out all the facts and figures of how working together could do us both better than working apart, and eventually Norman came around. In fact, once he was convinced, you'd have thought it was Norman pushing the merger instead of us. He agreed to things Bobby was sure he wouldn't just because he didn't want to hold up the paperwork."

She glanced at her watch, then excused herself to visit the restroom and call Bobby. "I'll tell him we're here. We might as well stay for dinner if you don't have anything else going. They have great steaks."

"Fine," I said.

As she walked away, I signaled the waiter.

"Another round of the same, only make my Bloody Mary a virgin."

I didn't have a husband coming who could drive me home if I went over the limit. And if I drove off the edge of the road on the way back to town, I didn't want it to be because I could blow an eight.

"Whoa!" said Joyce when she returned to find a fresh martini before her. "I need food if I'm going to have another drink. Bobby was already on the way. Want to split an appetizer while we wait for him?"

"Sure," I said and steered our choice toward the fried mozzarella sticks, figuring we wouldn't get many and that they would be salty enough to keep her sipping from that cocktail glass.

I was right on both counts. Not that I really needed to ply her with gin. Joyce was too gregarious not to talk freely.

"It must be awful for you and Bobby," I said. "Losing two friends like this."

"And in our own house." Sadness mingled with indignation. "With one of my own candleholders."

"Any ideas as to who wanted them dead?"

She shook her head. "I've been over it and over it in my mind and the only person who might have had it in for both of them is Simon Proffitt. Remember him from Monday night?"

I nodded. The dueling fiddler.

"Carlyle and Norman wanted to buy him out and use that lot for something more in keeping with Cedar Gap's image since it's right there at the town entrance. They wouldn't take no for an answer either. He said they were worrying the heart and soul out of him and if they didn't quit it, he was going to take ol' Jessie to them."

"Who's ol' Jessie? His dog?"

"His twelve-gauge shotgun," she said

dryly. "Simon's a holdover from the old days, back when Cedar Gap was just another little hillbilly mountain town. Then Norman and some others got a whiff of the money that could be made if they beautified and landscaped and made it look exclusive. People were so poor out here that most of them were willing to do just about anything to attract big spenders."

"But Proffitt wasn't one of them?" I asked, nibbling on a cheese stick.

"To put it mildly. He rallied enough likeminded businesses to grandfather in what they had, but the rest of us — and yeah, Bobby and I were just as bad — fell right into line. And it certainly worked. The town is beautiful now, isn't it?"

"Yes," I said, and said truthfully, because she's right: Cedar Gap *is* beautiful — as beautiful as a Disney World re-creation of yesteryear and just about as authentic.

"Thirty years ago, there wasn't a house in the county worth more than fifty thousand dollars. Now you probably can't buy a cold-water shack for that little."

"Proffitt's not happy with the changes?"

"And I can't fault him for it. No, I can't. The way they hound him over all the new rules and regulations? He can't do squat without the town council coming down on him with a writ or a warning. He says it's like sitting bare-assed on a hornet's nest. Least little move and they pop him one. That's why I could see him losing it if Carlyle or Norman said the wrong thing at the wrong time, but still . . ."

Her voice trailed off and she shook her head. "I don't know, Deborah. Unless it's him, I can't think who else it could be. Sam Tysinger had words with them both, but Sam has words with everybody sooner or later. Doesn't mean a thing. And let's get real. Nobody's going to kill because they had to replace a big sign with a smaller one. Besides, that was six months ago. Now, if serious money was involved —" She hesitated, and then, with a what-the-hell shrug, said, "If Sheriff Horton didn't know for a fact that Bobby and I were down in Asheville when Carlyle was killed, I'm sure he'd think one of us killed Norman."

"Because of the partnership insurance on him?" Not by a flicker of an eyelash would I let on that I knew why they'd gone to Asheville that day.

Joyce nodded. "Short term, we really are worth a lot more today than we were three days ago, but long term? Norman was such a rainmaker. He charmed everybody. We don't have a single penny now that we wouldn't have had eventually if he'd lived."

She had caught our waiter's eye before and made a circular motion with her index finger. As she described the plans Osborne and Bobby had made to expand into the neighboring counties, the waiter arrived with another round of drinks. I sipped mine cautiously, unsure if this was the real thing. Joyce was now on her third martini and, except for the way she relaxed a little deeper into her wicker chair, I couldn't tell that it had any effect on her.

"How's Sunny doing?" I asked. "She must be devastated."

"Yes and no."

I raised an inquiring eyebrow and Joyce gave a baffled, palms-up gesture.

"It's weird. The way she's practically lived in his pocket these last two or three months, you'd expect her to fall apart completely now that he's gone."

"And yet?" I encouraged.

Again that baffled look. "Well, on one level she has. You saw them Monday night. That duet they sang wasn't just an act. They were crazy about each other and she's wild with grief that he's gone. At the same time, she goes ballistic whenever anybody tries to link his death with Carlyle's. It's like she thinks it somehow demeans Norman's death, if that makes any sense."

Her face suddenly brightened and she half stood to wave. "There's Bobby!"

Bobby Ashe's progress across the wide terrace was slowed by the many people who spoke to him and whose hands he paused to shake. His sandy hair and droopy sand-colored mustache reminded me of that big goofy cartoon sheepdog that was so popular when I was a kid. You had to smile just looking at him.

"Hey, purty ladies," he said, taking my hand and leaning over to kiss Joyce at the same time. "Y'all looked awful serious when I first came in."

"We were talking about Sunny Osborne," I said. "How she doesn't think her husband and Dr. Ledwig were killed by the same person."

His good-natured smile faded and he nodded thoughtfully. "I'm wondering if she's afraid Horton will think Norman found out who killed Carlyle and that's why *he* had to die."

"Now that makes a little more sense," said Joyce. "If Norman has to be dead, Sunny would want it to be that he was killed for who he was, not because he happened to get mixed up in whatever reasons there were for killing Carlyle."

"That would be Sunny all right," Bobby said as our waiter came over to see what he wanted to drink. He was the type of man who instantly becomes the host as soon as he sits down with two women, and he made sure that Joyce and I were fine for the moment before telling the waiter to bring him a Jim Beam on the rocks. "A double, straight up."

Then he noticed that Joyce's glass was nearly empty and said, "Hold up a minute there, son, till I find out whose turn it is to drive home."

Joyce smiled. "Your turn, honey."

"Better make that a single then," he told the waiter. "With a splash."

"How's it going down there?" Joyce asked.

"It's going." He brushed the ends of his mustache away from the edge of his mouth. "Norman's people are still in shock, but they're savvy folks and they've got it in gear."

I couldn't let it alone. "I don't suppose Sunny will have anything to do with the partnership once all the paperwork's done?"

"Lord, no," said Bobby. "She hasn't

worked real estate since their daughter was born."

"She said she wanted to get back in it," said Joyce, "but that was just because she got to where she couldn't stand not to be with Norman every minute. She was always such a take-charge person — athletic, played tennis or golf two or three times a week, sat on boards, volunteered at the hospital, and then, bang! Almost overnight, she turned into a kudzu vine. Like to've worried us to death, right, hon?"

"Oh, she was all right," Bobby said. "Y'all order yet?"

"All *right?*" Joyce rolled her eyes. "The way she was always there, asking questions, writing everything down? You were ready to strangle her."

"Now, Joyce, baby —"

"Well, you were, Bobby. No point in pretending you weren't just because you feel sorry for her now." She turned back to me. "I feel sorry for her, too, but you can't imagine what a nuisance she was. She wouldn't just sit and watch and listen, she kept jumping in the middle. There were a million details to take care of with this merger and Norman couldn't concentrate for her running her mouth every minute."

"And I say let's stop boring Deborah

and get this young fellow here to tell us about tonight's specials." He took a swallow of the drink the waiter had brought and leaned back in his chair. "What you got good, son?" he asked.

When our steaks came, mine was just the way I like it: charred on the outside and rare on the inside. Conversation became more general. Bobby clearly didn't want to gossip about Sunny and Norman Osborne. Instead, he'd heard rumors about the Tuzzolino trial and wanted to know if it was true that they'd really hired somebody to steal for them.

Joyce thought it was funny. "An ex-con for your personal shopper?"

I nodded. "She said that her husband was so down over his Parkinson's that beautiful and expensive things were the only antidepressant that worked."

"Sounds like they got screwed by his partner," said Bobby.

"Well, to be fair, he couldn't afford the buyout and the insurance only covered the senior partner's death."

"Isn't Parkinson's a death sentence?"

"Eventually, maybe, but these days drugs can keep you going for years. Clearly he wasn't going to die soon enough to take the burden off the younger guy."

"If the practice was that good, he should've sucked it up and worked his tail off to keep it going," Bobby said.

"Maybe he would've," I said, "except that Mrs. Tuzzolino was trying to hold him to the partnership's buyout agreement right away and he simply didn't have the money."

"Wow!" said Joyce as a personal application hit her. "God, Bobby! Think what it would've done to us if that'd happened to Norman."

"That's exactly why we both went for complete physicals, remember? The insurance people were a little worried about my cholesterol, but Norman was in perfect health."

"Was Ledwig your doctor?" I asked. "Carlyle?"

"Oh, no," said Joyce. "Carlyle wasn't an internist. His specialty was geriatrics."

She passed me the bread basket, but when I turned back the napkin, all those hot rolls were gone. I'd already had one and knew I shouldn't have a second, but I didn't protest when Bobby caught our waiter's eye and held up the basket.

I asked them what it was like growing up here in the mountains, and it sounded a lot

like my daddy's tales of his childhood —
privations, yes, but a sense of rootedness.
Hard work, where even children were expected to carry their share of the load, but
time for music and storytelling, too.

When I asked if they knew Richard
Granger or Hank Smith, Bobby began to
laugh.

"Hell, yes! You hear about Dick shooting
Hank's ear off last month?"

"They were both in my courtroom
today," I said. Since Granger's trial, like
the trial of the Tuzzolinos, was now public
record, I could speak freely about it.

"I hope you went easy on Dick," Joyce
said in quick sympathy. "He and his wife
are having it rough since he got hurt at the
chip mill. They're too proud to take
charity, but when she brought one of her
mother's quilts to ask me what I thought it
should fetch at the craft gallery, I did
manage to convince her to sell it to me for
about twice what it was really worth."

Bobby looked at her quizzically. "Did I
know this?"

"Oops!" she said with a smile.

"They don't have to live that close to the
bone," he said. "Dick and Sarah Granger
are living on one of the prettiest pieces of
land on Laudermilk Creek. They could sell

out tomorrow and live in ease the rest of their lives."

"Live where?" asked Joyce. "You know they'd die if you took them off that mountain."

"All the same," he said, "I believe I'll take a ride out there next week, see if I can interest him in selling."

"Bobby, no!" she protested.

"I know, honey, I know," he said soothingly, "but if not me, it'll be somebody else. Somebody who might not give him as good a price."

When I got back to the condo, all it really needed to be ready to rent were fresher curtains and a carpet cleaning. The kitchen cabinets sparkled with new enamel, and all traces of paint buckets, brushes, and drop cloths were gone. Fred and Beverly should be pleased about this much, at least.

I checked my e-mail again. Still nothing from Dwight. Well, what did I expect?

There was also nothing on television, nothing in the condo's selection of videos that I wanted to watch, and nothing I wanted to do.

Nobody to talk to either.

Good thing, too, said the pragmatist.

"The way you're feeling right now, you'd just be spoiling for a fight."

"Go to bed," said the preacher.

"Go to hell!" I told them both.

And went to bed.

Chapter
25

 With no paint crew to cook breakfast for, the twins opted to sleep in the next morning. Hard as they'd been working, I certainly couldn't blame them, and I tiptoed around quietly. Wouldn't hurt me to make do with orange juice and an apple after those rolls last night.

Besides, I knew that the usual carafe of coffee would be waiting for me.

"The way you and Mr. Deeck are zipping through the calendar," said Mary Kay, "it looks like tomorrow's going to be early getaway."

Now there was a thought. If I finished by lunch tomorrow, I could be home before dark.

Before Dwight left for Virginia.

Morning court was a brisk array of the usual, and at noon I went down to the Tea

Room and scrounged a salad from the twins, who seemed strangely uninterested in discussing the murders.

"Of course, Carla and Trish still want to know who killed their dad," June said, "but we were only asking around because Danny couldn't afford a real detective."

"And now that he's going to be off the hook —" said May.

"— we can leave it to the police," said June.

What mainly seemed to occupy their thoughts was where they were going to live after Parents' Day at Tanser-MacLeod College. Beverly was bringing up the new curtains she'd made, and a new couch and chairs would be delivered at the same time. Fred had already contacted the management office about renting out the condo for the tail end of leaf season.

"We were going to crash on friends at our old dorm anyhow, but that's just for the weekend."

I cast a glance up at the pressed tin ceiling. "What's up on the second floor here? Could you camp out up there?"

"Lord, no, don't even think about it," said May.

"It's jammed with all the junk that came

out of the ground floor," June chimed in.

"Dirty."

"Cold."

"Spiderwebs."

"I think I saw a mouse when we carried up the last load."

"And anyhow, there's no water up there."

"And no shower in the ladies' room down here."

"Besides, if the Health Department caught us —"

"— not to mention the zoning people —"

"— we could lose our restaurant permit."

"So where will you go?" I asked.

"We'll think of something," said June.

"Here, have a cruller," May said.

Afternoon court was a repeat of the morning, until shortly before three, when I was presented with a couple of judgment-impaired twenty-one-year-olds from Tanser-MacLeod College who had gotten drunk and disorderly in a Howards Ford bar, where they did six hundred dollars' worth of damage to the mirrors and bottles behind the bar. Both were white, both had that slightly arrogant stance of kids who were used to doing what they liked, knowing that their parents would clean up the mess. Indeed, Matt Dodson, an attorney I'd met at the Ashe party, presented documents that showed me that restitution had already been paid.

I listened to their guilty plea and their pro forma apologies and I heard what the prosecutor was recommending, then Dodson made a game plea for a low fine and community service.

Nice try, but I'd caught a good glimpse of the first youth when he swaggered up to the defense table in a preppy, long-sleeved rugby shirt, khaki shorts, moccasins, and no socks even though it was a cool fall day.

"Step out from behind the table," I told him when both stood to hear my ruling.

There on his leg, from his ankle to his knee, was a tattoo of an extremely explicit nude with her legs spread wide. A full frontal view.

"Do you really think that tattoo is appropriate for a courtroom?" I asked.

He shrugged and with a nod toward Dodson said, "Well, he did tell me maybe I ought to be wearing long pants today."

"You should have listened to him," I said.

At least his partner in crime wore clothes a bit more appropriate: long cargo pants and a navy blue sweatshirt that read, "If you don't love the South . . . ."

"Excuse me, Your Honor," the bailiff murmured, "but you might want to ask him to turn around."

The young man glared at the bailiff and then reluctantly turned around when I made a circular motion with my finger.

There on the back was ". . . then you can suck my Dixie."

Both had previous convictions for DWIs, so I fined them a thousand each with the stipulation that they pay the fines out of their own earnings and provide proof of it, but instead of suspending the full forty-five days as I might normally do, I decided that serving two days of it in jail this coming weekend might be a better attitude adjuster. I'm pretty sure I saw an amused gleam in Matt Dodson's dark eyes as he thanked me for my leniency.

"Jail?" snarled the tattooed one, angrily shaking off Dodson's hand when the attorney tried to restrain him. "Hey, I know my rights. My tattoo's protected under the First Amendment. Don't I have freedom of speech?"

"Absolutely," I said. "You have the freedom to talk your way right into a contempt of court."

"Hey, dude, chill," said his friend, which gave me a little hope for learning experiences.

"Sorry, Your Honor," said Dodson and hustled his clients out of the courtroom.

The last three cases of the day asked for continuances, which I granted. I signed a couple of show-cause orders, but there was nothing else on my docket so I adjourned court shortly before three-thirty.

Rather than go back to the condo and veg out, I dug into my purse for the card that Billy Ed Johnson had given me Monday night with his cell phone number. He was so proud of the work he'd done in the area that he'd offered to tour me around. "Anytime," he'd said. "Just give me a ring."

When he answered on the third ring, he sounded pleased that I'd called. "I thought you were just being polite."

I laughed and reminded him that I still had his ball cap from our drive up to the Ashe house.

"Aw, you don't need to give it back."

Remembering the raunchy logo on it, I assured him I did.

He told me that he was out near the Tennessee border at the moment, and we agreed to meet at a watering hole two ridges over from Cedar Gap, at a place called Eagle Rest. I gave him my cell phone number in case he got delayed and he gave me clear directions, which he made me write down and read back to him. He assured me that this was a can't-miss shortcut that would take me straight to the pub by four o'clock if I left right then, so I slid my phone back into my purse, put on my jacket, hung my robe on a hook behind the door, slung my laptop over my shoulder, and was out of there, calling good-bye to Mary Kay, who was still looking at pictures of the bailiff's new granddaughter.

A UPS truck was parked off to the side of the parking lot downstairs, and if I hadn't already told Billy Ed I'd meet him by four, I would have hung around to hear what Underwood had learned. Now I'd have to wait till tomorrow.

There was a moment of unpleasantness as I put my laptop in the trunk and un-locked my car door. Several cars over from mine were the two young men I'd just sentenced. The one with the obscene sweatshirt quickly looked away when my eyes met his, but the tattooed one — Barringer — glared back and gave me the finger.

More freedom of speech.

I shrugged and got in my car.

Ten minutes later, I was two turns off the main road, bedazzled by the fall colors blazing all around me as I topped the first ridge. I kept the speedometer well under the limit because there were no guardrails along this secondary road. It's crazy. I don't pay a lot of attention to Republicans, but I sort of remembered how one of the state senators from out this way — Virginia Foxx? — keeps trying to get Raleigh to put guardrails on all paved mountain roads. I guess there must not be enough voters up here to keep DOT on its toes and that most of them probably skid off the road every time the roads ice over.

At least the traffic was light here, and the few cars that were on this narrow road seemed to be locals, not leaf-crazy tourists, so when a black Ford Ranger riding high on oversize tires zoomed right up behind me, I assumed it was someone in a hurry to get home and moved over to give him room to pass.

That's when he bumped me.

Startled, I glanced in the rearview mirror and recognized the angry kid from court. What the hell — ?

He bumped me again, harder.

I stepped on the accelerator and my wheels squealed as I took a curve a lot faster than I wanted. He started to pass me, but then a car from the opposite direction appeared in the left lane and he swerved back in, grazing my rear bumper.

I realized that I couldn't let him get between me and the side of the mountain. The crazy way he was driving, he might push me off the road. The bottom fell out of my stomach as I stole a glance toward the side. No shoulder worth speaking of between the right lane and a sheer drop beyond. I hugged the center line as long as I could, till yet another car appeared and I had to move over, fighting the wheel as the curve tightened. Before I could get back to the center, he elbowed in beside me.

A Firebird's something of a muscle car, but with those monster tires he could climb all over me. Metal crunched on metal as he nudged me closer to the edge. I battled to hold my own car on the road, then, more in desperate instinct than rational thought, I sat on my brakes and he shot past me.

Frantically, I made a three-point turn and headed back up the rise, but the clashes had done something to my alignment and I had to struggle with the wheel. At least I now had the mountain on my side of the road.

My moment of relief was short-lived, because here was that shiny black Ranger in my rearview mirror again and coming up fast. The road took a sharp right curve, but I kept my right foot on the gas pedal and mashed it to the floorboard as I cornered.

At that instant, I felt a sickening jolt from behind.

A split second later, I was sailing straight out through bright blue sunlight. I stomped on the brakes, but there was only air beneath my wheels.

Sky and trees tumbled wildly in front of my windshield, then my world went black.

Chapter
26

THURSDAY, 3:50 p.m.

 "Hey, Mary Kay," George Underwood said as they met at the outer door on the lower level. "Playing hooky?"

"Just a little bit. We finished up early and Mrs. Vincent said I could cut out early, too," she said, referring to Lafayette County's clerk of court.

"Judge Knott's already gone?"

She nodded. "You missed her by about fifteen minutes."

Underwood experienced a twinge of disappointment. He was looking forward to telling her of their interview with the UPS driver, who was just now pulling his boxy brown truck out of the parking lot as they watched.

"You sure you remember that Monday?" they had asked him. "Could you maybe be thinking of an earlier day when Mrs. Ledwig actually did take delivery?"

"It was that Monday. That's when my radio station does the roundup of all the weekend baseball scores, and I wanted to see who the Braves might be going to have to face in the playoffs."

"And you're positive it was Mrs. Ledwig? You knew her by sight?"

"I didn't ask to see her birth certificate, but I'm pretty sure I've seen her before. Middle-aged? Blond? 'Bout as tall as me? She was coming around from the back to get in her car. Had the keys in her hand and looked a little like she really wanted me to move it 'cause the truck was blocking the drive. I just handed her the stuff and she went back with 'em the way she'd come."

Underwood looked at his notes. Tina Ledwig drove a silver Lexus. "What kind of car was it?"

The driver shrugged. "I don't keep up with the makes. It was a luxury sedan, though. White."

"I don't suppose you noticed the license plate?"

"Sorry. I don't remember the numbers, but the first three letters were S-U-N."

Underwood, who had been leaning back in his chair, came upright. "You sure about that?"

"About the letters? Sure, I'm sure."

Underwood swung around to his computer. "I'm going to type up your statement, and while I'm doing that, Detective Fletcher here will need to get your fingerprints so we can eliminate them from the packages."

Now, the deliveryman was on his way back to Asheville and Underwood took his signed statement into Sheriff Horton's office.

"You saying Sunny Osborne was at the Ledwig house that afternoon?" asked the sheriff.

"She's tall, blond, middle-aged, and the license plate on her white Lincoln has the word 'SUN' followed by the date she and Osborne were married. They say she swings a mean tennis racket, too," Underwood told him.

"Jesus!" said Horton. "You serious? You really think she killed Ledwig?"

"I don't know. All I know is that she was there that afternoon and she didn't see fit to tell us."

"Osborne's body's still in Chapel Hill. She do him, too?"

He shrugged. "Our DA and Judge Knott both say she was playing a dulcimer the whole time before Osborne went missing."

Horton's face brightened. "That's right. So if she didn't kill her husband, she didn't kill Ledwig. She was probably scared to say she was there. Afraid we'd jump to the same conclusions we almost did. You go talk to her, George. Be easy with her. I bet she'll tell you what really happened."

"I'll give her a call. See if I can run up there now."

On the way back to his office, Underwood paused at the dispatcher's station. "Any word on Proffitt yet?"

The owner of the Trading Post hadn't shown up yesterday morning, and when a deputy went to collect him today, he was not to be found.

The dispatcher shook her head. "Nobody's seen him since night before last. Faye says his shotgun's still there, but if he went hunting, nothing's in season for another week. Course that wouldn't stop ol' Proffitt, but his truck's still parked out back. You reckon he's skipped town?"

"In what?" asked Underwood. "Don't make it official, but I'll send somebody out to check his house, and you tell everybody to keep a stray eye out for him, okay?"

"Sure, Captain."

He went on down to his office and called the Osborne house. The housekeeper who answered said she thought that Mrs. Osborne and her daughter had gone to a funeral home in Howards Ford. "To make the arrangements," she said with a catch in her voice.

He left his number and asked her to tell Mrs. Osborne to call when she got back.

THURSDAY, 4:30 p.m.

The intercom on Lucius Burke's desk gave a preliminary crackle, then his secretary's voice said, "Billy Ed Johnson on line two, Mr. Burke."

He pressed the right button. "Hey, Billy Ed! How can I do you?"

"Well, I was just wondering if that lady judge is still around the courthouse?"

"Judge Knott? I'm not sure. You want me to have somebody check and see?"

"Well, I'd appreciate it. She was supposed to meet me up here at Eagle Rest, but looks like she's running late. Only she's not answering her cell phone either."

He gave Burke his number and said, "Call me back, hear?"

"Sure thing." Burke cut the connection and touched the intercom button. "Suanna? Would you see if Judge Knott's still in the courthouse?"

Out in the anteroom, that young woman rolled her eyes, but pushed back from her computer and went down the hall to the courtroom the visitor had used today. The lights were out. The light was also out in Judge Rawlings's chambers, but Suanna was nothing if not diligent. She took the stairs down to the lower level and peered out over the parking lot. "Anybody know what kind of car that judge drives?"

Fletcher, on his way back from flirting with the evening dispatcher, said, "Captain Underwood might."

"Might what?" Underwood called, having heard his name.

"Know what kind of car your judge friend drives," Fletcher called back.

Underwood came to his doorway. "Who wants to know?"

"Mr. Burke." As the DA's secretary, Suanna usually took notes on his calls unless he specifically told her to get off the line. "She was supposed to meet somebody at Eagle Rest at four o'clock and she's not answering her phone, so they want to know if she's left yet."

"Eagle Rest? That's what? Eighteen, twenty miles?" Underwood went over to the wide glass doors and scanned the lot,

341

but didn't see her black Firebird. "Mary Kay Kare said she left around three-thirty. She should be there by now."

He accompanied Suanna back to Burke's office and was soon dialing the number Billy Ed Johnson had given Burke.

"How did you route her out there?" he asked when Johnson answered.

Within thirty minutes he had retrieved her license plate number from Motor Vehicles, and as the sun sank low in the west he had three units prowling the roads Johnson had specified.

There might be a dozen reasons why she was late, but how many reasons could there be for not answering her cell phone? And maybe he was jumping the gun, but if it was Annie, he'd sure want to know.

With a sigh, he pulled out his wallet and found the number he'd scribbled on the back of a card three days ago, then picked up his phone and dialed the area code for Colleton County.

Deputy Ray Elkins was only twenty-one. He had joined the sheriff's department in July, shortly after finishing a two-year criminal justice course at the local community college, and he was very much aware of being the new kid with something to prove. Accordingly, he drove fast down the stretch of road he'd been assigned, looking for a black Firebird in obvious trouble — maybe something as simple as a flat tire or broken radiator belt.

Along the way, the young deputy stopped to examine a set of fresh skid marks on the outer lane at the bottom of the second long hill. There were shards of silvered glass on the pavement and he found a smashed side mirror that had been recently torn off a black vehicle and bounced over to the base of the mountain wall; but after walking fifty feet in either direction from the skid marks, he saw no sign that a vehicle had gone over the side.

He wasn't real sure if this mirror came off a Firebird, but he stuck it in the trunk of his unit anyhow and drove on.

When the quick and dirty failed, Elkins turned around at the end of his assigned stretch and drove back more slowly. As he came up the same hill and rounded a sharp curve, there, about fifty feet past the crest, he saw a short set of skid marks. They continued off the pavement and on across the narrow, leaf-strewn shoulder.

He got out of the car and looked down, taking care not to step on the torn-up weeds and dirt. The tire tracks were so fresh, the exposed dirt had barely begun to dry. If a vehicle had gone off here, though, into this thicket of head-high mountain laurels and hardwoods, it wasn't immediately apparent. Nevertheless, he climbed down to make sure, holding on to young saplings and laurel branches. Just as he was ready to turn back, a breeze parted the leaves and sunlight gleamed off black metal another twenty feet down.

A crumpled form lay in the bushes beyond the vehicle, and Elkins hesitated. The only dead bodies he'd seen in his short life were properly laid out in caskets in Sunday clothes. For a long moment, he stood there cussing the stupidity of people who don't buckle up automatically, before his training kicked in and he forced himself to walk over to the body, to squat down and feel for a pulse.

Nothing.

He located the victim's wallet and driver's license, then climbed back up to the road, where he thumbed his mike and radioed for help.

Chapter 27

My alarm clock was ringing — ringing with such infuriating loudness that I fumbled for it on my nightstand, ready to slap it across the room, anything to make it stop. I seemed to be lying on my left arm and it was half numb as if I'd slept on it wrong. My head throbbed like the worst hangover of my entire life and the front of my neck was so sore I could barely turn it.

And still the alarm shrilled, sending daggers through my pounding head. I cracked one eye and groaned. It wasn't even full daylight yet. The sky was the gray of predawn without a single rosy-fingered sign of sunrise. Why the hell had I set the alarm for such an early hour? And where was the stupid thing anyhow?

Abruptly it stopped.

Good.

Now I could turn over and grab another

hour of sleep. Get rid of this headache.

Except that I seemed to be all tangled up in the covers.

I struggled to free myself, every part of my body hurting as I clawed at the constricting sheets —

Sheets?

I opened my eyes and looked down. Not sheets.

Seat belt.

I was hanging almost upside down against the left door of my car. No wonder my arm had gone numb. The deflated air bag hung like a limp balloon from its space on the steering wheel and there seemed to be a white powder all over my jacket. I twisted around, and as I shifted my weight, the car gave a sickening lurch, then slowly rolled over, crashing through the undergrowth. My head socked against the window and I blacked out again.

When next I came to, it was even darker. Remembering what happened the last time I moved, I slowly lifted my head and looked around. The car seemed to be slightly canted on its right side now so that I still hung in the seat belt like a trussed calf. The front end pointed down the side of the mountain at what felt like a forty-five-degree angle. To my infinite relief, though, it appeared to be blocked from further slippage by the sturdy trunks of two large maples, not to mention that I was jammed in by so many laurel bushes that I could barely see the sky through all the thick leaves and the shattered windows.

At first I couldn't understand where I was or how I had gotten myself in such a fix, then, as my head cleared, I remembered the tattooed kid from court, the black Ranger, the whole terrifying incident.

I tried to push myself upright and discovered that the car roof was now several inches lower, almost even with the top of my headrest. Dwight's always complaining about the cramped interior. He'd go ape boxed in here now.

I strained to reach the cell phone that had been thrown into the well on the passenger side, but my seat belt kept me too far away. Between the jackhammer that pounded through my head and the pins and needles in my arm, it was difficult to concentrate, yet I did realize that my first order of business was to get out of this seat belt.

Easier said than done. Even pushing against the floor with my feet to take a bit of the tension off, nothing happened when I pressed the release. I tried again and again, moaning with frustration at each failure.

Jammed.

It was so dark down here under this canopy of leaves that I could barely make out the numerals on my watch.

6:10.

I was two hours late for my meeting with Billy Ed, the only one who knew where I was headed. Would he assume I'd changed my mind? If he thought I'd decided to blow him off, he might head back over toward Tennessee without saying anything to anyone. I could dangle here forever.

The twins wouldn't be home till midnight. If they noticed I was gone, the way their minds work, they'd probably think I was in bed with Lucius Burke somewhere. I couldn't count on a search party until tomorrow morning when I didn't show up for court.

If only that guy with the jackhammer would knock it off, take a cigarette break, sit down on the curb for two minutes so I could think. I tried to press my temples with both hands. That's when I noticed that my left arm didn't want to track with the right. Broken?

I tentatively squeezed along the top of my forearm with my right hand and it hurt like hell. Fortunately, the pain felt more like a bad surface bruise than something deeper.

I assessed my damages. Sore arm. Banged head. A burning area on the front of my neck where the seat belt must have rasped me. No nausea, though. No blurred vision. Nor did I feel an overwhelming urge to sleep. If I was remembering correctly everything that nurse had said when I was seven and fell off a barn roof where I wasn't supposed to be climbing, then I probably didn't have a concussion.

With the top of the steering wheel blown off by the air bag, I couldn't seem to locate my horn, but at least the light switch was in its usual spot on the dashboard.

I turned the knob. It got me nothing except more darkness.

There was barely any wiggle room. I could get my arm free, not that it did me any good. Not when the roof and seat kept me from eeling out. It was like being strapped into one of those MRI machines. All the same, I scrunched over till most of my weight was on my other hip and pressed the seat belt release again.

Still jammed.

There was a nail clipper in my purse, but my purse was down there with the cell phone. Both might as well have been in China for all the good they were doing me.

The console yielded up Johnny Cash tapes, a nearly full plastic bottle of water, a wad of gas receipts and fast-food napkins, scraps of notepaper, a ballpoint pen, and a foam coffee cup. Safety glass is all well and good and has no doubt saved a lot of lives but it meant no sharp shards. Why hadn't I brought a regular mug? Something I could break and use as a knife.

Knife? I automatically reached for my keys before I remembered.

After 9/11, the penknife I used to keep on my keychain had been confiscated the first time I went through an airport safety check. What about the keys themselves, though?

They were still in the ignition. I pulled them out and felt the shafts till I found one that was sharp and crisp — the key to the front door of my house, a brass key I'd maybe put in the lock once just to make sure it worked because nobody in my family ever uses a front door. Everyone pulls up at the back and enters through the kitchen.

I shifted around till the seat belt was as

taut as I could make it, then, using that key, I began to saw at the tough woven nylon just above the metal clasp. I kept it up till my hand cramped and my body ached, then I relaxed so that the belt went slightly slack, and examined the spot I'd been working on with the tiny light on my keychain. The edge of the belt was barely starting to look frayed. At this rate, it was going to take me hours.

"Well, it's not as if you've got anything else to do," said the pragmatist over the pounding in my head.

Chapter 28

"Jason Barringer? And he's got a Tanser-Mac student card?"

The name on the victim's driver's license did not register with George Underwood, but the bailiff had started hanging around the sheriff's department past quitting time after his wife died the year before, and he was standing at the dispatcher's station when Deputy Elkins radioed in. As soon as he heard that name, he poked Underwood's shoulder and said, "Ask him if he's got a tattoo of a naked woman on his shin."

Underwood relayed the question to Elkins.

"Affirmative," came the reply.

"Well, hell!" said the bailiff. "He was in court this afternoon. Him and his buddy busted up a place down in Howards Ford, and the judge, she come down on 'em

352

pretty hard. Kid had a real attitude."

The lawmen looked at each other apprehensively. They knew about kids with attitude. What was this particular Tanser-Mac student doing on that road, the same road Judge Knott had taken? It was miles out of his way back to the college.

"Shit!" said Fletcher. "He followed her."

"No sign of Judge Knott's car?" Underwood asked Elkins.

"Negative, sir, but Alpha Unit just arrived and one of us will keep looking."

By the time Underwood and his team arrived, the third patrol unit had been there long enough for the three deputies to form a working theory. They were aided by a second body, that of a deer that lay mangled and torn a few feet down the slope from Barringer. Scraps of bloody fur were caught in the Ford Ranger's grille, and blood spattered the windshield.

"Elkins found a mirror that could've come off the judge's Firebird," said Deputy Carter. "About eight-tenths of a mile further on, down toward the bottom of the hill. If Barringer was trying to force her off the road, it probably happened somewhere past where the mirror was. We haven't yet found the spot where she actually went over, but from the skid marks, we can tell she was going west toward Eagle Rest. We figure he runs her off the road, then he turns around and is heading back toward Cedar Gap and Howards Ford when he comes around the curve too fast here, sees the buck right there in front of him, and just automatically swerves to miss it."

"Sniffing for a doe in heat," Sheriff Horton grunted. "Damn things are all over the roads. Be glad when hunting season opens."

Officers walked the shoulder of the desolate road from the point where Elkins had picked up the mirror all the way to where the road teed into another two miles beyond. Three houses stood at that intersection and none of the residents had seen or heard anything unusual.

"If she got this far, she'd've driven right into one of them yards with her horn blaring," said Horton.

Underwood nodded. "Too bad the state won't give us guardrails. Cars could go over anywhere and we'd never know."

By the time the sun had fully set, the moon was rising fat and orange in the east, and they came to the reluctant conclusion that finding Deborah Knott and her car was going to be a lot harder than they'd hoped.

Sheriff Horton, who'd been through many of these searches over the years, called for a helicopter and had the dispatcher notify the various fire stations that they needed all the volunteer help they could get.

"Temperature's supposed to go down into the mid-thirties tonight." Even as he spoke, Underwood's breath made little puffs of steam in the chill night air. "Maybe that'll help the heat sensors," he said, reaching for all the silver he could find on this black cloud.

"Damn deers are gonna screw 'em up anyhow," Horton said pessimistically.

Underwood's cell phone rang and he pulled it from his jacket pocket.

"Captain Underwood? This is Sunny Osborne."

Her voice sounded drained to him, but then picking out caskets can do that, he thought.

"You left a message for me to call you?"

"Yes, ma'am. Could you hold for just one minute?"

He held a broad finger over the mike. "It's Mrs. Osborne."

"Ain't nothing more you can do out here

right now till the chopper comes," Horton told him. "Might as well run on over there and get her story."

Reluctant as he was to abandon the search even for an hour, Underwood knew that Horton was right. He moved his finger and put the phone back to his ear. "Mrs. Osborne? I was wondering if I could come by for a few minutes?"

"Has something happened?" Her listless voice quickened in sudden hope. "You've found who killed Norman?"

"I'd rather discuss things with you in person," he hedged. "I can be there in about twenty minutes, if that's all right with you?"

"Yes, of course," she said.

"Let me know how it goes," said the sheriff.

Underwood nodded and walked back to his car. Before switching on the ignition, though, he gave Judge Knott's cell phone one final try. It rang twice, then a pleasant digital voice said, "We're sorry. The customer you have called is currently unavailable. Please try your call again later."

Chapter
29

As long as I kept sawing at the seat belt with that key, I generated enough heat to stay warm, but whenever I paused to rest, the chill burrowed a little deeper into my bones. I had a couple of layers on my upper body, and my guardian angel must have cast an eye in my direction this morning when I chose to wear slacks today instead of the short skirt I'd contemplated. Too bad it hadn't nudged me toward wool socks instead of knee-highs and two-inch heels. Fortunately I wouldn't have to hike out of here in those heels. Assuming I ever got out of this seat belt, I do keep a pair of sneakers in my trunk for brisk walks at lunchtime.

But jeez! Who knew seat belts were so damn sturdy? It took me a full five minutes just to fray past the edge, and even then the material didn't want to cut. It merely fuzzed up. I had to make my aching left hand hold the tiny gap apart so that the jagged edges of my key kept in contact with new threads instead of futilely rasping against old fuzz. Over an hour later, I was barely halfway through, and a blister had formed at the second joint of my index finger where I grasped the head of the key.

Dumb of me not to have realized it sooner. I groped for those napkins in my console and wrapped one around my finger like a bandage. It helped my blister, but slowed the sawing.

By now I was tired and hungry and I'd been sparing of my sips of water for obvious reasons. I can go hours without a bathroom break, but there was no point in pushing it till I was free from this seat belt.

As I mechanically sawed the key back and forth, my mind jumped on and off a dozen trains of thought — the Barringer kid for starters. I wished I could be there to see his smartass face when he learned I wasn't dead.

— Dwight. Who didn't call and didn't E, and was it going to mess up our friendship, not to mention the marriage we'd arranged, if he heard I'd kissed Lucius Burke?

— Lucius Burke. A no-fly zone.

— The twins and what Beverly and Fred were going to say or do when they realized what was going on.

— Tina Ledwig's collapsing alibi. Her lack of grief over her husband's death.

— The tears in Sunny Osborne's eyes when she'd sung, *"You'll never know, dear/ How much I love you."*

— My name on Osborne's notepad and a question mark beside "Judge."

— His short-lived partnership with the Ashes.

— The Ashes. Bobby and Joyce's worthless son. Legal bills. Medical bills. And that crack Tina had made about shrinks for their daughters. Shrinks don't come cheaply either. The insurance on Norman.

— Sunny. How almost overnight she'd gone from strength to utter dependence. How she'd followed Norman out to the terrace when he was talking to me. How she panicked when she realized he wasn't in the room. Menopause, said Lucius, yet she'd sat there playing all evening and I never saw a single hot flash.

— Ledwig's abrupt call to Norman Osborne the night before he was killed even though Trish thought the two men had been estranged since the end of summer.

★ ★ ★

I thought about the timing of that call. Ledwig tells his former pal, "It may be legal, but it's not ethical" and "I can't stand by and let you do this to them."

And the very next day, he's dead.

Could Osborne have been the killer?

But then who killed Osborne?

Cui bono?

All the things I'd heard or seen swirled around like shifting patterns in a kaleidoscope.

I'd never met Ledwig, but I had met Osborne and something he'd said or done that night must have triggered his death. He'd been pleasant, genial, hail-fellow-well-met. Expansive and pleased about his new partnership with the Ashes. As defensive of Ledwig's bigotry as if there'd never been a rift in their friendship. He'd cited Ledwig's continuing gifts to Cedar Gap — oh, wait. No. That was Sunny who thought Ledwig had left a bequest to the new senior center. Mistakenly thought, according to what Tina told me Tuesday.

Nevertheless, something about that conversation . . .

I replayed the scene in my head, trying to remember every word. Liz Peters, one of the attorneys, and that guy who owned

360

several gem mines — Tysinger? Yeah, Sam Tysinger. They had criticized Ledwig's position on race, until Osborne had said, "You're bad-mouthing a good man who's not here tonight to defend himself." Then he'd talked about all the good Ledwig had done for Cedar Gap, ending with that comment about building a new senior center. Tysinger had sounded surprised by that, and Sunny had said, no, not another new center but a bequest to build onto the one so recently built. "Or so we heard."

Now, who would have told her that? Not Tina and certainly not their attorney since it wasn't true. So why would Sunny say it?

And why would Osborne agree with her? Unless . . . ?

And if that phone call made them afraid that Ledwig would tell . . . ?

And if that was true, then Sunny could have been the woman the UPS deliveryman saw. Both were blond and athletic with similar hairstyles and —

A loud roar almost rocked the car. If I hadn't been strapped in so tightly, I'd've jumped three feet.

I strained to see through the leaves jammed up against my cracked windows. A helicopter hovered off to my left, about a half mile away, further down the mountain.

Slowly, deliberately, it began to move back and forth, up and down, casting a beam of bright light through the trees.

The cavalry had arrived!

I waited for them to come back my way and prayed that the leaves around me would let them see my car.

My black car.

Damn!

I swore right then that my next car was going to be white. Black might be cool, but cool don't cut it, baby. Not when you're stranded on the side of a mountain.

As I watched, the helicopter moved further away.

Huh?

How come they were working down there and not up here?

Patience, I told myself, and my mother's voice came singsonging through my head: *"Patience is a virtue. / Have it if you can. / Seldom in a woman, / Never in a man."*

I kept sawing with the key. More than half an inch to go, yet the helicopter was even further away now, sweeping the area with its cone of light. Desperately, I paused and flashed the light on my keychain. Pitiful. The tiny bulb was meant to give just enough light to see a keyhole, not to signal rescuers. There was a flashlight in the glove compartment, though, and if I ever got out of this seat belt —

I sawed frantically. Oh glory! Here came the helicopter back up the slope again. I urged it on. Come to mama, baby. A little more, a little more — shit! Nowhere near me and now it was turning to hover over the same area.

My fingers were cramping. I felt the blister pop and I didn't care, just pushed aside the fuzz and kept sawing.

Suddenly the last few threads parted with a jolt and I was free!

All my bangs and bruises protested as I lunged for the glove compartment and found the flashlight. The brightness almost blinded me when I flashed it off and on toward the helicopter.

I almost howled in frustration as it flew slowly back down the mountain.

Belatedly, I remembered my phone. Yes!

I had to wriggle over the console to the passenger seat and then fumble around on the floor before I found it.

As soon as I flipped it open and pressed the menu button, the dial lit up. Lit up, but no little service symbol appeared on the screen.

I couldn't believe it. I'd heard it ring before the car rolled again, and surely I hadn't rolled very far. All that effort, only to find I was in a dead zone?

I slid back over to the driver's seat and pushed on the door handle. The car had landed at an angle that would require me to push the door's entire weight up and away. Even bracing my back against the console and pushing with my feet, I couldn't get enough leverage to open the door more than a crack. I knew this model had heavy doors, but this was ridiculous.

At this rate, I could flat die here.

And then, miraculously, the phone chirped and I looked down to see the service icon. Just moving from one side of the car to another had been enough.

Carefully, gingerly, keeping all the stars in alignment, I dialed 911 and held my breath.

Chapter
30

"Captain Underwood?"

The blond who got up from the piano and came forward when the housekeeper showed him into the music room was a younger, plumper version of Sunny Osborne.

"I'm Laura Osborne. My mother will be down in a minute."

She was not as attractive as her mother. Her sweater was too tight to flatter her overly generous curves, her hair was cut too short and tufts of it stuck out as if she'd slept on it wrong, but her voice was bewitching when she asked if she could get him something to drink.

He shook his head, waiting for her to speak again, and when she merely stood there with a quizzical look on her broad face, he blurted, "I'll bet you sing like an angel."

She laughed, a rich chord of descending notes.

"Thank you. Some people have said so." Her voice softened. "My father thought so."

He looked at the sheets of music on the piano and remembered what the housekeeper had said when he called this afternoon.

"You're choosing music for him?"

She nodded. "And it's harder than I thought it would be. He was bluegrass and gospel, I'm Purcell and Bach. He's definitely not Bach, but bluegrass sounds really dumb when it's sung by a trained contralto."

"Please don't let me interrupt you, then," he said, half hoping that she would sing a few lines as she sorted through the music.

"That's all right. I — Ah! Here's Mother."

"Sorry to have kept you waiting, Captain," Sunny Osborne said. She crossed the room briskly to take his hand. "What can you tell me?"

"Is there some place we could speak privately?" he asked, with an apologetic look at Laura Osborne.

"No problem," said the younger woman.

"I'll be upstairs if you want me, Mother."

She pulled the door to when she left.

"What is it that Laura shouldn't hear?" Mrs. Osborne sat down on the sofa and waved him to an adjacent chair.

"The day that Dr. Ledwig died," he began.

"*Carlyle?*" Her bright face darkened with anger. "I've told you and told you. Carlyle's death has nothing to do with Norman's. Nothing! Why do you people keep saying it does?"

"The day that Dr. Ledwig died," he repeated firmly, "were you there on the deck?"

"I beg your pardon?" She sat very still and her blue eyes regarded him steadily.

"Were you on the deck the afternoon that Dr. Ledwig died?"

"Does someone say I was?"

"Mrs. Osborne?"

"Oh, very well. I suppose it was that UPS man?"

"Yes, ma'am. Why didn't you mention it to us before?"

She shrugged. "No one specifically asked me."

"You knew we were asking anyone who'd spoken to Dr. Ledwig that day to come forward."

"And if I'd had anything to contribute, I would have. But I didn't. I felt like a game of tennis and I stopped by to see if Tina wanted to play. When no one answered the front bell, I heard hammering and went around to the rear."

"Dr. Ledwig was still alive?"

"Well, of course he was! I asked him about Tina. He said she was already at the club and I left." She gave a wry smile. "At least I would have left if that UPS truck hadn't been blocking my car. He assumed I was Tina and handed the stuff to me. It seemed like more trouble than it was worth to tell him differently, so I carried it back around and Carlyle told me to put it on the table by the door. And then I really did leave. You can ask at the club. I was there before three."

"You saw no one else as you were leaving?"

She shook her head.

"Who do you think killed him, Mrs. Osborne?"

"That boyfriend of Carla's, of course. He was there. He had the motive."

"And if not him?"

She shook her head. "Then I don't have a clue."

"I see." He stood to go. "Thank you,

Mrs. Osborne. I'm sorry I had to bother you tonight."

"That's it?" she asked, surprised. "You came all the way out here just to ask if I saw Carlyle that day? What about Norman? Don't you have anything new to tell me?"

"I'm sorry, ma'am. Soon as we know, you'll know."

"It's not fair." Tears filled her eyes. "Norman's dead and the only one you worry about is Carlyle?"

"No, ma'am," he said gently. "We worry about both of them."

To return to the road Deborah Knott had disappeared on, Underwood had to go back almost to the main state highway, then head west up over the ridge. As he drove, he checked in with the dispatcher. "Any word yet?"

"Negative, Captain. ETA for the chopper is about another twenty-five minutes. Volunteers from two fire stations are already there, with three others on the way."

"What's taking the chopper so long?"

He heard a snort of laughter across the airwaves. "They were changing the oil filters on it when we called."

★ ★ ★

Underwood pulled up at the bottom of the hill where they assumed the judge's car had gone over just as the helicopter came over the ridge. A welcoming cheer went up from the men and women who'd turned out to help search.

Deputy Fletcher sat in a patrol car with his radio tuned to headquarters and his walkie-talkie set to the chopper's frequency. First it made a sweep with the heat-sensing elements.

For a moment, they thought they were going to get lucky right away. Infrared showed them one warm body that didn't bolt and run the minute they got near. They swooped lower toward it and suddenly a ten-point buck bounded up from the rhododendron bushes and raced straight down the mountain.

"So we do it the hard way," someone said.

With the lights from above turning the mountainside into day, the volunteers fanned down across the slope, all eyes alert for a black Firebird.

They had been at it almost an hour when the Lafayette dispatcher broke in excitedly. "Captain? You there? I got her on her cell phone! Patching her through to

370

y'all. Go ahead, ma'am."

The signal was faint and wavering, yet Deborah Knott's voice itself sounded strong. "I keep losing the signal so I'll talk fast. I can see a helicopter about a half mile to the right of my position. West of me, I think. I was heading back toward Cedar Gap when that bastard Barringer ran me off the road with his truck near the top of a hill. Hey, is anybody hearing this?"

"Loud and clear, ma'am!" Underwood said happily.

"George? Is that you?"

"Yes, ma'am."

"I can't get out of my car. The door's too heavy, but — Oh, good! Finally! The chopper's heading my way. Tell them to keep coming . . . keep coming . . . down the slope more . . . *yes!* They're right overhead."

"Hang on, ma'am. Somebody'll be with you in a minute. You okay?"

"Just banged and bruised. And, George?"

"Ma'am?"

"I want to swear out a warrant against Barringer."

"We'll certainly talk about that, ma'am." Underwood put his car in gear and joined the parade up the hill. Why she was going in this direction was something else to talk about. Time enough to tell her that Barringer was dead once she was back on level ground.

A rope line was stretched down to the car and an EMT team went down with a stretcher, but Judge Knott insisted on walking out by herself.

"She's a pistol," one of them told him later. "Made us get her sneakers out of the back and wait till she put them on. Told us if we wanted to carry something, we could grab her guitar and her laptop, but nobody was strapping her into anything unless we gave her a pair of scissors to hold."

"Welcome back, Judge," Underwood said, reaching out a hand to help her around a rock.

There was a bruise on her left temple that extended up from her eyebrow and another on her neck, but her smile was radiant. "If my arm didn't hurt so bad, George, I'd hug you here and now. Please thank everybody for me."

She waved to the television camera and to the circle of people who wanted to see her for themselves. "Thank you!" she called. "Thanks for helping. I really appreciate it."

Underwood had a feeling she would have

gone over to shake every hand there and thank each volunteer searcher individually if the EMT team hadn't persuaded her to let them take her on down to the hospital.

Chapter
31

 "I'm fine," I kept telling them.

"You probably are," the medical technician agreed, "but until you get checked out thoroughly, you can't be sure. You've got a contusion on the side of your head. There may be chipped bones. That arm could be fractured."

"George!" I entreated.

He gave a heartless smile. "I'll follow you down and see you at the hospital."

Resigned, I lay back on the stretcher and let them strap me in.

"There's a pair of scissors in that locker beside your head," said one of the medics with a chuckle.

"You laugh," I said darkly, "but I'd like to see you get out of a jammed seat belt without some."

At the hospital, they made me strip off into one of those godawful gowns, and a doctor went over all my extremities, pushing and flexing and "This hurt? How about here?"

I was advised to put ice on my temple and left arm for the next seventy-two hours. They gave me an ointment for the belt burn on my neck and they bandaged the raw place on my finger where the key had rubbed it, otherwise, it was exactly as I'd thought: I was bruised and battered but unbroken.

"How long before this one goes away?" I asked, looking in the mirror at the side of my face. Every time I took the ice pack away and checked, the bruise seemed to be darker and was passing from purple to black even as we spoke.

"About three weeks," said the doctor.

"What?"

"With a little luck, regular makeup will cover up the worst in about a week," chirped the nurse.

Damn that Barringer! I could just imagine some of the things those courthouse smartmouths down in Dobbs were going to say when they saw me next.

Glumly, I went back to my cubicle and was half-dressed when I heard the nurse say, "Sir? Sir! You can't come in here."

"The hell I can't," someone snarled.

"Deb'rah? You back there?"

I zipped up my slacks and poked my head out of the curtain. *"Dwight?"*

He strode down to my cubicle. "You okay?"

"I'm fine," I said, stunned to see him here.

He gently turned my face and looked at the bruise. His own face was grim.

I pushed his hand away because I couldn't meet his eyes. Not when I was feeling so uncertain about our future together, not when it was possible we would have no future. "It looks worse than it is."

"Glad to hear it," he said with the first trace of normality, " 'cause it sure does look like hell."

"I'm happy to see you, too," I said tartly as I pulled on my jersey and slipped my feet into my sneakers. My voice sounded shrewish, even to me, with none of the easy banter that usually flowed between us. "What are you doing here? I thought you weren't due up in Virginia till Saturday."

"Underwood called me."

"He did? When?"

"I don't know. Around five-thirty?"

I looked at my watch. It was only a little after ten now. Amazing.

This wasn't Jeff Gordon or Dale Jarrett.

This was Dwight Bryant, a man who drives so slow that everyone says he's going to get T-boned by a turtle someday, yet he had made the trip in less than five hours. "How many times did you get pulled?"

He gave a sheepish grin. "Only once. He was cool about it."

I.e., no ticket.

He held my jacket for me and we walked out into the waiting room. To my surprise, George Underwood was still there.

"I need food and drink," I told them both. "And not necessarily in that order."

Five minutes later, we were in a booth in a little Mexican place on the far side of the hospital.

I was running on adrenaline between my harrowing evening, Dwight's sudden appearance, and the conclusions I'd reached about Ledwig's death. Most of all, though, I was still furious about my own near death. George kept putting me off whenever I asked, but as soon as we were seated, I said, "So what about Barringer? Did you arrest him yet?"

George looked at Dwight, who put his hand on mine and said gently, "He's dead, shug."

"*What?* How?"

The bottom fell out of my stomach as

George told me about the dead buck they'd found and how it must have happened right after he ran me off the road. I felt my eyes fill up with tears. The waste of it. Yes, he had been full of the arrogance of privileged youth. Yes, he had almost killed me. All the same, he was still just a kid. Okay, a stupid kid. But he'd had a whole lifetime before him, time to learn, time to change. And now in the blink of an eye, all his time was up.

"He didn't deserve to die," I said shakily.

"Neither did you," said George.

Our drinks came and they left me alone to deal with my thoughts while they talked of mutual acquaintances across the state, each getting a feel for the other by whom they admired or considered a showboater or thought was abusing his power.

Eventually, I came back to them and looked around the restaurant. It was neat and clean but decidedly downscale in appearance. The frozen margaritas were pleasantly tart, though, and the nachos supremo were wheat-flour nachos, not cornmeal. The clientele seemed to be mostly Mexican — day laborers, domestics, and hospital custodians — yet I did see several white doctors and nurses sprinkled around.

"How did a place like this slip under the zoning radar?" I asked.

"Dr. Ledwig," George said. "He argued that if these people were going to come up here and work for us, they deserved a place they could relax in, a place they could afford. As you see, though, no garish neon outside, no calling attention to itself. He wasn't that liberal."

"I'm pretty sure Sunny Osborne killed him," I said, licking a fleck of salt from my fingertip.

Underwood almost choked on his drink. "Huh?"

"I had plenty of time to think about things while I was sawing my way through that seat belt," I told him. "What did the UPS driver tell you?"

"That the woman was driving a vanity plate with 'SUN' on it."

"Sunny, right?"

His nod confirmed my theory. "Yeah. And tonight she admitted it."

"She admitted killing Ledwig?"

"No. Just that she was there. Stopped by to see if Mrs. Ledwig wanted to play tennis and left him alive and well."

I shook my head. "I really, seriously doubt that."

"But you're her alibi for Osborne's

death," he protested.

"Yes."

"Who's Osborne?" asked Dwight. "And how did you get to be somebody's alibi? I thought you said you weren't going to get involved."

"I'm not involved," I said. "Not really. But people tell me things."

He gave me a sardonic look. "Maybe if you didn't go poking around, asking questions . . ."

George smiled and Dwight just shook his head. "Okay, tell me."

Anything to take my mind off Jason Barringer. Together, George and I brought him up to speed on the two deaths.

"What you might not know," I told George, "is that Ledwig called Norman Osborne the night before he was killed and warned Osborne that he wouldn't stand by and let him do something that was legal but unethical."

"Which was?"

"Ledwig and Osborne used to be tight, right?"

George popped a nacho in his mouth and nodded.

"Then sometime late in the summer, Osborne started avoiding him. At the same time, though, he decided to accept Bobby

Ashe's offer of a merger. In fact, he pushed it through so fast that the Ashes got a better slice than they expected, according to Joyce. They kept the merger so quiet that even Ledwig didn't get wind of it till the day before he was killed, two days before the final papers were signed that would make the partnership a done deal. Bobby and Joyce had stopped by the Ledwig house, and she told me Bobby let it slip. Trish Ledwig says that as soon as the Ashes were gone, her dad called Osborne and said, 'I can't let you do this to them.' "

"Do what?" George asked. "The merger? Hell, that was good business for both of them."

I shook my head. "Not anymore. Not if Norman was going to stop being a rainmaker and become a drain on any partnership." In my mind's eye I saw again the tears in Sunny's eyes when they sang together. Love had been there, yes, but also grief and pain.

"He was sick? I thought they both had physicals before the insurance company would write the policies."

"They did. His trouble wasn't physical. It was mental."

"Oh, now, wait a minute. Norman

Osborne was one of the sharpest, savviest —"

"*Was,* maybe, but that night at the party, he kept saying things that didn't compute. He spoke about Ledwig as if they were still close friends, as if Ledwig was still alive. He referred to the senior center Ledwig was *going* to build because he'd forgotten that it was already built. He forgot my name and wrote it down on his notepad so he'd remember."

George and Dwight were both looking skeptical.

"Carlyle Ledwig was a gerontologist who specialized in the aging process," I said, carefully loading a nacho with guacamole. "He would have picked up on any symptoms long before anyone else except perhaps Sunny. I think that's why Osborne started avoiding him and that's why he rammed through the merger."

"Okay," George said, "but even if he was starting to lose it a little, Bobby Ashe wasn't born yesterday. Why didn't *he* notice?"

"Because Sunny didn't give him a chance." I described to Dwight how Sunny Osborne suddenly — conveniently — became menopausal and had everyone convinced that she was so wigged out that she couldn't stand to have Norman out of her sight. "She was driving Bobby and Joyce nuts with all her questions and writing things down and making them explain. Those questions weren't for her own benefit, though, they were for his. She was turning herself into his backup memory. Just last night, Joyce said Bobby was getting fed up with the way Norman couldn't seem to concentrate because of Sunny's distractions. It was her distractions that covered up his growing inability to concentrate."

"So when Ledwig found out about the merger, he would've tried to get Osborne to pull out before the Ashes got burned."

"And they would have been burned bad. If it's a standard policy, the partnership insurance they had on each other wouldn't pay out for debilitating conditions, only for death. The Ashes would have had to front the buyout of his share of the partnership from their own pockets or else keep paying him a big part of their annual take as long as he lived. That could've been years. Osborne must have figured that this was the best way to protect what he'd acquired and secure his and Sunny's future at the same time, a future that was nothing but a long and expensive descent into total senility."

"Alzheimer's?" asked Dwight.

"Or dementia."

I spoke from experience, the experience of dealing with distraught adult children who came to me to seek a power of attorney for a parent when I was in private practice. Often, the parent seemed as clearheaded as ever. He could speak cogently about the running of his businesses down to the smallest detail. Then I'd ask him what year was it? Who was president? What did he have for breakfast? And he'd look at me blankly.

"I think that Ledwig threatened to tell the Ashes. I think Sunny went over there that day to try to persuade him to keep quiet for just two more days, and when he refused —"

"And he would refuse," George said grimly, as if remembering his wife's uncle.

"— then she smashed him with his own hammer and pushed him over the side."

"But when did she kill Osborne?" asked George. "Everybody says — Hell! You said it yourself. She was playing her dulcimer right beside you when he went missing."

Again I shook my head. "She could never have hurt him."

"But — ?"

"What you said before, bo," said Dwight,

who sometimes knows the way my mind works. "This Bobby guy. He wasn't born yesterday."

"The last time I noticed Norman Osborne," I said, "he was standing at the bar talking to Bobby Ashe. He probably said something that gave the game away and all the pieces dropped into place for Bobby, just as they did for me, only in Bobby's case, he was looking at probably two or three million out of pocket. It was a case of 'If it were done, 'twere well it were done quickly.' "

"Huh?" George flicked a puzzled look at Dwight, who shrugged.

"Sorry. My former law partner used to quote Shakespeare all the time. Bobby must have realized he couldn't afford to let Osborne's condition become general knowledge or he'd be the first suspect in any murder case."

"So he carpayed the damn diem."

"Well, that's one way to put it," I said.

Chapter
32

 Although I had been on an adrenaline high, the margarita brought me down to earth with a bang and suddenly all I wanted was to go to sleep.

"C'mon, shug," Dwight said when my head drooped against his shoulder. "Time you got to bed."

"My laptop," I said. "My guitar."

"In my car," said George.

Dwight paid the bill and we walked out together. Every inch of my body hurt and I was so weary that my brain seemed to be fogging over.

"He won't confess, you know," I told George as Dwight took my things and stowed them in his truck. "And there's no hard evidence."

"Worry about that tomorrow," Dwight said. He shook George's hand with great ceremony. "Thanks, buddy."

"Anytime," George said, giving Dwight's shoulder a pat.

Men are sweet the way they bond.

I managed to direct Dwight back to the condo. The twins weren't due in for another half-hour and he helped me to the bedroom, where he eased my clothes off my sore body. It felt so good to lie down.

"Thank you for coming," I said formally and then I was gone.

Sometime later — it could have been five minutes, it could have been an hour — I felt a cool ice pack against my temple, but I couldn't make my eyes open.

When I awoke in the early dawn hours, Dwight was not there beside me. In fact, he hadn't been there at all. I sat up and was so stiff and achy that it was a true act of will to get out of bed. The doors to both bedrooms were closed. Out in the living room, there was enough light to see that the couch had been opened into a bed and Dwight was there sound asleep. I watched him for several long minutes, filled with turmoil and feeling strangely unsettled by the steady rise and fall of his breathing. Then I turned and went back to bed.

When next I woke, it was to a drizzly

gray day. I looked out the window and the horizon was gone, whited out by fog. Only the nearest trees were visible and even they looked like artsy photographs taken through gauze.

Matched my mood.

I smelled bacon and coffee and heard Dwight's voice mingled with the twins'. The nurse had said ice packs for seventy-two hours, so a hot shower probably wasn't recommended. Nevertheless, the water seemed to soften and ease my muscles, and by the time I dried off and dressed, I could almost move normally as long as I didn't push it.

May and June were all over me when I entered the kitchen.

"Omigawd! Your face!"

"I've seen it," I said. "Don't remind me."

They touched me gingerly, giving me soft little pats instead of hugs.

"Are you okay?"

"You could have been killed."

"Should you be up?"

"We were going to bring you breakfast in bed."

"Did you know Jason Barringer?" I asked them.

"Just by reputation," said June.

"It wasn't a very good one," May added quickly.

They seemed to intuit what I was feeling.

"Here, have some coffee," they said and gave me more reassuring pats.

Dwight eyed the way I was dressed. "You're not planning on court, are you?"

"Of course I am," I said firmly. "If someone will drive me, that is. I don't have a car anymore and I bet there's no place closer than Asheville to rent one."

"We'll work something out," Dwight told me.

At the courthouse, we both stopped by George Underwood's office first. I wanted to know what, if anything, was being done about my car. Dwight had promised to retrieve all my personal items from it, including the title and registration. I had already put in a call to my insurance agent back in Colleton County.

"The wrecker's out there now pulling up the Barringer kid's truck," said George. "Soon as I let them know where you want yours hauled, they'll come back and get it, too."

When Dwight said he'd take care of it, I didn't argue.

I left them discussing logistics and went on upstairs, where Mary Kay greeted me with sympathy for my bruised face and coffee for my sore spirits. Everyone knew what had happened and several stopped in chambers to express concern and regret for my ordeal. I thanked them all politely, but it was a relief to get back into the courtroom and have the bailiff call the place to order.

Friday is usually cleanup day for the odds and ends that were delayed earlier in the week, the emergency orders, the documents that need a judge's signature before they could be put into play. Today was no different. With William Deeck prosecuting, cases moved along at a brisk clip.

I took only a minimum break in midmorning, and Mary Kay came back bringing the freshest gossip. Sunny Osborne had been questioned and had sent for her lawyer. Rumors were starting to circulate about Bobby Ashe, and about Simon Proffitt as well. Deputies had been looking for him for three days now, but he seemed to have vanished.

"They'd be out with search parties except that his truck's still parked by the Trading Post and his shotgun's there in his office."

It all felt very anticlimactic.

Unfortunately for my plans to be finished by lunchtime, we hit a few snags, and when it became clear that there were at least another three hours to go, I adjourned for lunch at twelve-thirty.

There was no sign of Dwight downstairs, so I took the elevator back up to the first level and walked along Cedar Gap's pristine Main Street down to the Tea Room. The fog or cloud or whatever it was had retreated from the higher peaks, but the lower elevations were still swathed in white and the damp air definitely held a touch of coming winter.

As usual, there was a line, but by now Carla Ledwig was so used to my walking in and out of the kitchen that she just gave me a wave and kept on with her hostess duties.

"You should have called," said June. "We'd have brought you lunch."

"I need to walk," I said. "It helps with the stiffness."

I watched them fix me a salad, then said, "Is Simon Proffitt your landlord?"

"Where on earth did you get that idea?" asked May, not quite meeting my eyes.

"Something Carla's mother said Tuesday. She said she was glad her husband hadn't known about this business venture because he couldn't stand Simon Proffitt."

"Well, yeah," May admitted. "It's his building."

"Did you know that he's been missing ever since Captain Underwood asked him to come in and answer some questions about his threats against Ledwig and Osborne?"

"Simon didn't kill them," said June. "The sheriff and the DA are just looking for somebody to hang it on now that they don't have Danny anymore."

I held up placating hands before they could gather a good head of protective steam for the Trading Post's elderly proprietor.

"It's not official yet, but he doesn't have to worry. They know it wasn't him."

"Really?"

"He's a feisty old guy, isn't he?" I asked. "Bark worse than his bite?"

"Exactly!" said May. "He's really a sweetie, Deborah, and at his age, he doesn't need to be hounded by deputies."

"At his age, wherever he is, don't you think he'd probably be more comfortable in his own bed?" I cast a jaundiced eye toward the pressed tin ceiling, beyond which lay nothing but spiders and mice and dirty old junk were one inclined to believe what they'd told me yesterday.

They both looked at me sheepishly, but before they could blitz me with more twin-speak, Carla came through the door with a dazed expression on her face. "I just heard someone say that Sunny Osborne killed Dad! She and Mom play tennis together. Why would *she* kill my dad? Was she sleeping with him?"

By the time I adjourned court for the week, the buzz was all over town, and George confirmed it for me when I stopped by his office and found Dwight there.

"It was like you thought," he said. "Ledwig arranged for Osborne to be tested down in Winston back in August and the tests indicated the onset of early dementia. That's when he planned the merger so that he could maximize his holdings. The way his condition was deteriorating, he knew he wouldn't have time to liquidate everything himself and he'd have had to take a huge loss with the economy so soft right now. The easiest thing was just to stick it to the Ashes. When Ledwig heard about the merger, he called Osborne and told him to cancel it or he'd tell Bobby Ashe. Osborne was in such despair that Sunny went over to Ledwig's the next day to try to persuade him to keep quiet. When he wouldn't back off . . ."

"Sunny told you all this?" I asked. "Her attorney let her?"

"He couldn't stop her once I laid it all out. All she cares about right now is helping us build a case against Bobby Ashe for killing her husband. She's still trying to protect him."

"What about Ashe?"

"Claims he didn't have a clue, doesn't know what Sunny's talking about, and, on the advice of counsel, has nothing more to say."

I shook my head. "He's going to get away with it, isn't he?"

"Unless we can find someone who saw him follow Osborne out onto that terrace Monday night, we don't have a real case. No fingerprints on the candleholder. No proof that he knew what Osborne had done to him." George gave an exasperated sigh. "Sloppy work on our part. We should've confiscated the shoes and clothes he was wearing that night, checked them for blood spatters. There's another search team up there right now, but he's had four days to dispose of anything in-criminating."

"Tough luck," Dwight said sympatheti-cally.

As Dwight and I stood to go, I hesitated. "Jason Barringer. Is he from around here?"

"Louisville, Kentucky. We couldn't get hold of his parents till late and they're driving over today." George looked at his watch. "Should be getting in anytime now."

"Do they have to be told how he died?" I asked. "I mean, yes, of course, they have to know he lost control when his truck hit a deer, but do they have to know why he was up there? It's bad enough to lose a son without hearing he tried to kill somebody."

George nodded thoughtfully. "I'll pass the word," he promised.

Chapter
33

Driving down from Cedar Gap was an unsettling experience. Visibility was about three inches in front of the grille on Dwight's truck. We couldn't see behind us. We couldn't see ahead.

Which was pretty much how I was feeling.

It took us almost an hour just to get to the Tennessee border, and we were past Johnson City, heading north on I-81, before the fog dissipated into misty rain. Not that I noticed. By then, I had made myself a pillow with Dwight's jacket and slept most of the way.

At the east juncture with I-77, we pulled off to find a place to eat supper.

"You sure you want to do this?" Dwight asked when I picked out a motel at the same juncture.

"I'm sure," I said. "Halloween's right

around the corner, and if Cal saw this face, he'd think he's getting a real witch for a stepmother. Besides, it wouldn't be fair to cut in on his time with you. You need to focus on him this weekend and I need to veg out for a couple of days, sleep off this soreness, do some serious thinking."

"Not *too* serious, I hope."

His voice was light, but the truth was, we were awkward with each other. Our old-shoe easiness had evaporated.

Along with the passion.

He had slept on the couch last night and he'd barely touched me today. Even when he carried my things up to my room at the motel, he merely set them inside the door, brushed my forehead with his lips, and told me that he'd see me Sunday.

More like one of my brothers than a lover.

I slept twelve hours the first night, took a midday nap on Saturday, and slept another ten hours that night. By Sunday morning, even though my bruises were in full flower, it seemed to me that the deep blue-black places were slowly turning purple.

My body might have been healing, but my spirit was still sore. I found a country music station the first night that played real bluegrass — all the old cheatin', hurtin', lyin' songs that you seldom hear on commercial stations anymore. The music drifted in and out of my troubled dreams all weekend. Some time in the early Sunday morning hours, I came awake to hear Waylon singing "Brown-Eyed Handsome Man" and realized that I had been crying. Lying there in the darkness, I finally opened my own eyes and took a hard honest look at the whole worrisome situation. What I saw left me even more unsettled because it wasn't something I could hide from Dwight, yet telling him was probably going to cost me his friendship.

I had planned a logical and decorous scenario, and then Dwight caught me unaware by showing up two hours earlier than I'd expected while I was still in the coffee shop with coffee and the Sunday paper.

"I couldn't remember if checkout time was eleven or noon," he said when he found me.

"It's one," I told him as he slid into the booth across from me. "Want some coffee?"

"Sure." He signaled to the waitress.

"How's Cal?"

"Fine. It was his first football game last night."

"How'd they do?"

"Lost, but he scored a touchdown, so he wasn't too disappointed."

"That's nice."

"So," he said, when the waitress had brought him his coffee and been assured that no, he didn't want anything to eat, "you feeling better today?"

I nodded and braced myself for the worst. No point in putting this off any longer. "Look, Dwight, I have to know. Do you really want to do this marriage thing?"

"Is that the serious thinking you stayed here to do?"

"Yes."

"I'm still game to go, but I told you two weeks ago that if you changed your mind or if someone else came along, I wouldn't hold you to our agreement, remember?" He stirred his coffee and I couldn't read his face. It was like being back in that mountain fog.

"There's no easy way to say this."

"You don't need to," he said.

"Yes, I do. Because things have changed." I was too nervous to meet his eyes. Instead, I focused on the ring he'd given me. "Did you meet Lucius Burke Friday? The DA for Lafayette County?"

"Yeah. What about him?" Dwight's voice was grim.

"He brought me home from the Ashe party Monday night. We had dinner together on Tuesday night and he kissed me."

Across the table, beyond my own hand, I saw Dwight's tighten around his mug until his knuckles showed white through his tanned skin.

"He kissed you or you kissed him?"

"Well, he made the move and I didn't stop him."

"I see."

"No, you don't. Because nothing happened. No sparks, no tingles, and that's when I started to realize — I mean, even when I've been in other relationships, there were always sparks and tingles whenever another good-looking, available guy came on the scene, but not this time." I looked at him helplessly, feeling myself on the verge of tears again. "I'm so, so sorry, Dwight. I didn't mean for this to happen. I know we agreed that our marriage would just be a practical arrangement. Good friendship, good sex, and nothing more, but I seem to be in love with you and I don't think I can keep hiding it. So if that's going to be a problem for you, if it's going to make you uncomfortable, we don't have to do this wedding. Honest."

I had to look away again from his steady brown-eyed gaze; and his voice, when at last he spoke, was flat and unemotional. "You're in love with me."

I nodded.

"And you still want to marry me."

"Yes," I whispered.

He took a deep breath. "Okay, Deb'rah, since we're being so open and upfront here, want to know why I joined the Army instead of going off to Carolina to play basketball?"

"Why?"

"Because I couldn't trust myself to keep my hands off you if I stayed in the area."

"What?"

He gave a rueful shrug. "I've been in love with you since I was nineteen."

"But you never said — You never —"

"You were a kid, for God's sake."

"Listen, Dwight, I haven't been a kid for a lot longer than I care to admit. Why didn't you tell me?"

"When the hell did I have a chance?" he asked indignantly. "Every time I came back to Colleton County, you were either over the moon for some guy or else swearing off men forever. Do you know what it's been like these last two weeks, making love to you and you just calling it good sex? Trying to play it cool, trying not to come on too strong because I was afraid I'd scare you off? Dammit, Deb'rah! You have any idea how I felt when Underwood called me? To know every mile of the way that you could be dying?"

He glared at me across the table until the full import of his words finally sank in. I don't remember if I was laughing or crying when I got up and went around to his side of the booth and into his arms. That part's a blur.

What I do remember is that there was absolutely nothing brotherly about that kiss.

Nor the ones that followed.

I could have taken him right there in the booth, but hey! I still had a room, didn't I?

And checkout wasn't till one o'clock, right?

We made it with five minutes to spare.